Praise for *The* ...

"This is Lemann at her witty best, showing us the quirky mannerisms beneath the manners and leading us through a world that through its exaggerated gestures, reveals both the charms and danger of our own."
—*Chicago Tribune*

"Nancy Lemann's baroque voice channels the elegant phrasing of another era; playful stateliness ensues. As the Stewart family leaves a famed resort in Virginia for an episodic tour of the splendid ruined cities of the Ottoman Empire, one hears beneath the author's stylized nostalgia a *genuine* nostalgia—for home, for honor, for romance with 'dash.' " —*Elle*

"Another gorgeous winner from Lemann." —*Vogue*

"Nancy Lemann has so many gifts as a writer it feels odd to point first to her generous heart. But that is where it all begins: the romanticism, the affectionate humor, the elegant locutions that echo another era, and, of course, her ceaseless devotion to the South." —Amy Hempel

"What makes *The Fiery Pantheon* such a pleasure is Nancy Lemann's fey, delightful writing, as nonsensical as it is precise, full of the unexpected turn of phrase and as incantatory as light verse." —*Anniston Star*

"Lemann writes as if P. G. Wodehouse, Stevie Smith, and Eudora Welty had been distilled into a single sensibility and voice."
—*The Commercial Appeal*

"Lemann can evoke feelings of nostalgia for the fading traditional Southern family with her charming prose as no other writer can."
—*Charleston Post & Courier*

"Like [Joan] Didion, Lemann has a deadpan wit, an eye for the telling detail, and a wonderful sense of place." —*The Cleveland Plain Dealer*

"If you enjoy savoring language that creates a mood and atmosphere, this one's for you . . . a timeless dedication to the South comes through in the flowing words of the author." —*Baton Rouge Advocate*

"A slyly comic book . . . Lemann unleashes her buoyant prose and trademark wit, bringing with her an unassuming air and a devilish perception of Southern idiosyncrasy." —*Austin Chronicle*

"Her novel has a kind of insouciant, offbeat charm that is quite distinctive." —*The Christian Science Monitor*

Also by Nancy Lemann

LIVES OF THE SAINTS

THE RITZ OF THE BAYOU

SPORTSMAN'S PARADISE

THE FIERY PANTHEON

Nancy Lemann

SCRIBNER PAPERBACK FICTION
PUBLISHED BY SIMON & SCHUSTER

With special thanks to J.B.,
whose standards of excellence formed the definition of heroism

SCRIBNER PAPERBACK FICTION
Simon & Schuster Inc.
Rockefeller Center
1230 Avenue of the Americas
New York, NY 10020

Portions of this novel appeared in altered form in the *New York Observer.*

First Scribner Paperback Fiction edition 1999
SCRIBNER PAPERBACK FICTION and design are trademarks of Jossey-Bass, Inc., used under license by Simon & Schuster, the publisher of this work.

DESIGNED BY ERICH HOBBING

Set in Granjon

Manufactured in the United States of America

1 3 5 7 9 10 8 6 4 2

The Library of Congress has cataloged the Scribner edition as follows:
Lemann, Nancy.
The fiery pantheon / Nancy Lemann.
p. cm.
I. Title.
PS3562.E4659F53 1998
813'.54—dc21 97-28222
CIP

ISBN 0-684-84114-2
0-684-85205-5 (Pbk)

For my mind is full of forlorn hopes,
death or glory charges, and last stands.

C. S. Lewis

PART ONE

Virginia

1

It was a rambling old place, a mountain resort, in Virginia. Grace had to admit it was a little boring there, but the old place was beautiful, and they had an orchestra at five for tea. "The pace is quickening," said Mrs. Stewart when a couple (of whom most were aged) stopped for tea. The place had huge empty drawing rooms and writing rooms, with old camellia paintings and chintz armchairs. Robert E. Lee would not have raised his sword against it. At dinner there was an orchestra and dancing. It was the kind of place where fathers danced with their little daughters on the dance floor. The children and their parents did a conga line. You had to get dressed up for dinner. No one could walk around the hotel after seven without a coat and tie—formerly tuxedos.

During the day the pace quickened whenever someone walked down the Great Hall of the hotel, which was rare. Despite the fact that General Lee would not have raised his sword against it, the place seemed Northern. There was no hint of the tropics, or of the Stewarts' customary Gulf Coast environs. It was American more than Southern, this genteel old Virginia; it could have been the Adirondacks. There was no hint of the blazing tropic sun. A view to the mountains and the white-painted wood of some columned mansions in green groves, seen from the rambling verandas and turrets and spires of the Virginia Hotel, showed the hills and valleys that were once the haunts of the Confederates. But the place was neutral now.

The big moment came every day at five at tea in the Great Hall with the orchestra. Several people turned up.

A young man lay strewn on a chair in the hall. His eccentric posture seemed inconsistent with the genteel tenor of the old hotel—also inconsistent with the form and function of a chair. He sported a rather unkempt and yet dashing appearance, and despite his attitude of enervation, there was a curious air of purpose in his eyes. He was dark, and you would have to call him handsome, but the striking thing in the young man was, again despite his apparent attitude of relaxation, a quiet tensed energy.

He coughed. It was a feeble cough. It was the cough of a man who is testing a cough, to see how it sounds, and who would cough more robustly if he felt that more people were around to hear it, whether to disturb them, horrify them, or revolt them—it would be hard to say. He actually did seem to be slightly feverish. And if you could have read his mind you would have found it filled with forlorn hopes, death or glory charges, and last stands; and on that battlefield—if of his own devising—he never flinched.

Grace looked over at him skeptically. She regarded him as a crazed individual. He went over to the bar and started swilling cocktails.

He was very tall and wore Bermuda shorts and made innuendos to young women, making him unpopular with some of them and popular with others.

Grace was one of the ones to whom he made innuendos. With her this had made him popular. But since at twenty-eight she considered herself to be a prehistoric fossil buried in an antiquated stratum of the earth's core, and he was a crazed young man of twenty-five, she didn't give him much thought. Other than perhaps to revel in his lecherous glances, which at her advanced and doom-laden age she found to be flattering.

He was an odd type to have been found at the staid Virginia Hotel. People came in families there. No one came alone. Except for the crazed young man, who drifted aimlessly yet purposefully around running into people he knew, or making acquaintances such as with the Stewarts, sometimes achieving the mode of a hilarious family vacation—he enrolled in the wine-tasting class, he went for nature walks, he could be seen doing knee bends at the nature trail wearing ill-fitting jogging shorts. Other times he would gulp down vodka tonics in a disturbed manner and make sardonic comments. Some strangulated human essence emanated from him.

Yet he cut a strangely dashing figure, with his rather long black hair, piercing blue eyes, and tall stature.

He had proven to be a vague acquaintance of the Stewarts. He was from New Orleans, as were they. No one knew exactly what he was doing at the Virginia Hotel; but he seemed to be hanging around sort of aimlessly, causing disturbances, or hoping to cause them, or at least hoping to encounter them. He was a stockbroker at Merrill Lynch, a strangely normal position for him to have held, Grace thought, since he looked as if he spent his time wreaking havoc whenever humanly possible throughout the world.

He became engrossed in conversation with a woman at the bar, gazing fervently into her eyes. Grace had to admit that his eyes were ardent and intelligent and kind.

Grace was a beautiful girl of twenty-eight who apparently had tried to make herself plain, but had not succeeded, for she had a certain dashing air herself. She had a quiet unpretension, noticeable in the curious effort she had made to make herself drab.

The effort had not effaced her beauty, but it was noticeable in her general lack of adornment that an effort to efface her beauty had been made. The young man in the hall had found this inexplicably enticing, though he could not have then said why.

But it was not for him that she had made this enticing failed attempt to be drab.

* * *

The Stewart family, consisting of a spectacular array of relatives including Grace and three brothers, their wives, and their children, were at the Virginia Hotel celebrating their parents' fortieth wedding anniversary, their father's seventieth birthday, and Grace's somewhat unstable engagement to be married. Grace's attitude toward her intended bridegroom seemed to be becoming rather iffy, or sort of volatile, or deeply troubled. But her mother was anxious to begin planning for a large and elaborate wedding. Worry was beginning to consume her on this point.

Worry was beginning to consume her on a lot of points. She trained a troubled gaze on the turbulent-looking young man in the hall. He seemed to provide a lot of fodder for worry. After studying him for signs of turmoil and disintegration, which were numerous, she resumed her study of the other guests. From a strategically positioned chair she had an excellent vantage point of people and events.

She noticed that the people at the next table were in some sort of crisis. A middle-aged man came down and said, "She's gone. Disappeared. No sign of her. Gone since last night," with great indignation to a family of very indifferent listeners. Apparently "she" referred to his teenaged daughter. The rest of the family seemed especially bored by the news. Then another man sat down.

"Any sign of her?"

"No. None. She's gone. Vanished."

Mrs. Stewart had not been able to determine whether the missing person ever returned, and was considering calling the police, until a laconic youth showed up and announced, "Parnell has gone to North Carolina."

The resolution of this crisis occupied hours of analysis in Mrs. Stewart's mind.

There was also a desk clerk with a thwarted chin who troubled her, and Frank the doorman seemed to be engulfed in depression. Many people at the hotel seemed to have drinking problems. Perhaps they should consider professional help. Then there was the crazed young man in the hall. He should consider therapy. Then there was her daughter. Her engagement seemed to be in crisis.

In short, as Mrs. Stewart darkly observed her family, the hotel, the guests, the staff, and the entire state of Virginia as if it were one vast psychiatric ward, she found that turmoil and disintegration were as usual predominating.

On the other hand, Mrs. Stewart was probably the only person in the world who could find the genteel Virginia Hotel to be ominous, hopeless, and menacing.

That was her well-trained vision of the world.

Mrs. Stewart had a post on the front porch of the hotel in a patch of sun from which she watched the guests arrive. They drove up in their cars and took out clothes on hangers from the trunk instead of suitcases and then huge bottles of whiskey. Gallon jugs of vodka.

Mrs. Stewart held dominion over a vast field of worry encompassing not only her family but hotel guests and staff. Vast waves of worry emanated from her at all times. She was worried about each and every one of the guests arriving in this manner, how much they were drinking, why, and where it would ultimately lead. Each one was in deep, deep trouble, in her opinion, and their families should consider institutionalizing them.

Mrs. Stewart had been trained as a psychologist. Because she was a psychologist, she seemed to feel that everyone was mentally ill and should be institutionalized.

That morning she had also procured a New York tabloid at the hotel which stated that the earth was on a collision course with a comet that was currently hurtling toward it angrily from outer space. Mrs. Stewart was perusing this with interest.

If the earth was going to explode, as long as it did so after Grace was safely married, Mrs. Stewart would not have cause to complain. Perhaps it would even be a suitable conclusion to everyone's problems.

A small group of elderly ladies from New Orleans appeared at her post on the porch. Mrs. Stewart knew them in passing. One of their husbands, Mr. Cosell, a man of matinee-idol handsomeness, often described his wife's habits.

"Florence didn't sleep well last night," he informed the ladies. This was greeted with a palpable lack of interest. Interest in Florence's habits did not generally run very high. Undeterred, he went on to describe her customary habits. Usually Florence slept late. Then he would get the groceries and fix lunch for Florence later.

"Where's Muriel?" said one of the ladies. "Have you seen Muriel? She's the one who's always complaining. I'm sort of nursing her along." The speaker was eighty if she was a day.

Mrs. Stewart asked Mr. Cosell how he liked retirement.

"Oh, it's wonderful. We do absolutely nothing and don't have time for anything else."

He kept talking about how they did absolutely nothing and yet it was incredibly hectic.

"Florence doesn't travel well," he confided.

Florence was disintegrating, it was very plain. At least it was very plain to Mrs. Stewart.

Mrs. Stewart's companionship was like being in a sanatorium dense with Viennese psychiatrists. As if her own family did not present a rich array of psychiatric ailments, and avenues of worry, she now had the hotel and all its occupants to diagnose.

She was also quite concerned about her daughters-in-law, who provided striking examples of insanity such as overdressing and being late for dinner, and about the doorman at the hotel, Frank, a singularly gloomy individual, who seemed to be in a clinical depression.

That morning Frank the doorman had spoken to her for the first time. He spoke to tell her that it was Armistice Day and that he had almost been blown to bits in the Pacific by the atom bomb. His message thus delivered, he fell back into his customary furious silence.

Mrs. Stewart continued to gain insight into her fellowmen. As far as she could tell, one characteristic was shared by all. They were disintegrating before her very eyes.

Her extensive training was going to come in very handy.

At this point, the crazed young man walked past with a cigarette hanging out of his mouth. Periodic sightings were made by Mrs. Stewart of his unlikely and unwholesome apparition.

"This Walter person seems to be sinking into a tar pit of rage and depression," observed Mrs. Stewart with dark interest.

"I don't know if I would call it a tar pit," said Grace.

"He emanates anguish," said Mrs. Stewart.

"I think he has a cold," said Grace.

"Grace, he's *somatizing,*" said Mrs. Stewart.

"Who?"

"This Walter character," said Mrs. Stewart, referring to the crazed young man in the hall. "He's *sublimating.*"

"Well, what's he sublimating?"

"That's what I'm trying to find out, Grace," said Mrs. Stewart. "I haven't *probed* it yet. He seems *darkly hopeless.* It's as if he's *extinguishing* himself."

"He is? What? Walter? I think he's O.K."

"No, Grace darling, he's not *O.K.* I don't think he's had an *O.K.* day in his whole life. I don't think he'd know *O.K.* if it hit him over the head. I don't think he's ever experienced *O.K.* There's an intense *hopelessness* about him. He's *tremendously* pathetic. He's—"

"O.K. O.K., I get it."

"He looks as if the life is being *drained* out of him."

"I don't know, Mother. He looks pretty lively to me."

The apparition of Walter was actually nothing more nor less of course than grist for Mrs. Stewart's mill. "I regard him as a madman," she said happily to Grace.

The matriarch of a vast and spectacular array of relatives, Mrs. Stewart thrived on crisis. She had been ecstatic at her last Thanksgiving dinner because every single person at her table was in a huge life upheaval. Her nephew was getting divorced, her daughter was engaged to be married, her niece was pregnant with twins, her brother-in-law was remarrying, and her other brother-in-law's marriage was disintegrating.

Mrs. Stewart was constantly on the lookout for disintegration. Humanity provided ample candidates. Grace and her brothers and their wives and children composed a frayed domestic panorama on the battlefield of the matriarch's psychiatric analyses of doom.

Her brothers-in-law were a particular source of material to Mrs. Stewart. Mr. Stewart's brothers were Good Old Boys. They were always out hunting and fishing—or "killing," as Mrs. Stewart called it, and going to sumptuous New Orleans parties. The world was warm with liquor. They came home ecstatic after hunting trips—"because they've been killing things," as Mrs. Stewart put it—or from parties. "If the Civil War had been fought with parties, the South would have won," said Mrs. Stewart.

Mr. Stewart, though himself very circumspect, had a soft spot for the black sheep of the family. Cousin Malcolm was his favorite. When he was a boy, his father would say, Why do you want to go to Cousin Malcolm's house, he's the black sheep of the family. Exactly. He's the most interesting one, Mr. Stewart would reply. Grace felt the same way about it. As a kid growing up, her aunts and uncles were the most exciting—they smoked and drank all day and wore housecoats and bathrobes and got in towering arguments and called each other kiddo. They got diseases but they still had joie de vivre and drank three gigantic martinis every night. Grace always preferred the cousin who was constantly getting into trouble, going missing for days at a time, with drunk guys calling her up. For some reason Grace felt a deep bond with her, even though Grace was as sober and studious as her father before her. The wild hold a fascination for the sober.

Thus Mr. Stewart, the patriarch, was a man of serene and in fact oblivious calm, in striking contrast to his wife.

But even he was not excluded from her dark envisionings. The only person who was not disintegrating, so far as she knew, was Grace's intended bridegroom, Monroe. She was crazy about Monroe. In fact she had just gotten the harebrained idea into her head that Monroe could serve as a role model for Walter, the crazed young man in the hall, whom she had secretly conceived the burden of reforming.

❧

Tea had drawn on to cocktails. The pace was quickening, as Mrs. Stewart noted. The field was full for study.

A little boy sauntered up to Grace and Mrs. Stewart on the porch. He was wearing a coat and tie. Grace asked him his name. It was George. She asked where he was from.

He screwed up his face in a torture of thought—an agony of contemplation, thinking, trying, searching. Minutes passed. Naturally she was going to tell him it was O.K., he didn't have to know where he was from. But finally he came up with it.

"Rye."

"Rye, New York. How old are you?" she asked.

"Five." He contemplated. He squinted off into the distance, pondering his (limited) knowledge. "I used to be four."

Noting George's little coat and tie, she commented, "You had to get dressed up?"

"Yes, but I can make my tie go like this," he said, pulling one end of it until it choked itself into a strangled knot at his neck, disrupting his collar and face into a horrible contortion.

Their friendship thus cemented after this formal exhibition of trust, George suddenly raced off into the wild blue yonder.

❧

After dinner George raced back over in his little coat and tie. Mrs. Stewart noted George had the manner of a little New York boy. When you asked him a question he clutched his head, he gesticulated wildly, he struggled, he searched for knowledge. As Mrs. Stewart pointed out, he was sarcastic and dark and world-weary. He was world-weary, at five. He had a raspy voice and seemed very sophisticated, if not very knowledgeable, since knowledge tended to elude him.

Grace asked him how old his brother was. He screwed his face up into the questioning glare, which it was accustomed to mount when searching for the answers. "Five, six, seven . . ." he posited, searching, wondering.

"He looks like he could be eleven or twelve," said Grace.

"Eleven, twelve, maybe ten . . ." wondering, searching.

"Maybe he's nine or ten," suggested Grace.

Finally the elaborate shrug of absolute lack of information.

"I hate my brother because he pushed me against the car door and I had to get stitches," he said wrathfully. (This had apparently happened on the drive from New York to Virginia.)

His knowledge was very limited but his demeanor was very sophisticated and world-weary in his little coat and tie. A little New York boy.

"What school do you go to?" Grace asked.

"Midland," he said with infinite world-weariness. "It's in Rye," he knew after coming up with that earlier.

He said he was leaving tomorrow but Grace did not put his word as very reliable because he was very mixed up. He said he was going to his grandmother's in Narragansett. He definitely knew his grandmother's was in Narragansett. Grace asked him what he was going to do there.

The massive, world-weary shrug. Grace guessed that part of the little boy's quaintness was the energy he put into the massive world-weary shrug.

A small but volatile orchestra composed of melancholy Hungarians played fox-trots. There were potted palms, cane chairs, and forty-five-foot ceilings. Massive colonnades of white columns with Corinthian capitals and elaborate architraves. The place was very spruce.

It had served as military headquarters for the Confederacy during the War, and Lee had composed the Surrender there. Some columned mansions in green groves could be seen from the back porch. These groves were once the haunts of the defeated. Now they were the golf resorts of the triumphant. Grace noted men in tuxedos wandering around with their cigars, but they didn't seem doomed. Her mother seemed to think the place was doomed. But doomed Southerners were not to be found. Unless maybe you counted this Walter character.

It was customary to sit in the Great Hall or at the edge of the dance floor after dinner for an hour. George was seen straggling along behind his mother in the Great Hall on his way upstairs to bed. Grace noted that his mother admired a dress in the shop window on the way through the hall, asking her husband, "Do you think this would be good for the White House?" And George, in reeling off the names of his brothers and father, kept repeating the middle name of Delano, so it was speculated that maybe they were a political family or related to someone in office.

This was discussed and analyzed from all angles by Mrs. Stewart during after-dinner drinks.

* * *

"And we're on a direct collision course," Grace heard her mother saying.

The comet, someone's marriage, someone's drinking, politics, or what potential crisis?

"Well, when is this going to happen?" asked Grace. But Mrs. Stewart was already light-years ahead of her.

"I don't want to use the word Mafia, Grace—" she heard her mother saying.

"But you're using it, Mother dear. Mafia."

"Grace, you're tuning out," said Mrs. Stewart. "Every time I'm talking to you I can tell you're in another world."

"I'm not tuning out," said Grace. "I heard every word." This was not quite true. But it had something to do with the gardener. Mrs. Stewart was now getting her information from the doorman, Frank.

Mrs. Stewart looked at her daughter closely. "Grace, you just don't have enough clothes," said Mrs. Stewart tragically. "You dress as if you're trying to *erase* yourself," she added.

Here she hit a nerve. Grace had always tried to be drab. She felt that she didn't have enough room in her brain or time in her life to spotlight her physical appearance. Less penetrating souls than Walter, the crazed young man in the hall, would not perceive the stalwart effort that had gone into her self-effacement.

However, the truth was also that her old flames lay in demented heaps throughout the world, despite her attempts to be drab. The truth was that she would have batted her eyelashes at anything in shoe leather, although for some reason her attitude to Walter was strangely disinterested. The truth was also that she was a crazed young person herself, and one facet of crazed young people is that they are very self-lacerating. In this she was very keen.

"Grace, do you think this Walter character is happy?" asked Mrs. Stewart, sighing deeply. Grace thought it over.

"I think he's in deep, deep trouble," said Mrs. Stewart, answering her own question.

"But, Mother, you do have a tendency to exaggerate."

"I'm afraid this Walter character is going to have to be institutionalized before all this is over," said Mrs. Stewart.

"We can't all be institutionalized, Mother."

Walter perambulated into view.

"I am haunted by Walter's wraithlike appearance," said Mrs. Stewart.

"He's just a kid," said Grace.

"Why is he hanging around here? I wonder."

"He's finding himself," suggested Grace. "He seems to be some sort of a hypochondriac," she commented.

"And what about you, Grace? What about Monroe? Is it on or is it off?" said Mrs. Stewart.

"Of course it's on," said Grace.

"Are you sure?"

"Of course I'm sure."

"And is he coming here?"

"Of course he's coming here. He's coming here tomorrow night. You know that."

Mrs. Stewart again sighed deeply. "Promise me you'll wear lipstick," said Mrs. Stewart and gave her daughter a penetrating, tragic stare.

"O.K. O.K.," said Grace. They were dancing an old dance.

"I saw Monroe's mother at the beauty parlor before we left, you know," said Mrs. Stewart to her daughter. She stopped dramatically. "Some suspect it isn't the only beauty parlor she goes to," said Mrs. Stewart fiercely.

"She's committing the tragic sin of going to two different beauty parlors," said Grace.

"Grace, every night I lie in bed repeating over and over to myself, 'It's none of my business. It's none of my business.'"

"Yes?"

"You're marrying one of the Colliers. And I think some of the Colliers are in deep, deep trouble."

"But they're not the ones I'm marrying."

"And I don't think there is a cure for what Claude Collier has."

"You don't have to be Fellini to figure that out," contributed Walter, who had walked up and hurled himself dramatically into a chair.

"But I'm not marrying Claude. I'm marrying Monroe," said Grace.

Walter interpreted this remark as an opening to change the conversation to a more suitable topic: himself.

This was a wide-ranging topic encompassing vast avenues of problems that could not be evaluated in a brief time period. He started raving about his problems, and what to do with his life, making Grace very glad that she was not twenty-five anymore. Young people are very vague and they are constantly in a frenzy about their problems and what to do with their lives.

Although she was only three years older than Walter, she regarded him as a crazed young person and herself as a world-weary matronly figure.

But that's the great thing about young people, she reflected from the vast pinnacle of her doom-laden twenty-eight years. You ask them what they want to do or are interested in and they ramble on about their problems, and hopes and dreams, and you can't understand a single word of what they say.

He was wearing Bermuda shorts although it was quite cold, dark sunglasses, and a faded madras jacket that looked like it was about a hundred years old. He continually sported an overly informal and eccentric appearance at odds with the genteel tenor of the old hotel.

He never sat in a chair like a normal person. He was always strewn across a chair, as if he had just been deposited there by a tornado.

His rueful gaze lurked somehow menacingly among the populace, and came to rest on Grace. He was like The Man Who Came to Dinner, and then never left, as he had attached himself inexplicably to the old hotel and various guests, notably the Stewarts. They did not know how long he had been there. He could have been born there, for all they knew. He lay supine and gazed at Grace lecherously.

Then he revealed that a "channel of fire" was trapped within his chest. Grace deduced from this that he had caught a cold.

"Well, if you have a pillar of flame in your chest then maybe you ought to go up to bed," suggested Grace.

"It's not a pillar of flame. It's a channel of fire," said Walter.

"Oh. Sorry. Right. A channel of fire."

Then he rambled on about his problems, should he get an apartment in Milan, should he leave Merrill Lynch, should he go to law school. He wanted to quit his job, go to Australia, kill himself—he wasn't sure which.

Despite the fact that a disproportionate share of the Hot Springs pharmacy over-the-counter drugs were waging war with his ailment, it had not abated.

He had grown a goatee. It looked ridiculous. But that's young people for you, thought Grace. They're always in a frenzy about what to do with their lives, or growing a goatee, or struggling, searching for the answers.

Somehow extracting himself from the unique horizontal position he was able to attain in a chair, he looked around tragically, sighed, said good night, and walked off.

Mr. Stewart, an uncommonly dapper white-haired man in an uncommonly old blue suit, shook his head with bemusement. The matriarch was no longer able to restrain herself.

"Grace, his world is *collapsing,*" said Mrs. Stewart, in a stage whisper.

"What's that?"

"This Walter character. His world is collapsing."

"I don't know if I would take it that seriously, Mother."

"Well, you heard him, Grace. You heard how he talks. He's disintegrating before our very eyes!"

Mr. Stewart had been listening to the conversation bemusedly all evening, smoking his cigars. He gently took it as the foible of his wife to look into the dark side of a question, and it seemed to even comfort him somehow, that someone would. There was a dream of honor in his head, of probity and decorum, at odds with his wife's dark envisionings. But he heard her dark envisionings with some amusement. It was as if his wife was forever poised on the precipice of disaster. No real disaster had as yet occurred. But perhaps it would.

His wife had looked at him throughout the years with a clear-eyed gaze, not idolizing him as some others did, and he appreciated it; she knew his own foibles, such as they might be. There was, he suspected, a certain final truth in even her dark vision.

Mr. and Mrs. Stewart's arrival in Virginia, at the appointed hotel, had been made in a dramatic panorama of illness, Mrs. Stewart arriving in a wheelchair due to an onset of rheumatism, but dressed to the nines in pearls and furs. They were immediately swept into a whirlpool of solicitude. They made an appearance of helpless frailty combined with dapper formality that created a certain stir of decorum. They were anachronisms.

Mrs. Stewart had a different pair of gloves for every color in her wardrobe. Her canes were of fine mahogany. Usually she was dressed to the nines in pearls and furs and gloves. She made a picture with her husband, dapper as ever in his crisp blue-and-white-striped shirt, white bucks, gray suit, and his grandfather's watch chain and black ribbon, Mrs. Stewart frail but indomitable.

Every year Mr. Stewart took his many relatives on a hilarious family vacation. On these occasions his daughter, his great-aunt, his sons, their wives and children composed the vast domestic panorama on the battlefield of his wife's psychiatric analyses of doom. Mr. Stewart was accustomed to traveling abroad. But what with the many members of his family—aged relatives, retainers, invalids, dogs, grandchildren, sons and daughters-in-law, and his wife's decaying health—he had had to lately abandon that and stick to America.

For the hilarious family vacation of the previous year, they had gone to Florida, on the suggestion of some of the children. It was not a raging success. Mr. Stewart kept asking his wife if she had ever seen anyone wear a necktie in Florida. Decorum was the rule of his life.

Mrs. Stewart, following her natural search for pathology, found Florida ominous, threatening, and menacing. It would be a cruel torture to have to live in Florida. Everything was ominous and pathological in Florida. People were constantly plotting coups and overthrows of Latin American dictators, and she kept pointing out houses of drug dealers. But Mrs. Stewart of course saw the dark side of things. To Grace, for example, Florida was a green frivolous place, warm and beautiful. To her mother it was ominous, hopeless, and menacing.

Mr. Stewart was obsessed with whether or not there were sidewalks (there were not always sidewalks in Florida), why no one was wearing a necktie, dendrology (an interest he shared with his old friend in New Orleans, St. Louis Collier), and was ultimately transported to ecstasy at the tropical garden due to his love for trees. He saw a baobab tree at the tropical garden, which he said was a tree he had never seen before in his entire life and had always searched for.

Returning to Miami on the last night of the hilarious vacation before flying back to New Orleans, they went to dinner at a stylish French bistro in Coconut Grove. Mr. Stewart was much impressed.

"There's nothing like this in Miami," he said.

"Where do you think we are?" said his wife.

"We're in the Coconuts," he happily replied.

Later the restaurant became very crowded and Mr. Stewart complained of the din.

"It's gaiety," said his wife.

"One man's gaiety is another man's noise," said Mr. Stewart. Traveling with Mr. Stewart in America was like watching a man take the first flight to Mars.

There had also been a recent trip to California. This to Mr. Stewart was even more like Mars. But strangely enough, he liked it better than Florida. He had spent the first sixty years of his life vowing never to go to California, and yet after he had been forced to go there, he now wanted to see more of California than anyone ever had.

But Virginia was judged to be more of a success than either Florida or California, as the hotel was stiffly formal, everyone wore a necktie, and the place reminded him of Baden-Baden and the Black Forest in Germany; also the lake reminded him of Como, glimpsed in its refreshing beauty from the green curving road to the hotel.

The Stewarts were staying at the hotel for one week. Their party came up from New Orleans except for Grace, who came down from New York, her current place of residence. Apparently this Walter character lived in New York too.

It was a chilly early spring. The month was April. In New Orleans it would be hot. In Miami it would be sweltering. In Virginia, fires still had to be built in the hearth. Palm trees were not to be found.

Grace had a mania to compare everything with the tropics, for they comprised her point of origin. To her, Virginia was a somewhat bland and neutral place. Though Southern it was not the South she knew, of palm trees, hurricanes, and torrid heat. It was not the beleaguered bemusing hopeless South she knew. She was obsessed with New Orleans. Virginia was below the Mason-Dixon line and Robert E. Lee would not have raised his sword against it, but it lacked palm trees and a dilapidated air of hopelessness. It lacked a green boulevard, high dormer windows in the night, the old architecture crumbling in the overgrowth of her hometown, the place where she had spent more than half her life. There was this sense of hopelessness about the tropics which bemused her—perhaps she could afford to be bemused since she didn't live there now. The tropics induce mood swings—one minute you are in ecstasy that the temperature is eighty degrees and there are palm trees and that bemusing hopelessness—but of course the next minute the hopelessness has gotten to you, or it is overcast and depressing, or gets too hot to do anything, and you get a bad mood swing in the opposite direction. You turn a corner and suddenly you want to jump out of your skin, the weather changes and suddenly you are demented. But it was the tropics that claimed her heart. She loved them, they quickened her blood and rested her heart.

"Every man carries within him a world which is composed of all that he has seen and loved, and to which he constantly returns, even when he is traveling through, and seems to be living in, some different world."

As happened every morning in the inevitable march of human events, Walter walked past with a cigarette hanging out of his mouth and the goatee looking none too dainty.

"Grace, he's filled with *rage,*" said Mrs. Stewart.

"Who? Walter? He is? Well, what is he enraged about?"

"I don't know yet, Grace. That's what I'm trying to find out. Don't you see he's constantly *running away* from everything? He's a *lightning rod* for the emotionally downtrodden!"

"Well, where does that put us?" said Grace. "I mean, we're the ones he's drawn to."

"We've gone normal," said Mr. Stewart.

It was his way to kid his wife.

She cast him an angst-ridden glance.

"If you ever want to put me in a home," said Mrs. Stewart to her daughter, "just do it. Just put me in."

"You always talk like you're about to keel over, Mother dear," said Grace.

"I give you my permission to institutionalize me, Grace."

"Now, now."

"I may have to be institutionalized before all this is over."

"Before all what is over?"

"For one thing, Walter's complete and total disintegration. You hear how he talks, Grace. At least one of us should probably be institutionalized."

Walter was raving about his crises again. The main problem seemed to be centered on the question of where to stay in Milan. Apparently he went to Milan a lot on business. Usually he went to Milan with his boss and stayed at grand hotels. He no longer wanted to stay at grand hotels, for some reason. Maybe he wanted to stay at seedy hotels. But you couldn't really make sense of the problem, which focused on the apartment in Milan, maybe something to do with a girlfriend in

Italy, though he tried to deny that the girlfriend was serious, and then he tried to deny the reality of her human existence. Also, it had something to do with sky diving in New Zealand.

"He's very vague," admitted Mr. Stewart.

No doubt that is a huge trait of crazed young people. The world is still vague to them.

"You might have noticed that I wasn't here yesterday," said Frank, the clinically depressed doorman, in a rare moment of loquaciousness. He had taken to reporting to Mrs. Stewart every morning at her post on the porch with news of the day's doom-laden events. "I was attending services for a guest who plummeted from the fourteenth floor."

He gazed at them darkly.

And yet he was supposed to be the "greeter" for the hotel. He was supposed to be hilarious.

Frank seemed inexorably drawn to Mrs. Stewart.

"I'm an alcoholic," he said. "I only drink on the weekends, but don't kid yourself. I'm an alcoholic. Last week I blacked out for four days. Didn't remember a thing."

After delivering himself of this hilarious admission he again fell ominously silent, as was his wont. It seemed ironic that he should choose Mrs. Stewart, a trained psychologist, of all people, to confide in. Perhaps he sensed her prowess.

Mrs. Stewart found this very gratifying. She would perform some therapy on him. She was longing to perform therapy on Walter, who was "darkly hopeless."

The conversation reverted to Monroe.

"Are you happy, Grace?" asked Mrs. Stewart. "Are you *thrilled*?" she said fiercely. "Are you *sure* you want to spend the rest of your *life* with him? Is *he* sure?"

"You're prosecuting again, Mother."

"Just answer the question, Miss Stewart," said Walter, who had hurled himself into a nearby chair.

"Just don't *wound* him, Grace," said Mrs. Stewart thoughtfully.

"I'm not going to *wound* him, Mother," said Grace. "Why would I *wound* him?"

"Grace, I happen to know that you would bat your eyelashes at almost anything in shoe leather."

It is true that she would have batted her eyelashes at almost anything in shoe leather. But then, it wouldn't even have to be in shoe leather. She would bat her eyelashes at a friend, a relative, a building. She would have batted her eyelashes at a dog. This is the pathos of the incorrigible flirt.

The incorrigible flirt is not necessarily a woman who wears a certain kind of clothing. It is not necessarily a frivolous soul. It is not necessarily someone who cares about clothes and the surface impression. It is someone who would bat her eyelashes at the Tower of London, the Thames, the Pyramids—yes, hoping for a response.

Grace strolled to the lake. It reminded her of Switzerland. She had a mania to recall different places in the world and how they resembled one another. So the hotel reminded her of Switzerland, being on what seemed a green Germanic lake with boaters and Bavarian cupolas among the firs, cool and green and foreign.

Things were a little worse off with her engagement than her family knew. She strolled somewhat tragically around the lake. She had a mania to think she was a failed and tragic figure. She had a lot of manias, some no doubt related to her mother's ceaseless plea for turmoil and disintegration. She felt that she was sinking into a quagmire of crisis and decay. But she would not confide these tortured ideologies to her mother, only to fulfill her mother's vision.

She felt a nameless anxiety. It was not too hard to search for its name, however. For the sake of her engagement she had given up her job in New York to go on an extended trip to celebrate the engagement; she had given up her apartment in New York in view of then returning to New Orleans to plan the elaborate wedding with her mother and make arrangements to realize her dream of living the rest of her life there. It was her ideal but not perhaps her destiny. It was like jumping off the high dive and realizing midway down that the pool had been drained.

But she had an ideal of Monroe. She had an ideal of decency and decorum and the honorable estate. She wanted to conclude and fulfill all obligations she had undertaken. She had a sort of ideal of Southern Living, which Monroe represented. She had a nostalgia for a life that she had never led. That life was to be married and reside in New Orleans and watch football games with people wearing pink and yellow sweaters and green golfing slacks and on weekends revel in the bemusing hopelessness of Florida.

She glimpsed this life sometimes when returning to New Orleans. It was a life you could not lead in New York. It was too genteel for New York. It may have included certain moments of oppression, but that is the price you pay for gentility.

But she had seen another life, and it was only that other life, genteel and bemusing, that enabled her to live the one she led in the vast metropolis.

Then there was nostalgia in reverse, for escape. Venice, Istanbul, North Africa. Palermo, Cairo, Tunis. A cathedral in the Adriatic lagoon which showed the green of Paradise, the legions of the blessed, and the angels unfurling the starry sky of night to the end of time.

Grace completed her tragic stroll and came back up to the lobby. Mrs. Stewart cast her a darkening gaze.

The orchestra played fox-trots. The children danced with their fathers. Fires burned in the hearths. This was a false front, however. Mrs. Stewart detected darker things beneath the surface, not the least of which was the decline of Florence and Walter's ever-imminent disintegration.

The piercing strength of her vision was made the more impressive when contrasted to the weakness of her own position. At sixty-seven she was plagued with arthritis, rheumatism, and osteoporosis. These she bore with considerable bravery and a certain gallantry; being fierce and indomitable, she refused to give up; but it is well known that the subjects of physical pain may become irritable, crusty, and intolerant. The very fierceness of her personality increased in proportion to her pain, as indeed she fought her pain with her very fierceness. From a wheelchair she looked out on a decaying and disturbing world.

But it was not that as her illness increased, she was proportionately inclined to chronicle the disintegration of others. She had been just so inclined in her youth, and this steadfast personality far overwhelmed her physical frailties.

"I'm looking forward to seeing Monroe," said Mrs. Stewart. "He's so dear. So healthy. So *normal.*"

As if in contrast, Walter lurched in with his hair sticking straight up as if he had just been electrocuted. His entrance was greeted with stunned silence. He retired to the men's room and restored his hair to a somewhat normal appearance. He kept wearing Bermuda shorts despite the dress code and no matter what the temperature, wishful thinking since it was a chilly early spring. Then he hurled himself into a chair and instigated a lengthy discussion about his problems.

Cocktails drew on to dinner. Walter lagged behind.

"Aren't you eating?" asked Grace.

"Well, no, usually I don't eat after 1 P.M. because of my personal problems," he came out with.

"Personal problems?" she inquired.

But he lurched off into the night. The next morning she noticed he was more cheerful, and joined the nature group, who admired woodpeckers in the park.

An ever-present orchestra played fox-trots. The orchestra consisted of a number that reached seventeen members at its most robust and sometimes dwindled down to five. On breaks they rambled up and down the halls smoking European cigarettes or got into explosive arguments. They had outmoded monocles and cigarette holders and wore decrepit-looking white tie and tails.

The program started out with melancholy Balkan waltzes. A straggling crew of children and their parents attempted a conga line, but the music struck a note of Serbo-Croatian hopelessness similar to that of the doorman, Frank. Perhaps a certain lugubrious gaiety could be said to have prevailed, but that might be stretching it.

Mrs. Stewart felt that they needed therapy. She was hoping to administer it soon. Perhaps noting the lack of enthusiasm it was generating, the orchestra switched back suddenly to the fox-trot. The orchestra seemed to be having an identity crisis. It would fluctuate between a sort of Austro-Hungarian-European flavor and then, as if noting the lack of response, a Virginia reel.

Grace and Mrs. Stewart sat on the porch observing the scene. Beyond the Virginia Hotel was an uncrowded green road along the lake, which was masterful and majestic and moody. There were nearby inns and restaurants that were very old and very empty and some in ruins from another time, a gayer time, like the 1920s.

Occasionally an old bridge loomed across the river. There were lookouts to vast valleys and green mountains. The sprawling old hotel was on the green Germanic lake, with vast porches and deserted colonnades.

"Maybe he's happy. Maybe he's bored," said Mrs. Stewart.

"Who are you worrying about now, Mother?" said Grace.

"I'm worried about this Walter character, of course."

"It's fruitless to worry about him, Mother."

"Yes, but he seems to be sick."

"I told you, he's a hypochondriac."

"He says that a column of fire is trapped inside his chest."

"It's not a column of fire. It's a channel of flame," said Grace. She stopped herself. What was she saying?

"It's not good for him to just lounge around all the time, Grace. I mean he's always just lounging around."

"If I were you, I'd worry about somebody else."

This was not too difficult.

The group of elderly ladies from New Orleans was sitting nearby. Muriel was being needlessly provocative, Florence was dozing in the corner, and Mr. Cosell had taken to incessantly videotaping the scenery for his children. The scenery consisted of Florence. His svelte elegant form could be seen around the hotel incessantly videotaping Florence in varying attitudes of repose.

"It must be wonderful to be so obsessed with your spouse," said Grace.

"I sense tension," countered Mrs. Stewart.

"But really now, it would be hard to be tense while you're asleep." Which is how Florence spent most of her time.

Mrs. Stewart was already light-years ahead of her, however, worrying about someone else.

The very concept of worry, dark and constant, that dominated her mother's character was passed on to Grace in some way or other. Grace felt that there was actually much more than a grain of truth at the base of her mother's remarks, but that it would be too gauche to seem to publicly agree.

3

The Stewarts were now on their way to the neighboring resort in White Sulphur Springs for lunch.

Walter was in the backseat complaining. He seemed to have been adopted in the family as a disturbed young person of some sort. This presented to Mrs. Stewart many startling diagnostic possibilities.

Being on vacation she was surrounded to a greater degree than usual by pathological inactivity. Everyone she encountered seemed to be a drifter. The transition from drifter to criminal could be virtually instantaneous.

She kept pointing out people on the road who looked aimless. Aimless, drifting, without purpose. Grace pointed out that they were vacationing, they were supposed to be aimless. Mrs. Stewart insisted that they were indolent. She cast a significant glance at Walter.

"What is it exactly that you do, Walter?" asked Mrs. Stewart as Walter hurled himself into a rocking chair at the neighboring resort. It too was a storied former haunt of the Confederates in Virginia.

Hurling yourself into a rocking chair is no simple matter. It's not like hurling yourself into an armchair. An armchair stays still when you hurl yourself into it. A rocking chair, by contrast, catapults you back out of it if you hurl yourself into it. So then he paced around.

"What do I do? I lounge. I look at woodpeckers."

Mrs. Stewart looked at him despairingly. She was a puritan surrounded by drifters. Perhaps group therapy could be arranged.

He was wearing a neck brace. Apparently he was the victim of crippling back pain. But not crippling enough to prevent hurling himself into rocking chairs.

As a cautionary tale Mrs. Stewart told her audience about an actress who wrote a book about how she pulled her life together and lost a hundred pounds and then her whole life fell apart again when the book came out and she had to be institutionalized.

"You're tuning out, Grace," said Mrs. Stewart.

"No, I'm not, Mother. I heard every word. But really now, she couldn't kill herself twice."

"What, Grace?"

"You said she hung herself on the day of her father's second wedding and then you said her father shot her on the stairs."

"Now, Grace, this proves my point. You've been tuning out. I can hear it in your voice. I can hear it in your silences. You're a thousand miles away."

"Don't try to understand it, Grace," said Walter. "It's one of those things you can't keep up with. It's like the war in Afghanistan. I don't keep up with it."

"Well, it's over, Walter," said Mrs. Stewart.

"What?"

"The war in Afghanistan. It's over. It ended twenty years ago."

The thing about Grace's mother that rent her daughter's heart was her combination of being fierce yet frail.

"Tell me your life story, Mother," said Grace. "After all we're traveling on a long trip together. Now is the time."

"My life story is this," said Mrs. Stewart fiercely. "I wanted to study philosophy. I wanted to know: What's life for? I wanted to know the answers. I wanted to know what it all meant. So I took philosophy in college. But philosophy didn't provide the answers. It was all sort of rhetorical. For example Spinoza's concept of free will . . ." And the next thing Grace knew, her fierce yet frail mother, dressed as ever to the nines, a study in infirmities at sixty-seven, was talking incessantly about Spinoza. Now that was something you would not find in many Southern matrons, and it rent Grace's heart.

A harried motherly solicitude had crystallized over the years into a fierce consuming sense of trouble. At one time Mrs. Stewart had been almost vague and gay and solicitous and mild. But she had had three sons and a daughter and spent many years tending to their care, nattering on about the boys, sewing name tapes in their shorts, taking them to the store, where they writhed in agony while she made them try on clothes. Thirty years passed, and she yearned back to her days at Radcliffe, and her style became more fierce and elegant. She saw her children married, producing grandchildren, but among the weddings of her sons it had never of course been her place, until now, with her daughter, Grace, to be at the helm of the thing, the general of the campaign.

Fierce discussions of the wedding occupied many hours of their time.

Cheese straws, napkin rings, corsages, were discussed as if they were the tragic subjects of World War II summit conferences.

"Grace, how can you take this so lightly?"

"I don't take it lightly, Mother," said Grace.

"Grace, I am talking about the rental of an infinite number of the most exquisite cocktail napkins a person could possibly conceive of!" said Mrs. Stewart.

One minute Spinoza, the next, cheese straws.

"But I do have other things to think of, Mother. Such as Monroe, the person. The man. Things like where is he."

"Don't worry about a thing, kid," said Mr. Stewart, magnificent, suave, tossing aside his newspaper.

"If there's one person we don't need to worry about, it's Monroe," said Mrs. Stewart confidently.

Despite her worries, however dire, Grace felt the period of engagement was a fond one after all. Marriage would satisfy abstract concepts of Duty and Obligation. She would set her star to a course of Decency and Decorum. The engagement was a period of hope. She was ready to take on the mantle of responsibility, walk under the tree of heaven, and join the honorable estate.

Walter's view of marriage, which he volunteered, differed rather drastically.

"It's like being chained together like two mad dogs," said Walter.

4

Grace returned to her room to restore order out of the chaos engendered by Walter as well as by the world at large.

She incessantly cleaned her room, even though it was a hotel room. When the maid came, she should know that the occupant of this room, at least, was not a hellish laggard sinking into chaos and torpor with her personal effects flung heedlessly at random, which characterized all other hotel guests all over the world. Not to say which traumatized the maids of hotel rooms all over the world. The hotel maids would not be able to experience any disgust on her account. She frequently pondered the disgust which the hotel maids must encounter on everyone else's account. Grace would not contribute to their revolting burdens left by heedless inmates.

She stopped to pick up an infinitesimal speck of dust on the floor, and make sure that all drawers in the bureaus were closed, as otherwise they would drive her crazy.

A desperate compulsion for order characterized her as much as did a compulsion to make herself drab. Her hotel room would present as neat and modest an appearance as herself. She would present a plain and unobtrusive appearance through which the attributes of her soul must show unvarnished.

She insisted on wearing a barrage of shapeless layers of clothing successfully concealing her perfectly voluptuous form (which should not be shown disgustingly on display). At night she wore long underwear, a camisole, a nightgown, another nightgown over the first nightgown, and socks, and did not think that this was anything strange. It was a matter of honor to her that she should present an unobtrusive and drab appearance at all times. Yet in New Orleans she had grown up to be the belle of the ball, despite her attempts to be drab. She was curiously unconscious of her appeal, and found anyone who would cast her a lecherous glance to be virtually insane and deeply surprising, since she was so very drab. But this sent them reeling in confused admiration and landed them in demented heaps around the world.

She pulled on the variegated layers of clothing which comprised her boudoir attire and lay down to take a nap. She heard a whirring noise. It started to drive her crazy. She decided not to take a nap. Naps were for the weak and the lame and the enervated. She had better things to do.

She decided to take another tragic stroll around the lake. Except it wasn't that tragic. The stroll, the lake, herself—none were really that tragic on this occasion. She batted her eyelashes briefly at the lake, succumbing to its beauty. It is true that she would have batted her eyelashes at the Blue Ridge Mountains, or Park Avenue on a snowy night; she would flirt with a city, she would flirt with a concept, a dream; she would have batted her eyelashes at honor itself. It was true that her engagement did not prevent her from batting her eyelashes at the entire state of Virginia. It had nothing to do with her feelings for the intended bridegroom. She would have batted her eyelashes at a dog. The only thing she would not have batted her eyelashes at was Walter. Returning to the lobby, she was able to find other avenues of flirting than he, and batted her eyelashes at the orchestra, composed as it was of fascinating tortured Europeans.

"Sweetheart!" screamed a man to the waitress at the next table, drowning out the orchestra at tea. Grace looked at him curiously. It was the father of little George, the little New York boy. But the man was plainly Southern or else he never would have screamed out *sweetheart* in that cheerful, harmless way. Grace had it figured that it must be his wife who was from New York, and who had the political connections, and possible aspirations to the White House.

George had an illustrious name. George Delano Ladd. His mother seemed rather frosty but his father was a nutty character. His vocabulary was sort of quaint—he used old-time words, sort of a mixture of Southern and 1920s:

notions (the store sells notions)
motor car
moving picture
silver dime

He had a tendency to burst into song, old-time songs like "Fly Me to the Moon." When he wanted the waitress he screamed *"sweetheart!"* in a mad explosion.

Also he played solitaire. A lot of times he would just crash down in one of the chintz armchairs in the hall, scream for the waitress *"sweetheart!"* and then start playing solitaire.

Walter again perambulated into view. Shambled might be a more accurate description of his mode of transport. He presented his customary aspect of crazed youth, ill health, and exhaustion, casting lecherous glances at young women.

"Is this cigarette going to bother you, Walter?" said Grace politely.

"Not unless you plunge the lit end into my flesh," said Walter smolderingly.

Then he catapulted himself into a nearby rocking chair and slumped over as if dead.

"I'm a little subdued because I just got back from my wine-tasting class," said Walter, slumping further.

He had the ability to lie supine in a rocking chair.

Then he started raving about his crises again.

"I'm just trying to put one foot in front of the other," he concluded vastly.

"That's plausible," said Mr. Stewart. It was the patriarch's custom to give people the benefit of the doubt.

The orchestra was attempting a Cuban rumba, but it was overladen with Hungarian melancholy. Then they packed it in and went on their break, rambling up and down the hall smoking European cigarettes, talking effusively, and waving their arms around while making elaborate points in explosive arguments.

After this refreshing interlude they returned to their posts renewed, and pitched furiously into a Virginia reel.

The identity crisis of the orchestra seemed to mirror that of Walter. Grace's hair was standing higher and higher on end throughout the afternoon as Walter rambled on about his crises.

He kept calling her kiddo and casting her lecherous glances. Kiddo? She who was a prehistoric fossil buried in an antiquated stratum of the earth's core? Some nerve.

"Tell me about Monroe," said Walter. "Tell me of your plans for marriage."

"I plan to set a course to a star of decency and kindness and decorum."

"Is that what you want written on your tombstone?" said Walter. "Decency and Decorum?"

She cast him a murderous glance. This Walter character was extremely depraved.

"Tell me more about Monroe," he piped up again. "What's so great about him?"

"He happens to have integrity. I consider that to be the only quality that stands the test of time."

"Maybe he should have wings and a trumpet and be flying around in the sky," said Walter.

A murderous silence ensued.

"Although the drab, boring attributes of honor and compassion and kindness may seem drab and boring to you, Walter, I suggest that underneath the many layers of depravity that comprise your being, you have a few of them yourself," she commented. This seemed to impress him somewhat, and he sank into a vacant torpor.

Yet it seemed that Walter shared Mrs. Stewart's caustic, malevolent, and jaded vision of the universe. It seemed that she had met her match in him. A discussion ensued about one of Grace's brothers in New Orleans, whom Mrs. Stewart believed to be disintegrating.

"Do *you* think he's happy?" Grace asked Walter, testing the waters. Walter appeared to know a lot of things about a lot of people.

"I think his marriage is in deep, deep trouble," said Walter. "You don't have to be Emanuel Swedenborg to figure that out."

"So you think the marriage is in deep, deep trouble," Grace commented.

"This is it, kiddo," said Walter. "This is the end of the line."

"Well, I have to tell you I don't agree with you. I couldn't disagree with you more."

"Take it from me, kiddo," he said. Then he swilled his cocktail.

Grace felt that this Walter character did not know whereof he spoke. How could he get such a crusty, jaundiced tone at twenty-five, calling people kiddo, swilling cocktails at twelve noon, and constantly suffering from eccentric ailments? This Walter character was a completely crazed individual.

Apparently Walter was taking a sort of sabbatical from his job at Merrill Lynch in New York. It was still an oddly normal job for Walter to have held, Grace thought. Apparently Walter incessantly made incredible demands and ultimatums to his employers, which miraculously, they always gave in to, as if cowering in fear of losing Walter's services. His latest demand was for an eight-week sabbatical, based on the theory that he had worked very hard for the past three years and was tired. He seemed to be off on some sort of mad quest of his own.

Every six months Walter would go through a major reevaluation period, during which he would reevaluate the meaning of life and whether he ought to stay at his job and what incredible demands and ultimatums he could make to his employers. You could tell when the big six-month reevaluation period was coming on because very often the goatee would make its appearance at these times. The general connotations of a goatee, Grace felt, indicated that the bearer was someone searching and struggling for the answers, and sort of veering off the track.

However, he did have a good job.

"I'm surprised that you're not worried about Monroe," said Grace to her mother.

"Monroe is a jewel. I don't need to worry about him."

But it had just come to light that Monroe was not coming. His father was sick. He was still hoping to join them later, for after all the trip was meant to celebrate the coming wedding.

"Maybe you ought to go lie down, Grace," said Mrs. Stewart.

"Go lie down?"

"Well, since we've just heard that Monroe is delayed," said Mrs. Stewart, "I thought maybe you'd want to lie down."

"Why? I'm not sick. I don't need to lie down," said Grace.

"You're supposed to lie down a lot if you're about to get married," said Walter. "You're supposed to go lie down in a darkened room."

"Why? I'm fine. I don't want to lie down."

"It's just the way it is," said Walter, "when a girl is about to get married. Nerves. Marital turmoil."

"Marital turmoil. I'm not even married yet."

"You're supposed to be delirious every night when he walks in the door."

"O.K. O.K. but we're not even married yet."

"So you're supposed to be wringing your hands and thinking about floral arrangements and napkin rings and dress styles."

"Maybe I ought to think about his whereabouts before I think about the napkin rings," brooded Grace.

The subject of Monroe's whereabouts and the delay of his arrival was momentarily dismissed in favor of a general discussion of Grace's marital status, accompanied by the melancholy Balkan waltzes with which the orchestra serenaded her. They seemed to sense the mood.

"Grace, there's a house across the street from us that no one lives in and you're welcome to move there if you want," said Grace's little nephew, Andrew.

"Grace, I have a garage," said Theo, age three, in his tiny voice. "You can live there if you want."

"Thank you, boys. I'll consider it. But don't worry, I have a place to live."

Despite the rather piteous vision of Grace as some stranded human soul bereft of dwelling, she had a glamor to the little boys, who viewed her as an inexplicably unmarried person amid the vast extended family and domestic panorama of the Stewarts.

The theme of the rest of the evening was Monroe, apparently a misanthrope. Being a misanthrope, he was perpetually absent. He was ensconced at his farm. He liked nature. He had a farm in the country across the lake from New Orleans.

He was like the perpetually absent character in a play who is always spoken of and analyzed ceaselessly. What would Monroe think of this? What would Monroe think of that? Monroe likes this. Monroe likes that. Monroe detests that. If Monroe doesn't take a shower in the morning he goes to pieces. He likes to take five showers throughout the day. He hates to go out. He likes to stay home.

But he was never around. Monroe had a lot of ailing relatives. He had to tend to them a lot. His family was prominent. He had to hold them together.

"Grace, there are six steps to marriage," said Andrew.

"Oh, really? What are they?"

"First you are friends, then you send postcards, then best friends, then you kiss, then you have love, then you get a ring, and then you are married, Grace," he concluded cheerfully.

Perhaps inspired by the missing fiancé, Theo kept talking about "Miles," supposedly another little boy staying in the hotel. But try as Grace might to come face-to-face with Miles, he had never materialized, although Theo talked of him incessantly, and Grace got the idea that Miles was imaginary. According to Theo, Miles had many friends but Theo was not one of them. Theo wanted to crash into Miles and bonk him on the head and crash him into his friends. Miles had a friend who was green whose name was January. Who *is* Miles? Grace asked Theo. He's Miles, Theo nonchalantly replied. His nickname is Mile.

Theo was not the only man obsessed. Walter seemed to have formed a fixation on Grace which was becoming much more robust after news of her fiancé's protracted absence. He sat next to her at dinner with his entire body sort of draped around her. He kept going through various personality changes as the dinner courses changed. Finally he complained of the "channel of flame" and staggered off.

However, Walter was not necessarily the heartthrob type. His last girlfriend had fled to Africa after going out with him.

Walter had responded by renting a helicopter and sky diving into the Ganges.

Walter was the type of person who was pictured in the society page with Arabian sheiks or African princes, no one knew how or why, usually Walter playing a background figure in a turban lying passed out on a horse, while the sheik's party made its way into the desert.

Mr. Stewart trained a bemused gaze on Walter. Mr. Stewart had a soft spot for crazed young people. Walter was a crazed young person incessantly wondering what to do with his life. But most crazed young people wouldn't have a job. Walter, Mr. Stewart suspected, did not have that luxury. He was not actually a stockbroker, as Mr. Stewart had ascertained. He was a securities analyst with Merrill Lynch's foreign offices in New York and Milan, with opportunities in their international investment bank. Like most crazed young people, Walter wanted to see the world. No fond patriarch would send him—such as Mr. Stewart would have done for his own sons. So he had seen it for himself.

Mr. Stewart found a good deal to admire in the boy, despite his crazed demeanor.

Mr. Stewart's attitude toward Monroe, Grace's fiancé, was not robust. But this was more of a reflection on Mr. Stewart's great love for his daughter than it was on Monroe's character. If a man has any feeling in him, there is very little that can more acutely try it than the parting from one so dear to him as an only daughter, and an adoring one, such as Grace. Mr. Stewart was in a sort of duel with Monroe, in his mind.

This Walter character could after all to some extent represent a pitfall strewn in Monroe's path, and Mr. Stewart, quite devilishly, was not altogether sorry.

If Monroe wanted to attain his prize, then he'd better get in the game. Because maybe this Walter character would have something to say about it.

On the other hand, Mr. Stewart knew in his heart of hearts what was indeed the truth: Grace had not the slightest interest in this Walter character, and she regarded him as a completely crazed individual.

After Monroe joined the Stewarts, they were planning to go to New York and embark for Europe, where they would travel in their extended entourage. They would return to New Orleans for the wedding. It was going to be a large and elaborate wedding.

Mr. Stewart gave Grace some advice on marriage. "Monroe has many admirable qualities. Keep them foremost in your mind and count your blessings for them. As for his deficiencies, which any man must have, recognize his limitations and adapt yourself to them. Then live your life—and keep decorum, courtesy, and kindness in your house."

5

Some places are in your destiny and in some places you are happy. It might be a world of decorum. It might be a bleak benighted dust-choked landscape. But you might be happy there. It might be that in a taxi driving in the night in Africa toward Tunis, across the flatlands and sea, Louis Armstrong comes up on the radio, and so you miss your country, and remember all the other places that have claimed your heart, and comprised your happiness, for they all come back to you. In the end they all bear some relation, whether in the contrast or in the similarity, to your native place.

Mr. Stewart had traveled to Europe every summer of his life, since birth. From his isolated, geographically remote, and sheltered existence in New Orleans, these trips constituted the refreshment of his life. When he was a child his parents traveled abroad formally every summer for a month. They took transatlantic liners to Russia, they toured the Pyramids, they went on African safaris. Perhaps from the remembrance of the more florid style of travel in those days, Mr. Stewart became somewhat quixotic in his vision. A snack bar was a dining salon, to him. People traveled with steamer trunks and fourteen suitcases. They were completely helpless without porters, and porters were very often nowadays, he had found, elusive. Traveling with semi-invalids was also much familiar to him. His mother with her lap rugs, wheelchairs, canes, on these trips in his early childhood, was what his wife would one day become.

Despite the modern lack of porters, porters seemed to naturally materialize when Mr. Stewart was around, with his helpless entourage, composed of aged relatives and vast family members; his travels were not conducted so very differently than they had been since his birth.

There was always a vast panorama of family members in Mr. Stewart's households. His father had had ten brothers and one sister. Numerous cousins and great-aunts populated the family home, some staying permanently, others visiting. They seemed to cleave to one another with an excess devotion. The sister, when she was twenty-nine years old, was leaving the family house to attend nursing school thirty blocks up St. Charles Avenue. On the eve of her departure, there was a gloom in the house similar to that following a funeral. Her father just sat there and stared into space. Her mother wandered around the house with tears flowing freely down her face. The great-aunts told the children to go outside and play. It was as if the sister were moving to the other side of the Indian Ocean. She was going thirty blocks away, and would be home on weekends.

Some members of the family were well-to-do, were mentally sharp, were members of the professions. Others were weak, or were ne'er-do-wells, but the family always took care of them. There was always a room for them.

Mr. Stewart's father was definitely one of the sharp ones. He was the great man who had to decline a Supreme Court appointment in order to look after his family. Cousin Malcolm liked to say that DeCourcy Stewart Sr. had a weakness for the racetrack and a fondness for cocktails, but that was probably because Cousin Malcolm had a weakness for the racetrack and a fondness for cocktails. The patriarch had a different profile to most others. The general attitude toward the patriarch was awe. Throughout the family of innumerable cousins and relations and retainers, fathers said to their sons, If anything happens to me, you go to DeCourcy Stewart.

When he died, it was a shock to Mr. Stewart, though his death was not unexpected. His death was a shock to Mr. Stewart for what it meant in the family firm. It meant that Mr. Stewart and his brothers would have to hold the reins. It meant that they would have to impress the clients with their ability, so that the clients would stay with the firm. The clients were the New Orleans Cotton Exchange and the Shipping Board and the Louisiana Bank, the newspapers and the utilities. Mr. Stewart was thirty-three at the time that his father died and, as a young man, felt the responsibility. He went into a family council with his brothers. He held conferences with patriarchs and scions. He had one request, one point to negotiate, and one thought above all. This was that he wanted to move into the office that had been his father's.

He had followed the family profession, he had a wife and four children, numerous daughters-in-law, grandchildren, and an antique live-in mother-in-law, who was the source to him of a great deal of inner angst.

He had a quiet unpretension, a quiet intelligence that you would take to be piercing. He had made keen investments but he was not really interested in business. His lonesome unpretentious soul had elegance. He said he was not a visionary or a person of great imagination. For this reason he would turn down invitations to speak to a professional audience. But in truth it was only his quiet unpretension, his modesty, and piercing intellect that prevented him from thinking of himself as out of the ordinary.

There was a haunting line in a story Grace had read, where a father laments that he had given his daughter nothing. Her father had been able to do the diametric opposite for her.

It was her father who had shown her the world. He took her to a cathedral in the Adriatic lagoon which showed the green of Paradise, the legions of the blessed, and the angels unfurling the starry sky of night to the end of time. This happened in her childhood. She would not forget. He took her to the grand hotels in Paris and Venice and Cairo, also the Grande-Bretagne in Athens, and others. He bought her a string of pearls at Bulgari in Venice and a black fan. It was touching to recall, when he had taken Grace there as a girl, the fourteen pieces of baggage and three "helpless ladies" (Grace and her mother and Aunt Stella) of his parlance. The three "helpless ladies" stood to the side in airports and at docks while he negotiated for the fourteen pieces of baggage. That was his vision of the world.

❧

Some of the Stewart party had already departed for New Orleans, where they composed a vast and spectacular domestic panorama. In Virginia they became somewhat frayed, under the ceaseless psychiatric penetration of the matriarch.

Grace would soon be left alone to minister to those aged relatives remaining in the party, including her mother. Several of Mr. Stewart's elderly relatives were to be taken along on the trip, and Grace attended to their many needs as they prepared for their journey. Aunt Stella required ancient baking soda in old-fashioned vials for unknown ancient purposes. Cousin Malcolm needed smelling salts. The possibility of swimming was discussed. "Anyone who saw Stella in a bathing suit would have to be hospitalized for post-traumatic stress syndrome," said Mrs. Stewart.

"Now, now," said Mr. Stewart. In his courtly fashion, he had raised his children to believe that Sundays must be devoted to visiting aged relatives, who were also to be brought along on trips. How well Grace could remember dark Sundays of her childhood devoted to Aunt Stella, even then, twenty years ago, a diminutive and retiring invalid living alone in a huge mansion on St. Charles Avenue in which a special elevator had been built to accommodate her very limited movements. Aunt Stella had changed little. She traveled with her wheelchair, and so far had not left her hotel room. Grace had barely seen her, except to perform mysterious errands and obligations oriented toward her needs. How Mr. Stewart proposed to get her around Europe, Grace did not know. Mr. Stewart visited Aunt Stella in her hotel room several times daily, but could not induce her to leave it. Mrs. Stewart herself was frail, and did not often leave the hotel. Mr. Stewart was accustomed to invalids. So had his mother been one. Not all of his aged relatives were so subdued, however. Cousin Malcolm, one of the aged bon vivants of the family, was a crazed 1940s cocktail type, still a gay blade now at seventy-five. He had had his heyday in the 1940s. His girlfriends had been Hollywood starlets. He was a flying ace in World War II, though his moment as a hero had not endured long. When he materialized in New Orleans after the war he put on Bermuda shorts and hung around the house all day with a cocktail weaving into the azaleas as if looking for something. He called people Lambsie and Sweetums and Kiddo. He golfed, he played bridge, he talked on the telephone all day, he read magazines, he stayed at the Beverly Hills Hotel when his girlfriends were starlets and talked to them on the phone by the pool, he watched the stock ticker at Merrill Lynch. It was thought that he would not make the transition to civilian life, that perhaps he had been traumatized. He went on a vacation after the war, except the vacation never ended. There was something about amnesia, a gold purse, the Riviera. He disappeared for five years at a time. But he always turned up in New Orleans, the permanent home of the family, no matter where the world had taken him.

All across New Orleans Grace's relatives sat in their various abodes, lavishly celebrating the cocktail hour every evening, ensconced in their apartments since many were invalids, reminiscing about their beaux and their numerous relatives. Dusk turned to twilight and pursued to evening while Grace's elderly relatives reminisced of long-departed members of their family, those whose hand they held when those others died, those who told them that they loved them, those who wore the hat with the cherries once in Paris, those whose beaux adored them, those whose brothers went astray, and those who lay ill with tuberculosis, among their cigarettes and cocktails.

Cousin Malcolm fascinated the sober and industrious Mr. Stewart. So did his brothers, the Good Old Boys, fascinate him, being bon vivants like most of the family. Even his father, the great man, was fond, it is true, of his cocktails, the racetrack, a Saturday night stroll in the French Quarter.

Mr. Stewart's father didn't understand him. His father kept wanting him to go to the Blue Room (local nightclub in the Roosevelt Hotel). But he didn't want to go to the Blue Room. His father did not understand his love of solitude. I don't have the key to him, his father would say.

But each man has his home. All Mr. Stewart really wanted was decorum. That was home to him. And he loved the law.

❧

Mr. Stewart was from a long line of lawyers. "They don't converse, they prosecute," said Walter. Mr. Stewart's father had been called the finest lawyer below the Mason-Dixon line in the 1930s. It was he who had raised the family law firm, in New Orleans, to prominence. The old man lived on the park, whose entrance, with its wrought-iron rail, looked through to the long green boulevard with gigantic palms and old green light standards in symmetrical rows. You could see that he was once a very handsome man, in his crisp white shirt and suspenders and his ancient gray trousers. His house had screened-in sleeping porches, where his boys had slept in the summer heat, and extensive gardens, where mosquitoes bred. His wife had died of tuberculosis at a time when there was no cure, and he had taken her to Saranac Lake on many occasions to the sanatorium there in an attempt to save her life.

He had three sons, comprising the current Mr. Stewart and his Good Old Boy brothers. The boys were still small when they lost their mother. Their father would take the boys to Audubon Park on Sundays for a ride in the swan boat. Often it rained. When it rained it was as if the whole heavens bottomed out and the sky was not only gray but black. He and the boys would go to the park anyway, all with umbrellas, and ride in the swan boat in the rain.

At night he put on his black tie and went to Antoine's or his club, in the beautiful rainy night.

Justice Algrant recommended him at this time to the President for an appointment to the Supreme Court. Stewart was skeptical, for he had meanwhile adhered to his principles in casting his vote as a member of the Committee on Rules of Civil Procedure in a manner that he knew would put him in the President's disfavor, thereby in all probability destroying his chances of the Supreme Court appointment. He preferred to stand by his principles and vote as he believed. Personal ambition did not enter into it.

But the President's annoyance was overcome by his admiration, and the seat on the Supreme Court was offered. Stewart was called to Washington and went to the White House. The President was drinking rum. Some of the other Justices who had grown fond of Stewart were present, in those days men of towering integrity and intellect, some of whom Stewart had known in the Harvard class of 1910, and who had formed voluminous correspondences with Stewart over his dissenting opinions. They were not advocates of judicial dissent but Stewart had long ago won their hearts, and they urged him to accept. But Stewart declined the appointment for personal reasons, after agonizing over it long and hard. He had lost his wife. His boys were still small. He did not want to be deterred by the consuming business of the Supreme Court from raising his boys. They had already been through enough.

And after all he had a very extensive family to look out for. He had to steer the ship.

❧

As a small child thirty years later Grace was taken to visit her grandfather on certain occasions. King, the butler, leaned on a broom in the hallway, singing in a rich voice the Nat "King" Cole song "Mona Lisa"—"Mona Lisa, men adore you." The nurse, Geraldine, took Grace home. They walked the seven blocks in which a very world was traversed, for the neighborhood changed greatly in that distance. There was a dilapidated little church on the corner. Could it be that anyone ever went to that church? It appeared to be closed at all times. The neighborhood was called the Black Pearl. It was one of the few integrated neighborhoods in New Orleans. There were parades with small black children dressed up in white clothes and dignified black gentlemen in black suits and dark sunglasses. As Grace walked with Geraldine the weather was warm and clear. Geraldine too sang a Nat "King" Cole song, "Unforgettable." There was a Nat "King" Cole craze then. There was a sense in the air that anything could happen, and that it likely would.

There were black men in old-fashioned shirts and panama hats and cigars in the steamy night with old Coca-Cola signs and neon signs and dilapidated nightclubs with names like Club Paradise. Ever after she could not but be as she had been, and whenever she loved a place it was because it reminded her in some way or other of this.

Her grandfather's work for the Committee on Rules of Civil Procedure and in several other connections continued to come to the attention of the Supreme Court Justices and in turn to the President, for her grandfather's was the sole dissenting opinion in several reports.

His integrity in this had long since prompted Grace to elevate him to the Fiery Pantheon occupied by the heroes of her life. She had seen his correspondence, containing many personal references and effusive declarations of friendship from the illustrious judges. I never part from you without regret, they said. Your friendship is one of my treasures.

At his death their eulogies came pouring in. Tell them that a Supreme Court Justice still remembers, one of them had said, will always remember, his modesty and self-effacement and his adherence to his principles. He was one of the ablest lawyers of his generation. But there are many able lawyers. Even if he had been a poor lawyer, he would have still been the same man to me.

Grace's father inherited the administration of the family estate. It was never rich. The estate consisted of sugar plantations in Louisiana, which had been ceded through mortgage defaults during and after the Civil War. There were other land holdings in Mississippi, on some of which oil was later and intermittently found, and a cotton plantation in the Mississippi Delta. His father had bought shares of the Ford Motor Co. and the Coca-Cola Bottling Co. in the 1930s. These last were his keenest investments.

The administration of the somewhat extensive but somewhat fruitless estate occupied about 10 percent of his valuable time. Like his father before him, his life had been spent chiefly in the practice of law. He drew contracts and wills, formed corporations, prepared bond issues, handled estates, considered tax problems, and above all, advised old clients on family problems, for he was, even more than his father had been, the old style of lawyer who is privy to the personal problems of the men they advise, and viewed as a sort of Delphic oracle.

He was extremely loyal to his friends. When Mr. Stewart gave his heart, that was it, he was bound. It could not be altered. His devotion to the old verities—honor, compassion, generosity—was in deeds, not words. The adherence to principle that his father had shown, the capacity for the dissenting opinion, oblivious to machination and calculation, ran in his blood, as it did in that of his daughter, Grace.

One night Mr. Stewart was up late working on the bankruptcy case of an old friend, which was causing a good deal of scandal in New Orleans. Grace asked her father about the case, as it seemed to be causing him heartache. She wondered what in his long years of the law he had learned, being privy to the secrets of powerful men. Her father shook his head. "Two things stand in stone," he said. "Kindness in another's trouble. Courage in your own."

Grace did not forget that vision of her father, the old lawyer who after a lifetime of hard work came up with that simple credo.

There was a dream of honor in his head. To Grace, her acquaintance with honor began when she knew him.

There are two kinds of people in the world, the kind that idolizes people and the kind that doesn't. It is a trait that says more about the person doing the idolizing than it does about the idol, perhaps, and connected somehow with idolizing people is something low in one's own self-esteem, this source would say. This source was Mrs. Stewart.

Mrs. Stewart's view of humanity was diametrically opposed to that of her daughter, Grace. But it had too been shaped by her vision of her own father. Mrs. Stewart's father had been an insurance broker in a family firm. One day at the age of fifty-six, in the middle of a stately career, he suddenly went on a bender and never was the same. One Saturday he was downtown at the office and one of the partners noticed him staggering down the corridor with a peculiar flush on his face and with his speech slurred; a few months later they had to send him away to a sanatorium. And he never was the same. He went on his permanent, quiet, inexorable bender. His family protected him, but his daughter did not respect him. His decline was somehow the event of her life. Perhaps it was thus that she obtained her dark envisionings and dark sense of worry. Perhaps she thought everyone was suddenly about to go on a permanent bender and ruin their life.

But in the case of Monroe, Grace's intended, it just so happened that Mrs. Stewart was crazy about Monroe. He seemed to be the one person in the universe excluded from her field of worry. Also, she had taken the crazy idea into her head that Monroe could be seen as a possible role model for Walter, whom she had single-handedly assumed the burden of reforming. She must probe, diagnose, and reform him. It would be no easy task, and it might require herculean strength, but once Mrs. Stewart got an idea in her head, she was, as they say, like a dog with a bone.

6

A ne'er-do-well is exciting, at least if he is still young enough, because you wonder what his potential will ultimately deliver. It seems imaginative of him to want to hang around all day in Bermuda shorts. He has balked against regular American life. Perhaps he will suddenly do something great, get an idea while hanging around in Bermuda shorts all day. But perhaps he will remain in Bermuda shorts for the rest of his life, like Cousin Malcolm. It could go either way. You are incessantly waiting to see which way it will go. The suspense is killing you. Or even if the suspense is not killing you, you wonder what it is about regular life that has disturbed him so much that he must always evade it, and hang around in Bermuda shorts all day. You probably wish you could hang around in Bermuda shorts all day. You envy him.

The connotations of spending most of your time in Bermuda shorts are surely generally accepted as "I am on a permanent vacation." Combined with the goatee, the message would generally be interpreted as "I am on a permanent vacation but I am also searching for meaning, trying to find myself. I may be an artist, and I spend half the day in my pajamas staring vacantly."

But to dispel the romance of Walter's exciting ne'er-do-well reputation, actually Walter did not usually lounge around in Bermuda shorts. He had gone to Wall Street straight from college several years previously. He had not had the chance to find himself. You could not ask the exciting question of him, will he or won't he find himself? He often worked eighty or a hundred hours a week in a grueling program to learn equity, debt, capital markets, and mergers and acquisitions.

Being a financial analyst as a young kid, Walter was milked by his superiors for all he was worth, which was actually a lot. Often he had to work until two in the morning. He lived in the neighborhood of New York known as Murray Hill, across the street from the old Bellevue Hospital, which looked like something out of Charles Dickens—an ancient red-brick structure with vines growing all over it and huge cast-off Corinthian capitals lying ruined in the garden behind rusted and imposing iron gates.

Living across the street from a hospital, the incessant sirens of the ambulances, contributed to the general air of catastrophe that pervaded Walter's life.

By contrast, the Merrill Lynch offices in the World Financial Center were of a sleek and new modernity, with a gigantic and untoward palm tree garden in the lobby.

And what had induced a young man from New Orleans to live in New York? One swift word: anonymity.

Walter's position was that of securities analyst. He was philosophically indifferent to his work, and yet, for three years he had performed it with great diligence. In fact he performed it with such diligence that his employers were willing to let him take a two-month paid sabbatical to agonize over his customary six-month self-crisis evaluation period, in hopes that it would pacify him.

They had in fact put an offer on the table to him in New York in yet another attempt to pacify him. They had offered him a job on the Italian desk in London working on European deals to bring over to New York. This proposition Walter was also contemplating during his paid two-month sabbatical.

Walter's philosophical indifference to his work seemed to be the cause of the frequent crises of his soul, causing the consequent reevaluation crisis period. But when he was on the job, he devoted himself to it with an energy and perseverance that would have caused him to excel in any line of work.

Monroe Collier may not have been aware of the existence in the world of Walter Sullivan, but Walter knew of the existence of Monroe. The Colliers were a prominent family in New Orleans and they were hard to miss. The older generation of the Collier family were distinguished by their works, and the younger generation contained some black sheep, as the younger generation always does, though Monroe was not one of them. He displayed the same attachment to his work that Walter did. It was this that Grace admired in him. She was not jealous of his work, she was proud of it. She did not repine if it should take him away from her, as it had many times. Her love followed worth, and was given to excellence.

Or so she believed from the vast doom-laden pinnacle of her twenty-eight years.

Nevertheless it was Walter, not Monroe Collier, who was vacationing with the Stewarts at the Virginia Hotel, celebrating Grace's engagement, and generally sticking to them like glue.

7

The women at the reception desk of the hotel all wore the same dress, not a uniform, but the same dress, like bridesmaids. Walter had made conquests of them. When he arrived at the hotel he was a day late, and had not guaranteed his room. "You were supposed to be here yesterday," said the girls at the reception.

"Yes, but I had to psychologically prepare myself to deal with three such beautiful women," said Walter, smolderingly, his eyes like hot coals burning into theirs.

"How long can you stay?" they asked.

Taxi drivers, hotel proprietors, guards in pith helmets, it was all the same. Everyone knew he was a character. You got that picture right away. Some people from the hotel took the bus to town with him one afternoon. When they came back Grace asked them where he was. They said the last time they saw him he was standing on the street reading *The Wall Street Journal* and then they chuckled and shook their heads in bemusement, because even to think of him standing in the street reading *The Wall Street Journal* was bemusing, once you knew he was a character.

But the remarkable thing about Walter was this. He had seen that Grace attempted to efface her beauty. He had seen that she attempted to be drab. He had studied her closely. Why would she try to efface her own beauty? Why would she try to conceal it? What was wrong with this girl? He had watched her closely. And all of this had shown him that she was a tortured soul, and it had filled him with concern. Surely in any man, much less in one so young, such a strange and compassionate reaction is rare. Beneath his crazed exterior was a solicitude and thus a decorum—though he would do his best to hide it—that contained all the pity and elegance of the world.

The truth is that he was attuned to suffering. He did not like her for her beauty, anyway. He liked her for her suffering. For the same reason, he liked her mother. Mrs. Stewart's need to psychoanalyze everyone within a ten-foot radius only showed him that she too was attuned to suffering, after her own manner. Mrs. Stewart knew the score.

8

"Tell me about this Flaming Pantheon of yours," said Walter.

"It's not a Flaming Pantheon. It's a Fiery Pantheon," said Grace.

"O.K. O.K. Tell me about it."

"It's a sort of sacred shrine my heroes occupy . . ." She gestured with her hand. "There they rage in the Fiery Pantheon and I adore them. My father, my brothers, the judge . . ."

"Tell me about Monroe."

"You're like he used to be. The youngest one at the firm. You probably are. The boss was his mentor. You're probably the protégé of a big cheese. Monroe's passed beyond that stage. Do you see?"

"Yes, I see. It's not that obscure."

"But you're just staring at me with a blank expression."

"Maybe it's the Column of Flame. Is that any relation to the Fiery Pantheon? Maybe the Column of Flame should be put into the Fiery Pantheon."

"I'm talking about the ideals that I cherish."

Walter contemplated the battlefield.

"I'm not sure this Flaming Pantheon of yours is such a hot idea," said Walter, while Grace looked at him with an odd expression.

"It's not a Flaming Pantheon. It's a Fiery Pantheon," said Grace.

"Is there a Fiery Annex or something? Maybe I could go there."

She cast him a glance meant to be murderous.

"I guess I'm parking cars at the Fiery Pantheon. I've got the parking concession at the Fiery Pantheon," said Walter.

A stony silence ensued.

"Don't these paragons ever behave like human beings?" suggested Walter.

"Like noble human beings."

"And what about you?"

"I'm just a sober character. The wallflower type."

"I'm not so sure about that."

"I fear to be too meek," she said.

"Meek. Well, when you inherit the earth, please save me an island," said Walter.

In this way he gruffly said good night, and went back to reading the biography of Winston Churchill, a possible member of the Fiery Pantheon, for all Walter knew. According to the biography Churchill started drinking Scotch at 8 A.M. and smoked ten cigars a day. Grandson of a duke, brought up at splendrous Blenheim Palace, defender of the British Empire, Churchill liked to encourage the rumor that he was the illegitimate son of a wacko British millionaire who visited him a lot at Chartwell.

The next morning, as usual, the waiter brought Walter two breakfasts. Walter protested that it was only him. "We thought the lady was spending the night," suggested the waiter, with delicately raised eyebrows as usual. Whether it was the girls at the reception desk or other members of the staff who took a shine to Walter, they seemed determined to get him a date—or more accurately, to get a girl to spend the night with him.

The atmosphere at the Virginia Hotel was one of lugubrious gaiety. A man had a heart attack in the restaurant. The proprietor came out and chatted with the guests. He said that the man with the heart attack didn't want to leave and refused to get on the stretcher. Later the stricken man came out rather jauntily with his tie askew, and consented to go in the ambulance.

This did not faze Walter. Grace hovered solicitously near the ambulance but Walter reverted to their previous discussion without so much as a raised eyebrow. Walter, so it appeared, had seen it all.

"This Fiery Pantheon of yours. Is there a Warm Pantheon? Maybe I'm in the Half-Baked Pantheon." As no clarifications were forthcoming, he asked, "Does it have anything to do with the Parthenon?"

He was interrupted by a strange and maudlin encounter. In the lobby there was a very tall man with a tiny daughter seated in his lap. He seemed a little seedy, in an ill-fitting old suit and awkwardly holding the little daughter, smoking a cheap cigar. In fact he dressed as if he were on the brink of being a tobacco auctioneer. Suddenly he called out to Grace. He seemed to go to pieces when he saw Grace. She was startled and went over and took his hand. He reeked of tobacco and alcohol, was seedy, divorced, and was taking his little daughter to a dance class. I didn't know you smoked, she said. An occasional cigar, he said, smiling seedily. Then they seemed to have a tearful reunion of some sort.

Who was he? asked Walter when they had passed on. Grace identified him as someone who was once "her darling everything."

"Your darling everything. Oh, I get it. Your darling everything. So I guess he's a member of the Fiery Pantheon?"

"Well, he's certainly in the Fiery Annex."

"What's so great about this guy?" said Walter.

He was a regular guy, a decaying American businessman. It was curiously touching to her that she should attract such a one, plus that she should value his acquaintance. Why? Because he was weak, because he was drunk, because he was a regular American, in whose dark American dream there is life.

"I'm a decaying American businessman too, you know," said Walter.

That's true. He was American, he worked at Merrill Lynch, and he certainly seemed to be decaying. He was a little young to be decaying. But he did a good job of seeming decayed. In fact, after he had one too many cigars he smelled like rigor mortis.

"So how about finding me a slot in the Fiery Pantheon?" said Walter.

"For one thing I've only known you for three days."

"Well, how long do you have to know me before I can get into the Fiery Pantheon?"

"It's really not a question of time. It's a question of your caliber. It's a question of your soul."

"Maybe I can get into the Uncomfortably Warm Pantheon," said Walter.

Mrs. Stewart appeared to be darkly familiar with the decaying American businessman.

"He looks like he's always brooding, but he's not," she said.

"But maybe he is," said Grace. "Brooding." She stopped. "I was ineluctably drawn to him, and yet inexorably barred from him," she theorized.

"And why were you drawn to him?" persisted Walter. "Because he's a fellow lost soul?"

"Grace is not a lost soul," said Mrs. Stewart. "She just aspires to be."

There was a stunned silence. It was an actual compliment from her mother. Grace stopped to revel in it. She did have a leading fondness for lost souls. That much could not be more true. It was the lost souls whose spectacle provided comfort among the successful, the driven, the happy, the functional.

Not everyone could get a place in the Fiery Pantheon. You had to have a contrast. And yet, lost souls came curiously close to enshrinement. They couldn't cope. It was comforting.

"What exactly does this decaying American businessman do?" asked Walter.

"Usually he stands on his porch in shorts and no shirt with a garden hose in one hand and a beer can in the other."

This guy apparently wasn't too high-powered.

Apparently he was an example of one of her old flames who lay in demented heaps around the world. After all she would have batted her eyelashes at the Blue Ridge Mountains, or Park Avenue on a snowy night, she would flirt with a city, she would flirt with an orchestra, she would flirt with an empire, preferably a fallen empire.

Walter pondered it all. He thought he saw a luminosity, from which he was barred entrance. Something shimmered on the far horizon. Something luminous. It was the Fiery Pantheon, and Walter wasn't sure he could ever get in.

And yet, all you had to do to get in was stand on your porch drinking beer in your underwear.

A waiter stole up and said quietly, "Will the lady be spending the evening, sir?"

"She's staying here too, you know."

"Yes, but will she be staying in your room?"

"I hope so. But I wouldn't count on it."

The next day they discreetly brought up two breakfasts.

All in vain.

Florence was dozing in the solarium when suddenly she awoke from her slumbers and spoke of her courtship. She said that when she married Mr. Cosell she told him there were two things she would never do: live in South America or live in Puerto Rico.

So naturally they had just been living in South America and Puerto Rico for the last seventeen years.

"Florence really isn't well at all," confided Mr. Cosell.

Big surprise.

"What's wrong with her?" asked Grace.

It turned out she had some strange phobia of everyday life materials, a phobia of rainwater, a chemical imbalance; certain aspects of everyday life made her nauseous.

He gazed moodily out on the garden.

"There's no lawn," said Mr. Cosell. "Just a garden. That's good. We hate lawns," he said.

But they did like their cocktails. "When five o'clock gets in the air, Florence starts thinking about her Scotch," said Mr. Cosell. Mr. Cosell started thinking about his Scotch too. In fact if a waiter did not materialize when they started thinking about their cocktails, a serious crisis was at hand.

"I think I know Monroe's family," said Mr. Cosell. "I just hope he doesn't destroy her," he whispered loudly to Florence.

"Your hair looks particularly awful tonight, Grace," put in Mrs. Stewart.

"Thanks a lot."

"If you would just use a *conditioner,* Grace," she pleaded.

"It would enhance your self-esteem," put in Muriel.

"I have self-esteem. I have inner self-esteem. I'm not featuring my outward appearance," attempted Grace. "I'm featuring the inner soul."

"You should wake up every morning and say, Goddamnit, I'm attractive," said Muriel.

Walter offered, "You should be like Carol Channing. You should get up every morning and say, I'm seventy-five years old, I've been playing the same role for fifty years, but do I doubt myself? Do I say, Should I still be playing this same role? Maybe I can't do it anymore? Maybe I don't feel so brassy anymore?—No. You just say, I'm Carol Channing, I'm brassy, I'm fabulous, I'm Auntie Mame."

Mr. Cosell looked significantly at Florence.

"Why would he *destroy* me, by the way?" said Grace. "First I'm going to *wound* him, then he's going to *destroy* me. I mean, what is this? I mean, we're engaged for marriage, not mortal combat."

Mrs. Stewart peered over her newspaper. This was perhaps more threatening than the headlines—TURMOIL IN BULGARIA, SUMMIT MEETING DOOMED—the daily rendering and confirmation of her own dark vision. Someone was wounded. Someone was destroyed. It was ominous, hopeless, and menacing. Mortal combat was involved. The situation had distinct possibilities.

The conversation continually reverted to the usual subject.

"If Monroe doesn't come soon, it's going to destroy her," concluded Muriel. So on the green lake ringed by mountains, at an old hotel rising like a Saxon palace, they cohered to ponder Grace's somewhat turbulent engagement to be married, and perhaps place bets on when it would destroy her.

10

Grace had met Monroe at the Democratic Convention in New Orleans, which he was covering and which she was attending with the judge she clerked for. In the tradition of her family, she had been to law school. But she had never practiced law, and as it turned out, she never would.

The judge she clerked for in New Orleans was eighty-nine years old. "What are you doing today?" Monroe would ask when he called her at her office.

"I'm taking the Judge to his eye doctor appointment."

"What is going on at the court today?"

"Well, the Judge is taking a nap."

"The Judge has to have some surgery at the dentist's today."

"The Judge is hallucinating."

The judge was on his last legs.

The courthouse had a daunting library where Grace spent most of her time, and echoing marble halls with potted palms in every bay, amid a great air of gravity and judicial slants of light.

At the time, she had just been to a number of parties with Monroe connected to the Democratic Convention. She had a special place in her heart for journalists. She was enraptured by their glamor. She romanticized them, she supposed. But it seemed there was a lot to romanticize.

She had always known Monroe's family. She had always known him in passing. Certain things about him over the years came across. He was always visiting his ailing relatives in Virginia. His terrain was always the South. He was the type of dyed-in-the-wool Southerner who is oblivious to the North, who may visit the North, but who is curiously untouched by it. Whereas Grace was torn. When she first saw the North, she had never seen before a like magnificence.

Monroe was the type of Southerner who, after graduating from college, when looking for his first job, asked himself, What is the most exciting city I could possibly live in? and came up with the rather startling answer: Mobile, Alabama. After cutting his teeth in Mobile for a year he decided rather unsurprisingly that it was not the most exciting place he could live in, and wondered where the next most exciting place he could live in would be, so then he came up with Tuscaloosa. You don't have to be Fellini to figure out that Tuscaloosa would not be the most exciting place to live in either, and just before someone could stop him from moving on to Pascagoula, his next ideal residence, he realized that his hometown, New Orleans, was no doubt the most exciting place to live in if you are going to live in the South.

Atlanta, Houston, Dallas—these did not occur to him. That was the type of Southerner he was. The New South did not occur to him. It was the Old South for him.

It was this quaint dedication to the South that she admired in him. For him the world began and ended somewhere between Biloxi and Myrtle Beach. Alabama was the source of all knowledge. Of course he was obsessed with the Civil War. The plantation of his ailing relatives in Virginia had been destroyed in the Civil War, but it did not surrender until it was destroyed, and what destroys you, you remember, long after the victors have forgotten. His ailing relatives had not forgotten.

She wished she could be that kind of Southerner. She wished that she could be so quixotic and honorable as to be loyal to the defeated party, the defeated place, the defeated purlieus of the Southern coasts, with tourists in lime green leisure suits, shambling toward further losses at the hideous gambling casinos of Biloxi, a doomed, defeated dream, the downtrodden South.

What she failed to take into account was that Monroe was probably the type of person who doesn't look at it that way.

He just lived his life. He didn't stop to think, do I choose the North or the South, shall I be faithful to a doomed, defeated dream, the downtrodden South, shall I denounce the larger world, the victorious North, etc. Monroe was very laconic. He watched football, the game of the South, among the green unfallen leaves, drinking beer. He drove around with his dog, sometimes visiting relatives in the Mississippi Delta, while the sky was almost as black as it was stormy and a light rain fell from a cool dark sky above a red band of the sunset. He wore khaki pants and an old muffler and seemed to represent everything in the South with his khaki pants and his dog and the cool dark sky. He visited his ailing relatives in Virginia. It occurred to her, if he was always visiting his ailing relatives in Virginia, why wasn't he here? It would surely be easy enough to come to the hotel while visiting his ailing relatives somewhere nearby. But then, his father was ailing, in New Orleans.

He could sit at his desk at *The Times-Picayune* all day without thinking to call, no doubt. He just lived his life. He drove to Baltimore once a year to visit the ancient nursemaid of his childhood, Canellia. He had dinner with his parents every Friday night. He had dinner with his sister every Wednesday. He played pool with his brothers on Saturday. He went to bed every night at nine. He took five showers throughout the day. On Sunday he did gardening. He raked leaves in the yard with his dog. All this she had romanticized into some teeming bastion of integrity, a shining beacon from the South.

In her vision of Monroe, which she seemed to view as the expression of her diametric opposite, the thing that fascinated her about him was what she perceived as his teeming integrity. Nothing fascinated her so much as honor.

* * *

She went on to clerk for another judge in New York. He was the epitome of judicial integrity and every time she saw him she wanted to drop to her knees and adore him. He was immediately submitted to the Fiery Pantheon. The relationship between a judge and his clerk was one that suited uncannily her penchant for idolatry, for it is intrinsically a relationship of adoration. The judge is an older and illustrious man, often fatherly, or grandfatherly, and the clerk sits at his knee to learn from the great man.

The judge in New York was a man who did not agonize over his decisions; he was swift and ruthless. He took Grace's measure, and he treated her with gruffness and austerity, but he could never complain of her diligence or devotion. He regarded his courtroom as a sewer which it was his object to sanitize of the deleterious elements permeating his many cases of corruption. He found in Grace an innocence whose magnitude he had not seen before, and for this he valued her opinions, although she had a sense of fairness and forbearance that was not altogether consonant with the letter of the law. Her innocence was a basic handicap to her, of which she was not proud, and she could not congratulate herself for her achievements. In her own opinion she had developed into a fairly meek character partly under the steady influence of her fierce mother. But in humoring her mother, in not tending to argue with her, Grace had only meant to be kind.

The two opposing influences in Grace were the stern sense of honor passed on from her father, and the deep sense of worry emanating from her mother. The latter was brought on by an intimate knowledge of human frailty, the former by an unusual innocence and rectitude. On the one hand was the Fiery Pantheon, inhabited by heroes who would never fall from grace, because they would be incapable of it. On the other was a land inhabited by the diametric opposite: a slew of human wrecks reeling in disintegration.

11

The orchestra was playing suave Depression 1930s jazz. The orchestra was ever present, ubiquitous, omniscient. Its Euro-Slavic members rendered entertainment with the inexorability of the advance of history. Mrs. Stewart felt that they needed therapy. But she had to admit that they were constant to their purpose. Incessant violins were heard amid deserted colonnades, for by the time the orchestra had pervaded its musical repertoire during the course of the afternoon, the audience had generally departed in search of bigger and better things. When bigger and better things failed to materialize, the orchestra played on.

"Did you notice anything different about Monroe the last time you saw him?" Grace asked her mother. "Did he seem different to you?"

"No. Why? Is it about the delay?"

"Monroe leads a very dynamic, vibrant life and he needs extra rest . . ."

"What's so dynamic about it?" said Walter.

"It's just so romantic," said Grace. "Hunting, fishing, shooting guns . . ." She trailed off. "His dog . . ." But she cast Walter a doom-laden glance. Actually Walter had a certain way of penetrating to the truth. It would be a joke to anyone who knew the slightest thing about Monroe's life to call it very vibrant or dynamic. It may have been many things, but it was not dynamic.

Monroe had ailing relatives all over the South. He frequently visited them, always driving, never flying, and they were always ailing. Many members of his family had never been outside of New Orleans in their lives, had never flown in a plane, had never been to New York. One pair of cousins in the country had decided to leave the family plantation and go on a trip. They packed many of their belongings into a car and decided to drive to Pennsylvania, for some reason. They couldn't stand it, and got as far as somewhere in Ohio, and then drove straight home.

But all this she admired. She wished she was that kind of Southerner. To her his quaint life in New Orleans was much more interesting than hers in New York. Soon she would share that more interesting life with him, never venturing farther than Baton Rouge, or possibly Biloxi or Gulfport, other than visiting ailing relatives in Virginia. They would vacation at the Grand Hotel in Point Clear. Slidell would be like the Bois de Boulogne to them. She would achieve her ideal of living in the South and being that kind of Southerner. That was her ideal. You might think it an odd ideal for a promising and after all somewhat cosmopolitan young woman to have. After all she had lived in New York for almost ten years. But the cosmopolitan can take many forms. The matriarch and patriarch of Monroe's family, for example, had, at the age of eighty, developed five different living rooms so that they could entertain more elaborately than ever before. Their invitations bore an embossed crest. They lived in the same house that the matriarch's grandmother had grown up in. Their entrenchment in society was deep. Some would say stifling. Maybe it was stifling to Monroe.

She remembered once about twelve or fifteen years ago she watched him leave some youthful resort of theirs in New Orleans, admiring the spring in his step. Maybe it was true that he had lost that spring now. But she would help him get it back.

Grace had also spent a stint at teaching. Her students were all crazed young people like Walter. They called her up to tell her that their houses were burning down, they wanted to kill themselves, they were building a Japanese pagoda in their backyard. They might as well have told her they were going to the desert to search for the Holy Grail. They wrote ten-page tortured letters about their squashed hopes and broken dreams even though they were only twenty years old. She recognized herself in them.

The most splendid of them were the shyest, and also the most tortured. They were humble to the point of torture. They had a sort of self-lacerating excess humility, as if they were all about to immolate themselves. Walter showed signs of this too, even as he showed confidence to the point of insanity. Flights of grandiosity alternating with bouts of self-loathing. His psychology was indeed a strange one. He was confident, and yet he was shattered.

Her soft spot for the crazed young people was somehow connected to her soft spot for the very old patriarchal white-haired gents who populated the Fiery Pantheon. So you either had a very young person struggling and searching in a vague morass of trouble for truth; or you had a slightly decrepit white-haired man possessed of dignity and the vast wisdom of his years, who was the great diametric foil of crazed youth.

She found this in her father, of course, and in his partners at the office, as in their rare elegance they contemplated the doom of honor, in their seersucker suits and white bucks and bow ties.

The more decrepit a man became, the more she honored him. She found in his age a knowledge and susceptibility that was unspeakably touching. It was a nameless thrill to cross the years, such as to communicate with the judge. There were more than forty years between them. It was not a small thing to her that she could look forward to a life in which she would be regarded as his friend.

She retreated to her room and rearranged the books on her bed table several times until they stood in an exactly uniform row. She repined for the doom of honor. Then she went downstairs.

12

A journalist appeared at tea who apparently was another old flame of Grace's. Apparently they had an electrifying reunion. Apparently she was frequently electrified. Walter asked about the old flame and she identified him also as someone who was once "her darling everything."

"Everyone is your darling everything," said Walter. "I mean it doesn't take much to become your darling everything. The cook will probably become your darling everything if dinner is good tonight. The receptionist is probably your darling everything. The Fiery Pantheon must be getting pretty crowded. They're going to need crowd control in the Fiery Pantheon. The Fiery Pantheon is like that closet on board ship in the Marx Brothers movie where everyone keeps piling in the closet like the maid with her ironing board and the telegraph operator and the laundryman and—"

He seemed to be becoming somewhat hysterical.

"The fiery pantheon," screamed out George's father in a tuneful refrain at the next table. He kept bursting into song. Often he would just make up the song from the last thing you said.

"Oh, you're a regular wallflower, all right," persisted Walter. "Do you run into these old flames a lot?" persisted Walter. "These darling everythings."

"Now and then."

"Now and then . . ." sang out George's father as if it were some old-time number. He kept bursting into song—based on the last thing you said. Just while sitting at the next table playing solitaire.

Grace's old flame went up to Walter and put his face about two fractions of an inch in front of Walter's and started saying over and over in a monotone, "I can't believe this day is happening. I can't believe this day is happening. I never thought this day would come. I never thought that this would really happen. I can't believe this day is happening."

"What day? What day is happening?" said Walter.

"The day she tells me that she's getting married," he repined.

He looked debauched and as if he were about eighty years old, Walter thought. He kept talking in this monotone over and over about how he couldn't believe this day was happening.

George's father suddenly came over and took Grace in his arms and waltzed her around. The orchestra was playing waltzes. *"I can't believe this day is happening,"* he yelled tunefully in a song, waltzing her around.

Her eyes were wild. She appeared to be losing her mind. Walter just had not thought of her before in quite this light, surrounded by electrifying old flames, all of whom appeared to be suffering from dementia. It was to Virginia that her old flames apparently repaired, hoping to mend their broken wills.

The Bosphorus, the Pyramids, Lake Como, they all might succumb.

Walter was accustomed to hard luck with women. He was accustomed to hard luck with women throughout the world. As mentioned, his last girlfriend had fled to Africa for two years after going out with him. Walter himself was thinking of escaping to Algeria.

Walter noticed that Grace's dress was on fire.

"Your dress is on fire," he said, going up to the dance floor. Then he put it out with a tablecloth.

Both the tablecloth and Walter were wrapped around her form, for several scintillating moments, during which some nightingales and angels began to crowd into his brain. Bands began to play. Civilization flowered. Wars were won. Peace reigned.

Then they went back to their seats.

Walter said he was experiencing back trouble.

"It's the injury *du jour,*" said Grace.

He had decided to go to a chiropractor.

"What exactly *is* a chiropractor?" Grace asked.

"It seems to be a man who talks incessantly while performing forms of judo on your body," said Walter. "'I'm just going to apply a little pressure here,' he'll say and then he takes a sledgehammer to you, or 'Now, this will feel a little uncomfortable' and then he drives into you with a Mack truck."

"So I guess it's not too pleasant."

"Apparently, no."

"Would you like more of this salmon, Walter?" she asked politely. They had gone in to dinner, where Walter draped himself around her from his customary position in the next chair.

"If I eat any more of this salmon I'm going to be swimming upstream," said Walter.

Walter had his charm, thought Grace. He had a certain insane charisma, she admitted.

An obnoxious conversation ensued about some of the many attributes of Monroe. At least it was obnoxious to Walter. Monroe liked to fish. Monroe liked to hunt. Monroe liked to shoot guns. On Saturdays sometimes he just got up and went to the shooting range because he felt like shooting guns. Maybe sometime Walter could go with him, it was obnoxiously suggested.

"I've never shot a gun," said Walter. "Do they play James Bond music while they're shooting guns? Maybe Monroe would want to shoot a duel. Can I wear a tuxedo while I'm shooting guns?"

"What does a man feel when he goes shooting? I wonder," sighed Grace.

"I don't know. What does a man feel when he goes bowling?" said Walter.

The ever-present orchestra came out again. It is true that Grace batted her eyelashes at it, as a matter of general habit. A rare tone of gaiety was struck by its habitually doom-laden members. They played an old Fred Astaire jazz song, which brought out her memories of New York. She batted her eyelashes at the orchestra, the music, and the whole place in general.

The only thing she would not have batted her eyelashes at was Walter, as a matter of honor—of some sort.

"You really should meet Monroe," she came out with. "He's romantic."

"What's so romantic about him?"

"Careening out in the bayous at four in the morning to go fishing. It's so Southern."

"I'm not sure I'd feel that same Messianic quality about him you do. Are you on acid or something?"

"I mean he's skating on thin ice right now, that I'll admit. But you really should meet him."

"Maybe I can touch the hem of his garment," said Walter.

Later it was suggested that they drink port after dinner.

"This is the first time I've had port," said Walter.

"Next thing you'll be shooting a gun," said Mrs. Stewart.

The orchestra started playing volatile Russian symphonic treatments—the violinist had a mad solo which he performed with fury. The orchestra was really going at it. It was impossible for attention at that moment to revolve around anything other than the small tortured band of Austro-Hungarian melancholics who composed the orchestra. For once the crowd went wild with adoration. The crowd demanded encores. One encore, a second encore, even a third encore ensued. Each time the violinist returned to the stage he was somewhat more disheveled. By the fourth encore his cummerbund was around his neck.

The audience finally allowed him to retire.

13

"Don't look now," said Mrs. Stewart suddenly, "but there's a person with a severe thyroid condition across the room. He really ought to be institutionalized. And there's a couple sitting right next to him who seem to be having severe marital problems."

Perhaps Mrs. Stewart's choice of psychology as her field of study had been inspired, again, by her father's strange behavior, in the middle of his life.

Walter was raving on about his problems, his ailments, and also the world's problems. Walter was obsessed with the major atrocities of mankind, and often talked about them at great length.

Mrs. Stewart was trying to determine whether Walter meant to stay on at the Virginia Hotel doing nothing—raving on about the major atrocities of mankind to whoever would listen—or where he meant to go from here, in general.

But whether Walter was ready to leave the Virginia Hotel—not that anyone had the slightest idea of what he was doing there in the first place—no one knew.

It was not the kind of place you would imagine him to go to for his own amusement, a staid family hotel, and his demeanor was at odds with his surroundings the entire time that he was there.

"If you could get him to stop talking about the major atrocities of mankind for about five seconds, then maybe you could find out what his plans are," Grace opined. "And I can tell you also that he said this morning he was sick again," she added.

It was true that Walter had as many ailments as the eighty-nine-year-old judge whom Grace had clerked for, if not more. Nevertheless they both seemed perfectly happy, if not ecstatic, about it.

"Walter seems perfectly happy to me," said Grace.

"But maybe on the inside he's a seething mass of turmoil," said Mrs. Stewart, hopefully.

Mr. Cosell was at the center of a somewhat inattentive audience describing Florence's ailments.

"Florence is not what she once was," he admitted.

"Which of us is?" asked Mr. Stewart, the patriarch, with his customary benevolence.

Mr. Stewart had a very strange quality of making you feel good about yourself even if you were not what you once were. Even if what you once were was pretty bad too.

Mrs. Stewart, however, disagreed with her husband's characteristically philosophical assessment of the Florence situation. Florence was somatizing. Mr. Cosell was an inverted narcissist. It was plain as day.

A waiter sidled discreetly up to Walter in the lobby.

"Will the lady be spending the night with you, sir?" he whispered.

"I'm afraid not."

"Will you be traveling with the lady?" he pled.

"I'm not in their party," said Walter.

"Can you get into their party?" he inquired.

Walter regarded his interlocutor.

"She's a lovely young woman," the waiter discreetly advised.

"I know that. There are lots of lovely young women."

"Shall I send up two breakfasts?" he whispered.

"No!"

"Just trying to be of service, sir."

Walter returned to his room in quiet dejection. He had a sore throat and he had run out of undershirts. A large mound of laundry lay strewn at the foot of his bed which he had forgotten to give to the chambermaid, the chambermaid with whom he was on pretty close terms. Actually he was on pretty close terms with the receptionists, the waiters, and Frank too.

He took out a pocket world atlas from his briefcase and looked up Algeria, which he studied with interest for a while. He was thinking of going there.

There was an ever so soft knock on his door. The intruder proved to be one of the waiters with whom Walter was on pretty close terms. He stepped discreetly into the room.

"Will you be checking out tomorrow, sir?" he murmured.

"I'm thinking of it."

"Will you be checking out with the Stewart party?"

"Look, we've been over this already. She doesn't like me. She's not interested in me."

"Sometimes it's O.K. to hang around with people who don't like you," observed the waiter cryptically.

"I don't think so." He held the door to indicate the visitor might retire. But he just kept standing there.

"Shall I send a car around?" he murmured.

"This isn't the British Empire, you know," Walter informed him. "We're in the twentieth century. People here in America don't talk like that. Now will you cut it out? What purpose would this car be for anyway?"

"Maybe you'd like to take the lady out this evening."

"You're not getting the message. I'm alone. She's leaving. We're not together."

Frank, the clinically insane doorman, appeared and joined the discussion.

"I've never been married," he informed Walter. "I'm seventy-three years old. I live alone in the attic." He settled down in an armchair, as if he were planning to stay, and sank into his customary doomed silence.

The receptionists dressed like bridesmaids fluttered up. Walter had previously made conquests of them, mostly by just staring at them while looking dangerous.

"She's not your girl?" asked Ivy.

"At least ask her to dance," said Celeste.

"When are you going to make your move?" demanded June.

"I wonder why my personal life is considered to be general knowledge in a public forum," mused Walter.

"They're checking out tomorrow," murmured the waiter, who with the others began to miraculously recede and vanish into thin air. "This is your last chance, sir," he echoed from the dust.

14

After dinner Mr. Stewart went to the reception desk to settle his extensive bill in view of an early departure the next morning.

Walter came downstairs and took note, while engaging in an obsessive discussion with George's father about his investments. George's father had gotten into several obsessive discussions with Walter about his investments.

Then George's father asked Grace to dance. He had reached an age that she adored in a man, sixty. That age in a man basically just gripped her heart. Also he danced in an old-fashioned way, with the arm up and out stiffly and widely and a strong lead holding you close.

Walter started gulping down vodka tonics in a disturbed manner causing brief bouts of hilarity punctuated by cavernous silences. Then George's father returned to discuss his investments. He appeared to be obsessed with an unfortunate land deal in the Outer Banks of Carolina. He had maps and charts of that region, which he would take out of his pocket and unfold and spread out on the table and study obsessively, madly drawling away. He was obsessed with his investments. Except the only investments he made were things like an ethanol plant in Wisconsin, or cattle. In other words—bombs. But it did not dampen his general air of enthusiasm. He apparently saw himself as some sort of wizard at the stock market, an investments genius, and he had spent two hours after dinner working on his stock market analyses every night for the past twenty years. There were notebooks, graphs, charts, shapes. When Walter asked him to explain it, it was incredibly esoteric and impossible to understand. It was as if he were applying astrology to the stock market. It had something to do with shapes.

This volatile discussion went on at the reception desk for about twenty-five minutes while Mr. Stewart settled his extensive bill. As he traveled with vast amounts of family members, the process was somewhat complex. Then Mr. Stewart walked over and shook hands with Walter, to bid him what Mr. Stewart thought, and at this point hoped, was an eternal farewell. The situation was getting out of hand.

Mrs. Stewart allowed herself a searching gaze into Walter's face and a warm admonishment toward vague forms of counseling she might mysteriously extend to him in the future. This seemed to please him. Grace looked at him skeptically and he smiled at her weakly. He meant to say something more, but George's father kept bursting into song—"Sometimes I Love

You," "Some Enchanted Evening," "Meet Me in St. Louis," "I Love You in Louisville." He asked Walter how he had liked the Virginia Hotel. It's etched onto my memory, said Walter. "It's Etched onto My Memory," George's father screamed out in a song, and collapsed into a chair.

15

At this moment an appearance was made by a laconic young man in a white summer suit. You can trust a Southerner to be dapper. Monroe was. He bore some resemblance to Mr. Stewart in his rather stiff demeanor of formality, and his suit, dapper as it was, looked as if he had been wearing it for several decades. But then he had only been alive for several decades. Well, it looked old.

He was greeted by a cry of joy from his prospective mother-in-law, some sort of guttural monosyllable from his prospective father-in-law, and a brooding misanthropic stare from the prospective bride. He was introduced to Walter, who did not lose his composure and in fact gave him the heartiest handshake that Walter had been hitherto known to possess, and a broad grin of truly Dionysian proportions, which was plastered across his face, where it remained frozen as if paralyzed.

Mr. Stewart persisted in directing some baleful stares at both Walter and Monroe; the latter succeeded in getting his arms around the prospective bride and kissing her on the mouth in full view of everyone, an event which Walter viewed with a crazed grin, nodding wildly, like a somnambulist.

Mr. Stewart smiled briefly and then returned to the *Decline and Fall of the Roman Empire.*

The prospective bridegroom disappeared into the quarters of the prospective bride, and the next day when the Stewarts left Virginia for New York—he was gone.

Walter, however, was not gone. He was brilliantly attired in a suit and tie at the reception desk, looking a thousand times more normal than anyone had ever seen him look before, his long black hair neatly combed straight back from his head, ready for Wall Street, ready for his fate, standing by his suitcase, apparently happy as a June bug in hay.

But it was a false front. Some detected in his normality-laden facade an elaborate construction of false cheer, and a dark undercurrent of doom.

Those who detected it—Mrs. Stewart by name—on this occasion decided to keep their own counsel.

16

Packed in Walter's suitcase was a tuxedo, which he carried with him to his seat on the plane. He was planning to change into it in the lavatory on the plane in mid-air, like James Bond. This was because Mrs. Stewart, unbeknownst to the rest of her family, had invited him to escort them to a black-tie charity benefit at the opera that evening in New York.

"Now, Walter, let's discuss this like mature, rational adults," she had said. "If you don't have time to go home and change, why don't you at least change into your black tie at the airport in New York, where the men's room at least will be larger and on solid ground."

But Walter insisted, perhaps promoting the similarity to James Bond.

A foreign-looking man in the next seat tapped Walter on the shoulder and asked in sign language for a pen and paper. Apparently he intended to communicate. Intently he wrote on the paper. Then he handed Walter the note.

"I don't know what to do," it said.

That's inconclusive, thought Walter. He noticed that the man's eye was twitching. He considered calling the stewardess.

The man passed Walter another note.

"Sometimes I mess up."

Walter again considered. This seemed like someone after his own heart.

Then the man winked, as if he were just an old cornball, and said nothing for the rest of the trip.

Walter always sat next to a lunatic on airplanes. Walter customarily consorted with lunatics. In fact Walter himself was a lunatic.

Now Walter had a purposeful, slightly antic stride, a striking young man in an old-fashioned suit and bow tie. In his line of work, you had to look conservative, even if it was the sheerest facade. Walter was dark, and you would have to call him handsome, but the striking thing in Walter was his quiet tensed energy.

He took some papers out of his briefcase and studied them as he prepared to meet the Stewart family in New York.

The flight proved to be turbulent. At the allotted time, Walter proceeded to the lavatory with his suitcase, attempting to look dangerous. In his mind he heard the music that accompanies James Bond as he emerges from sewer manholes in black tie. Then he was confronted with the wisdom of his mentor's words. First off, there wasn't room for his suitcase in the lavatory. All the seats were taken and there wasn't room to lay his suitcase on an empty seat and take out the tuxedo. The small sink of the lavatory was encrusted with slime, as was the adjoining minuscule counter. You couldn't really get into the lavatory with a suitcase. You could attempt this only by heaving it over your head from a stooping position with one foot in and one foot out. Then he was able to stand his suitcase on the floor on top of his feet and take out the tuxedo, then balance the tuxedo on the suitcase standing sideways. Then he found he could take off his shirt, but he couldn't really take off his pants because the suitcase was standing on top of his feet. This obstacle he overcame by discreetly opening the door of the lavatory a crack and setting his suitcase down in the aisle half naked, to the rather intense interest of the line which had formed there waiting to use the lavatory.

It wasn't easy to be James Bond. But it is pretty easy for a young man to change his clothes in a fairly short amount of time. So ultimately he emerged, looking more suave than you would think, and lurched in the turbulence to his seat.

As La Guardia came into view, the pilot announced that due to the traffic, they would be circling for three hours. After that, the pilot announced that they were being rerouted to Kennedy. Walter consulted his watch. The charity benefit would be starting. But he still held hope. After all his mind was filled with forlorn hopes, death or glory charges, and last stands. The Fiery Pantheon awaited. It shimmered on a far horizon, walled beyond its crazed inventor's luminous admiration. He wondered if he could ever get in. Or was he barred from entrance?

The plane finally touched down. Then it sat in a line for another hour waiting to find an open gate. Then a mechanical failure prevented the gate from being attached to the aircraft. When they finally got off the plane, the charity benefit at the opera had come and gone.

Walter was philosophical. His tuxedo hung limply on his frame. But his limp and flowing garment seemed to cause him to resemble Lawrence of Arabia after a long night in the desert, and keeping this in mind, as grandiloquent music describing sun-drenched exploits with the Bedouins played in his head, he staggered heroically to the curb, while formulating his next plans to find the entrance to the Fiery Pantheon and meet the Stewarts in New York.

Part Two

New York

1

Walter listened to the end of a Yankees game, which New York won against Chicago, on the radio in the taxi on his way home from the airport.

"What is that building?" asked Walter from the back of the taxi while passing on the Triborough Bridge.

"Prison for insane," came the answer.

"Where's Rikers?" asked Walter.

"There. I know it. I've been there."

"Pretty rough?"

"I tell you something. Twenty-five years to life—is no good. But eight months—is wonderful. Three meals a day, clean sheets. We play dominoes."

He sounded like Walter's type of person.

Walter was deposited at his apartment amid the sirens of Bellevue. He unpacked his clothes and formed them into a mound of laundry, which he extracted from his suitcase, along with his war-torn and world-weary tuxedo.

He lunged toward what he thought was the Fiery Pantheon. It proved to be the fire extinguisher. After accidentally getting tangled up in it he spilled a fresh pot of coffee on his world-weary tuxedo where it lay strewn on the floor.

Walter inspected the indignant memo that had just been slipped under his door. The elevator was always plastered with indignant memos from the tenants. Walter's signature was often sought for by the tenants on petitions, lawsuits, and court orders indignantly demanding improvements from the landlord. Walter could never share their indignation, try as he might. He was not innately indignant. He innately accepted disaster. It was the Southerner in him.

But the Southerner in him did not pine for the South. The Southerner in him did not brood over the Civil War. If he spent time with Grace, the Southerner in him might come to do these things. The Southerner in him might go fishing and duck hunting and might start shooting guns. The Southerner in him might start standing on his front porch wearing shorts and no shirt with a garden hose in one hand and a beer can in the other in the middle of a Monday afternoon. Maybe if he did all these things he would be considered for admittance to the Fiery Pantheon. But it was not his way to pine. He had work to do.

The porter, Carlos, knocked on Walter's door to give him some threatening notices from the elevator men. Carlos always wore a monogrammed blue uniform with gold epaulets on the shoulders provided by the management, which gave him a spurious elegance.

"Will there be a strike?" Walter asked.

"They make many piece of paper," scoffed Carlos bitterly.

It was his way to speak in thickly unrecognizable foreign locutions although he had been in America for fifty years, having arrived as a small child half a century ago from Argentina.

"How is your daughter?" asked Walter.

He replied cryptically in an unrecognizable conglomeration of syllables. He raised one eyebrow significantly. Significant of what, Walter could not know. They had many long unrecognizable conversations of this type. He stood at the door. Walter invited him in. He declined. "Crazy!" He shook his head at Walter's war-torn tuxedo before departing. "Crazy boy." On this point he was lucid.

Walter took a bath while looking at a gigantic world atlas. He studied the route of Hannibal across the Alps. He traced the borders of the Roman Empire.

Soon he was enthroned in his study. He had finished the biography of Winston Churchill. Now he was reading a biography of Alexander the Great. Among his books, which appeared mostly to pertain to fallen empires, was, however, an Ian Fleming novel. Strangely enough, James Bond was sort of lame in this Ian Fleming novel. The Chief was much more interesting. The Chief of the British Secret Service, otherwise known as M. He took four-hour lunches at the most exclusive British men's club in London, which gave change only in freshly minted coins of the realm, and whose omniscient headwaiter, Fairfield, reminded Walter of the hoteliers who tried to get him dates. His secretary, Miss Moneypenny, didn't know whether she loved him or hated him, but as she took dictation she knew that she respected him more than any man that she had ever known. Whereas James Bond was always changing into sandals. He had just been brainwashed by the KGB and maybe he was still recovering.

But by the end he was his old self, and stopped wearing sandals. He was in Nassau trying to wipe out a Caribbean gunman who was in league with the KGB, the Mafia, and the Cuban secret police. He did such a smash-up job that he got a cable from M requesting him for knighthood to the Queen. M always sent his cables in elaborate codes, using complicated covers and quaint phrases for the code. James Bond remarked to his secretary that this elaborate secrecy wasn't really necessary, especially for the import of the message in question, but M had the romantic streak of old-world Secret Service boys, and loved that sort of thing. James Bond did not romanticize things in that way. But he had to answer the cable with the intricate code directly to the Queen to accept the knighthood. Except James Bond declined the knighthood. He wanted to preserve his treasured anonymity.

James Bond had a secretary called Mary Goodnight, a most alluring creature. She started talking about how she would darn his socks and do his cooking. "At the same time he knew, deep down, that love from Mary Goodnight, or from any other woman, was not enough for him. It would be like renting a room with a view. For James Bond, the same view would always pall."

Walter read the end, impressed, and attempted to look crusty, dangerous, and solitary.

2

It was a little hard to look dangerous when you had to have emergency dental surgery. This happened on the following morning.

His ailments did not usually come to fruition quite so dramatically. He complained of a toothache and was recommended to a dentist. The dentist was in the Empire State Building. This seemed suspicious to Walter. It wasn't your usual ritzy East Side dentist. It was the world of the Empire State Building and Macy's and Penn Station and Thirty-fourth Street where all the sad clerks seem to be. On Thirty-fourth Street podiatrists and chiropractors peddled their wares on the sidewalk, with demonstration skeletons. The dentists in the Empire State Building seemed to Walter to be stooped, broken men with broken dreams.

The dentist took a look at Walter's tooth and said darkly, "It looks like you're going to have to have a root canal job."

"Root canal?" protested Walter. "I've never had a root canal before. I thought I'd be able to escape from a root canal in my life," he said.

"Death, taxes, and root canal," said the dentist menacingly. He shook his head. "Those things you can't escape."

"Will it hurt?" said Walter.

"I can't promise that you won't experience moments of deep, deep pain," said the dentist.

Gee, this guy really has a great bedside manner, thought Walter. But Walter couldn't really understand the problem because he wasn't a dentist. Only another dentist could understand. He thought of getting a second opinion, on the ritzy East Side, but there wasn't really time, and he felt he should go through the torturous series of emergency root canal treatments which the dentist had planned.

"What if I wait, since I'm about to go to Europe, and deal with it later when I get home?" said Walter.

The dentist looked at Walter.

"You're a walking time bomb," said the dentist.

He didn't know how true his words were.

Walter perked up. "I'm a walking time bomb?" said Walter. He liked the sound of it. "But I'm supposed to leave next week."

"It's impossible," said the dentist.

The dentist described the gruesome consequences of traveling by air with a half-done root canal job. He kept making dark predictions of pain instead of just having a good bedside manner and saying, No problem. He kept making dark predictions, of pain, of money outlays; he seemed like a broken man, among the sad clerks at Macy's. He was a stooped, broken man with broken dreams in the Empire State Building.

But dentists are a rare breed, reasoned Walter. They're very depressed people. We have all come across the ancient dentist who shakes and does everything at an interminable pace and is very, very elderly. Very possibly he drinks. Very possibly he drinks while performing root canal operations. There are many of those floating around. In fact we have all been related to one. We all have a cousin like that somewhere in the background, Walter reasoned. It could be worse.

So Walter went to the dentist for a period of five days straight. Each day the dentist would tell him what torture he intended to inflict.

"Today I'm going to carve into your gums to make room for the drill."

"Will it hurt?"

"I can't promise that it won't be deeply, deeply painful at times." The dentist paused. "And this stuff I have to put in your mouth tastes terrible."

During the fourth or fifth appointment Walter stopped the dentist during the operation and said, "Look. Every day I go to the dentist, I get incredible amounts of dental work done. I mean, this is my life. Can't you speed it up a little?"

And in fact the dentist did finally speed it up. But Walter suspected he had hurt the dentist's feelings.

"You're just using me," said the dentist. "First for the root canal you pressure me to fix it in three days and now you breeze in fifteen minutes late."

The dentist was snapping.

This pleased Walter. Anyone whom he could cause to snap, particularly if it was this dentist, gave him a secret relish. He went back down to Thirty-fourth Street with a spring in his step and stopped to watch the podiatrists and chiropractors in white coats set up on the sidewalk at tables with demonstration skeletons peddling their wares.

3

In between dental appointments Walter reveled in the experience of being a walking time bomb, and observed the ever-present novelty of his surroundings. His surroundings were a novelty even though Walter had worked for Merrill Lynch in New York for the past three years. His hometown of New Orleans was a burden that he always carried, whose memory was engraved onto his heart. It would always make New York seem novel. It may also have contributed to his fondness for the Stewarts. To have come across them seemed like a miraculous coincidence, a family from his old hometown. Thus he had held to them, perhaps as a steady anchor in the storm. There was beneath the crust of Walter's somewhat sardonic exterior a secret reserve of carefully guarded innocence.

But he was the type of Southerner who does not romanticize the South. In fact he was the type of Southerner who had to get away from it. It wasn't that he turned his back on it. Frequently he asked himself why he wasn't a vice president of the Bank of the South in Atlanta or why he wasn't wearing pink shirts or why he wasn't raking leaves and basically devoting his entire life to his dog. Maybe he should be a vice president of Citizens and Southern Bank in Atlanta. Maybe he should be having drinks at the country club and making deals with droll jocular Southerners shooting their cuffs. Maybe he should be raking leaves. No doubt Monroe did many of these things. And look where it got him. Straight into the Fiery Pantheon.

There was an article in the newspaper about the Egyptian President, who was having sycophantic meetings at doomed colonial palaces on the seaside. His eyes glittered. Perhaps he had come too much under Mrs. Stewart's influence. Anyone having doomed meetings at doomed seaside palaces was intensely fascinating. Perhaps he had acquired Mrs. Stewart's penchant for doom, her ceaseless plea for turmoil and disintegration. Sudden doom-laden attention was focused.

He was thinking about his career crisis. Merrill Lynch had a certain prestige, being a blue-chip or white-shoes sort of firm. Actually it was this that he disliked about it. Walter had no use for prestige—just as James Bond had no use for knighthood.

He had a secure job but safety and security did not allure him either. He would probably be made a partner in his department in several years, and he could stay there for the rest of his life, with an ample income. This did not allure him.

Men are not made anymore like Mr. Stewart, who stay in the same firm all their lives, joining it the day they graduate, and leaving it the day they die. Men are not that quaint anymore. It is not that simple.

Walter's boss was cheap, but Walter admired that in the person who was running the show, lacking waste, and providing good leadership; but as to what it does for you personally if your boss is cheap, that was perhaps the question.

On the other hand Walter wasn't interested in money per se. That is, he was not interested in getting as much of it as possible. His aim was not to make a killing on Wall Street. His aim was to see the world.

He was considering a move to the Italian desk in London, the international division of Merrill Lynch. He had spent a stint there in the previous year. The glamor of the Italian desk allured him somewhat but the Italians were volatile and Walter's boss would close down the operation if it didn't perform. This was a challenge.

He was not sure where the world would take him next. There was some talk at the Italian desk of a crisis in Palermo.

Packed in his suitcase would be the tuxedo, in case the need should arise.

4

He continued to ponder the Italian desk situation. If his troubles did take him to Sicily, he would have to start reading *The Godfather*. But he could not have guessed the importance that the Sicilian government would soon come to have in his life.

The "column of flame" was making a comeback in Walter's chest so he took to his bed while watching an old movie called *Johnny Allegro* about two people at a café in Miami who get in a motorboat in the middle of the night and pull up at the dock of an old mansion housing a maniac who raves on about how great he is.

This seemed to restore him. He ventured out. The New Yorkers were pretty sporting as they strolled through the park in the evening on their way home from work. The sky was pure. The air was cool and clear. The lights came on in the twilight. He could not forbear to think of Grace. It was not his way to be romantic, or to romanticize things, but New York had a different atmosphere to him to know that she was in it. Even the sirens of Bellevue seemed sporting.

He realized he had forgotten to go to his Sexual Harassment seminar. The culture of Merrill Lynch was sex-ridden. The traders had a stripper on the trading floor to celebrate someone's birthday. A week later Walter received a stilted, I-Have-a-Gun-to-My-Head letter from the head trader and chief participant, Leo Passaglia, apologizing to all the employees if sexual harassment had been caused by the stripper. Then a Sexual Harassment seminar was inaugurated. A lawyer gleefully related the most lurid examples of sexual harassment. The audience was soaked in sweat. But the traders could never quite get it right. They had the Dallas Cowboy cheerleaders performing seminude on the trading floor for the next person's birthday and the Sexual Harassment instructor had to be called in again, prompting another I-Have-a-Gun-to-My-Head letter of apology to the employees from Leo Passaglia.

A strange pounding centered somewhere in the vicinity of Walter's brain prevented further rumination. Walter could no longer forbear from again consulting a physician. He returned to his nemesis, the dentist, for his final treatment.

"The final treatment is sometimes the most painful," said the dentist darkly. But secretly it seemed to please him. "And I think I should tell you that a tropical storm is brewing out in the Atlantic and a tornado is headed straight for the Empire State Building."

Dentist of Despair, he ought to have been called. The entire treatment was oriented toward natural disasters in the community coupled with the devastation wreaked by root canal problems. He seemed accustomed to catastrophe, and had grown fond of his despair, warming to his role as doomsday statistician of the Empire State Building.

Walter stopped in at a bar in Herald Square. "What did you think of the fight last night?" said Walter to the bartender.

"It was a disgrace," said the bartender.

A New Yorker sitting two seats down corroborated. A Yankees game was playing on the television at the bar. Walter got the fellow started on the deterioration of the New York Yankees, and thus spent what was to him a pleasant hour, listening to the fellow tell his tale of woe. Walter had adapted to New York, despite its ever-present novelty to him.

Walter went to Saks Fifth Avenue to procure gifts for the Stewart women. He felt it was the thing to do. After agonizing at the costume jewelry counter, which seemed wrong, he decided on a silk scarf for Mrs. Stewart with the name of the designer dancing across the shocking colors of the background. It seemed a little loud, but he had a vague idea that such silk scarves were what women of a certain age and station liked. For Grace it was more difficult. He considered a shocking pink and midnight blue and royal green designer scarf, such as he had chosen for her mother. But that sent him reeling in confusion. It would not do for Grace. Even he knew that.

Then he got a cab. The driver rambled on about his problems, which were considerable. People often rambled on to Walter about their problems. This frequently happened at work, among the Wall Street deities. It had also happened at the dentist's, between the drills and treatments, until Walter had adapted to the brooding atmosphere in which the dentist dwelt, and it too became beguiling.

❧

When he got home to his apartment amid the sirens of Bellevue, his telephone was ringing. His telephone was always ringing. Walter was involved in a sort of imbroglio at the office. "What's happening with the Walter Sullivan situation?" yelled the Wall Street deities pacing up and down the halls of Merrill Lynch, even though Walter was but a mere crazed insignificant young person, and the fuss his intermittent crisis reevaluation periods created in the office seemed mystifying even to Walter.

It was the Head of Compliance at Merrill Lynch asking him to have lunch the next day with some other men from the firm.

So the next day he met them for lunch. "You think *you've* got problems?" they yelled when Walter talked of his customary reevaluation period. Then they told him all their problems.

They evaluated Walter's boss. "He knows the Street," they said.

Walter's boss sat behind his desk with his hands in a tepee under his chin and his eyes glittering while Walter talked of his reevaluation crisis period. He could see his boss's brain working through his glittering eyes. His boss brought out files showing future forms of financial remuneration that could in time come Walter's way if he stayed on. The office was decorated in a fireman theme. Old framed prints of New York firemen were lined up along the walls, with titles such as *Soldiers in a War That Never Ends.* Large portraits of nineteenth-century Wall Streeters hung in the reception room. The boss came later into Walter's office with more sheafs of papers and presented a financial analysis of Walter's prospective position. The boss was a hard-boiled rough fellow of fifty, a hard-drinking Irishman with six children and a beautiful wife, whom Walter had met at a party, where she and the boss drank tall glasses of straight gin. Then they made small talk. Walter asked them what was the key to marriage. "Three things," said his boss. "1) Good sex. 2) Good sex. 3) Good sex." Walter was scandalized. New Yorkers were blunt, more blunt than those in his magnolia-laden hometown. But he respected his boss, who ran a tight ship, was rather tightfisted, unphilosophical, and blunt.

Finally after days of discussion about Walter's reevaluation crisis, the boss sat down in Walter's office and said, "I want you to stay."

Walter's colleagues seeped into his office to inquire what Walter had decided. His father called from New Orleans to ask him what he planned to do. His mother called and talked about her own career difficulties at great length. His colleagues called him from airplanes and car phones to find out what the boss had offered, whether Walter had negotiated, whether he had accepted, and the nature of his destiny in general. Everywhere he went, people called, screamed, inquired, and sat on the edge of their seats wondering what Walter would do.

Thus his telephone was ringing customarily when he went home at midnight amid the sirens of Bellevue Hospital, as the world wondered at the nature of his destiny.

Three grueling years had preceded Walter's current crisis, during which midnight frequently saw Walter as a frenzied occupant of the World Financial Center. Quite frequently he also had to travel, as he was sometimes sent out to chase deals. Walter served such a variety of purposes at Merrill Lynch that he could no doubt accurately be called the hardest-working man in New York City. So ordinarily you would find him in his office in his suit and tie, with gadgets attached to the telephone and computer, crisply talking about deals, with the energy of all the young men of the world.

He bowed to convention enough to appear as a young man who goes off to his office every day to conquer the world. But he had enough of a spark about him to question its merits. Yet he had the somewhat rare ability to put aside his doubts for the task at hand.

At lunch with the Head of Compliance and others, Walter's boss was often discussed. "Does he squint until you can't see his eyes when he's talking to you?" asked one of Walter's colleagues. "That's a good sign. When he squints a lot it means he likes you."

When he squinted it actually meant that he liked, not you, but your ideas, and the more you talked and the more he squinted, the more it meant he was irritated that he didn't think of your ideas before you did.

While talking to Walter his eyes turned to slits.

In short, Walter was actually a success. But failure is more interesting than success, and of this he was well aware. Or at least it seemed to be more interesting to Grace. She liked lost souls. She liked men who stood on their front porch in shorts and no shirt holding a garden hose in one hand and a beer can in the other at one in the afternoon on Wednesday.

By contrast Walter cut a certain swath around the world. He had done his stint in London. That was when he had been in another reevaluation period and had thought of quitting. As usual, as if cowering in fear of losing Walter's services, his boss had sent him over to talk to the Italians and test him out in Europe, thinking he might like it better than New York, and that it would pacify him. The Italian desk in London, which was composed of volatile chain-smoking Sicilians, was causing Merrill Lynch a lot of problems. It was little wonder. The Italians were even more crazed than Walter. They got along miserably with the Americans, incessantly causing horrible fights and internal politics. The Americans couldn't make heads or tails of them. Rosetti, Franzi, Lorenzo—the Italians were but a group of demented madmen whose purpose was to destroy the European department of Merrill Lynch. So the Americans sent Walter over to see what he could do with the Italians. The Italians took a liking to Walter, and agreed to work with him for a trial period of three months. From the Americans' point of view, Walter would intervene and mediate in conference calls, memos, and meetings. From the Italians' point of view, Walter would be their spy.

So Walter took the Italian desk in hand for three months. Walter was the steady anchor in the storm. That Walter could play such a role was surely evidence of the volatility of the Italians.

Now that Walter was in his reevaluation period again, his superiors dangled the Italian desk in front of him as a fly fisherman would throw out a lure. The Italian desk had degenerated into a seething mass of turmoil without Walter. The proposition would be that the Italians would scour Italy for deals, and Walter would execute them in New York. He would travel between New York and London, and work with the Head of Compliance at Merrill Lynch, who reviewed the Italian deals with the Securities and Exchange Commission. Walter had started as an analyst. Now he would be a European investment banker. But did he really want to be a European investment banker? Walter wasn't sure.

But for the remainder of his sabbatical he would explore this possibility in London and Milan.

The next day he went to lunch with the Head of Compliance again. The Head of Compliance had taken a liking to Walter. At lunch the agenda was that a group of men in their fifties and sixties sat around screaming at one another—and especially at Walter—but in a friendly way deep down. That's how it was in New York.

So Walter cut his swath in the world, carrying the European market on his crazed young shoulders.

5

Walter was now reformulating his plans to meet the Stewart family, while studying a gigantic map of the Mongol Empire in the year 1205. In his briefcase was *The Fall of Constantinople,* describing that melancholy and embittered city in the year 1405. Fallen empires appeared to obsess him. He studied this for a while. Then he returned to Murray Hill to pick up his watch, which had been reduced to a constant state of disrepair by his watch repairman. The watch repairman, Ignatius Lewis and Sons, was a man of about eighty. The walls of his office were covered with photographs of satisfied customers in 1948, such as people like Fiorello La Guardia, with testimonials stating that they were satisfied with their watch repair.

Walter was not satisfied with his watch repair. The last time he picked up his watch it had stopped during lunch.

"Let me see your guarantee," said Ignatius Lewis when Walter brought it back in after lunch, even though he had just picked it up an hour ago. Usually his watch stopped within two hours of picking it up from Ignatius Lewis. But they had grown fond of wrangling, a custom in New York. What you do for kicks.

"Why isn't my watch ready?" said Walter. "It's been here six months."

"Let me make a phone call," Ignatius Lewis said. He went to an ancient rotary phone. "One-oh-five-one-six—fifth time. Is it ready?" he said into the phone. He got a puzzled look. "Was it a round face or a square?" he asked Walter.

"Round."

"Please relax in the lounge."

"You don't have a lounge."

"Let me call again."

"It's been here six months."

"Is it a round face or a square?"

"You've lost the watch, haven't you?"

"Please relax in the lounge."

"I've been relaxing in the lounge for three years," said Walter.

He went out to dinner. Oscar's at the Waldorf-Astoria Hotel is the type of place populated by an elderly woman from Mississippi with a heavy drawl, dressed like Gloria Swanson in *Sunset Boulevard,* including the turban, smoking cigarettes, making conversation in a world-weary familiarity with her neighboring diners and the waitresses as if she went there very, very often, as perhaps do the world-weary neighboring diners such as Walter. Still yakking about Mississippi genealogy after all these years. Chain-smoking away with a dark defiant self-destructive glamor. She ensnared Walter into conversation. If there was a murder in Mississippi this woman wanted to know the genealogy of the murderer.

You know the little old lady who constantly rings your doorbell trying to convert you to a Jehovah's Witness? When Walter was growing up in New Orleans, he would come home from school and the doorbell would ring and pretty soon that little old lady would be sitting in his living room, with Walter wearing a mildly pained expression, while she tried to convert him into a Jehovah's Witness. Most people wouldn't actually ask this person in. But Walter was the type of person who would not only ask her in but would sit there for an hour after school while she raved on about her beliefs.

So the elderly woman at Oscar's in the Waldorf with the turban dressed like Gloria Swanson in *Sunset Boulevard*, with her lost gentility, was familiar territory. Somehow she reminded him of the Jehovah's Witness of his childhood, a curiously genteel figure raving on politely about her ideas.

When he got home to his apartment amid the sirens of Bellevue, his cleaning lady was there. She kept eccentric hours.

"Walt, I'd like to talk to you about something privately," she informed him. She searched his face. "Why haven't you joined Price Club yet?" she said tragically. This was a store in New Rochelle selling items in vast quantities at huge discounts. Walter tried to put her off as he had other things to think about than getting vast quantities of household toiletries.

He had just purchased *The Godfather,* for one thing, and was reading the scene where the Sinatra character is about to beat up the movie actress except she says, "Not in the face, Johnny—I'm doing a picture," so he starts considerately beating her up somewhere else.

Walter picked up the book and tried to look like a thug, but the cleaning lady led him into the kitchen and displayed with ancient pride the most gigantic box of Cheerios ever observed by a human being. It came from the Price Club.

Then she called him back into the living room and said, "Walt, we need to talk. Privately." This insistence on privacy was of course ridiculous since it was a small apartment and no one was there except for Walter and the cleaning lady. But she had the flair for the dramatic of sixty-year-old women from New Rochelle who wear leather pantsuits and watch soap operas. She gave him a package. "This is for you, Walt." It came from the Price Club. It was a hideous powder blue jogging suit.

"Walt, it sickens me that you haven't joined Price Club yet," said Myrtle. "When I see you going to SeaTown" (his local supermarket) "I just feel sick. I feel physically sick."

"Well, if you're not feeling well, Myrtle, then maybe you should go home," said Walter.

"I'm not sick in the body. I'm sick at heart."

"But I don't want to go all the way to New Rochelle to get groceries," said Walter.

"I'll take you, Walt."

Sometimes you have a vision of a man and it later proves that your vision was wrong. In Virginia he might appear world-weary and glamorous in Bermuda shorts as if he had never been acquainted with a suit and tie. But he was not wearing Bermuda shorts now. He was wearing a hideous powder blue jogging suit, so as not to hurt the feelings of his cleaning lady.

Perhaps his trouble resided somewhere between these various opposing extremes.

Walter was now the proud possessor of two hundred and fifty garbage bags from the Price Club. He was seized with post–Price Club malaise. When he got home he realized, So now I have two hundred and fifty garbage bags. So? And I have just spent six hours in New Rochelle with a sixty-year-old woman named Myrtle. And I'm wearing a hideous powder blue jogging suit.

Something is amiss.

The next day it was the last straw. He found himself watching Myrtle's favorite soap opera. He felt like an idiot but perhaps there was a lesson to be learned in it all somewhere.

The lesson that he learned in it was this. The people lacked a sense of honor, and this deprived the show of drama. Even though one character had turned into a wino lunatic and another one was turning into a suicidal maniac, even though they had faked their own deaths, blown up each other's apartments, been abducted by maniacs and released themselves from Houdini-like restraints to foil their captors, later dating their captors, even that was not enough to relieve it of its listlessness. Only honor could have given structure to these people.

They ought to havc a Fiery Pantheon, thought Walter, as he could not forbear to think of Grace.

His fortunes appeared to be sinking. But they would soon pick up. He soon received a phone call from her mother, and was at last able to reformulate his plans to meet the Stewarts.

6

The Stewart family was embarking on its tour of the world as planned, although without Monroe. Monroe had been unable to come to New York, due to work, but was hoping to join the family at some point.

"What should I bring, Gracie, when we meet again?" he said.

"Just bring your heart," said Grace.

So Monroe would be absent at the start. Walter, however, would be present.

❧

Walter's sabbatical from Merrill Lynch still had a month to run its course. He had been invited by his mentor, Mrs. Stewart, who was trying to reform him, to join her family on their travels. Some might consider this to be an odd invitation under the circumstances. But the dog-with-the-bone syndrome was in full swing. It was Mrs. Stewart's quest to penetrate into the mystery of Walter's purported state of disintegration, according to her vision of it, which of course was actually correct. He was not the only beneficiary of psychiatric treatment from Mrs. Stewart that her family knew her to have taken up. So it did not surprise them. Many times her children had brought home their friends, only to find Mrs. Stewart asking dense, penetrating questions of them over dinner, later giving diagnoses pertaining to different forms of mental turmoil. Once she had taken a broken-down Egyptologist from Boston under her wing during a trip on the Nile and was not satisfied until she had brought about a reconciliation between him and his estranged wife in Luxor. She had brought her taxi driver home to dinner one night from the beauty parlor, and had later succeeded in enrolling him in an "assertiveness training" course. All the hairdressers in her beauty parlor were already enrolled in assertiveness training courses. The manicurists were in therapy. Everyone who came into contact with Mrs. Stewart was the beneficiary, in short, of some form of psychiatric treatment and, to be frank, most were the better for it. Walter's prospects under her mentorship therefore were not really bad.

Small children and aged bon vivants, a maiden aunt, and

several other relatives would comprise their party on the trip, so Walter was not the sole focus of his mentor's mind. There would be other human guinea pigs to work on as well as Walter. Before the trip was over, who could tell what human wrecks Mrs. Stewart might adopt? It was not perhaps the most flattering vision of Walter that had won him his invitation, but Walter was not concerned with such gradations of the impression that he made. He was happy to be on the move. Repair it by flight, as St. Augustine said. As to what was really troubling Walter, no one yet knew.

But some could guess.

Walter felt his certain fascination for Grace Stewart, if not for the Fiery Pantheon, and had done so actually for longer than anyone conceived. He knew of course that she was otherwise engaged. It was not in his concept of honor to interfere. He tried not to think about it. But he failed. The tragedy of human naturc is that sometimes you know in your heart what is right, and you cannot do it. However, Walter was able to justify his behavior by deciding that in this case it was right to interfere. The tragedy of human nature could be averted.

To Mrs. Stewart, Walter's attitude was knowing. He was amused by her fierceness. He also felt a nameless bond of emotion with one who was the author, as it were, of Grace. But Walter also knew the score. He knew that he was being psychologically analyzed by the matriarch. Walter had gotten the gist long ago.

As for the patriarch, Walter admired him, within reason. A certain amount of honor was due to the patriarch in the well-ordered society of New Orleans, within which Walter occupied the place of Crazed Young Person.

7

The hotel was on lower Park Avenue with a view to the last suave sight in New York, of the angels atop Grand Central. The Stewarts were staying there for two weeks. Then they were to fly to Istanbul, where they would embark on a ship. The ship would go out through the Dardanelles and the Aegean, up the Dalmatian coast of Yugoslavia and cross the Adriatic Sea to Venice. From there it would go down to Sicily and cross to North Africa.

Ironically the route described the borders of the Roman Empire. Ironic because the fallen empire was Walter's specialty and it was as if the Stewarts' route had been exactly tailored to his needs. The fall of Constantinople in 1453 was the catastrophic culmination of the decline of the Byzantine Empire, whose melancholy and embittered situation in the first half of the century led up to the sack he was now studying. It was a sack so brutal that it was almost painful to study. But it was not the only sack destined for Constantinople.

The party lacked Monroe, but he said he would try to join it in Istanbul. So the party consisted predominately of Grace and her parents, with a moderate amount of elderly relatives. It seemed strange to be spending all her time with her parents and elderly relatives, but she doted on them. It seemed lame that her whole life was now lived in hotels, though she doted on hotels. She neither lived here nor there. She lived in hotels. She didn't have a job. You couldn't have a job if you were always traveling. You couldn't follow a career if you were always doting on your relatives and performing obligations oriented toward their needs. She had given up her teaching job to go on this huge extended trip and then remove to a marital scope of matronly self-sacrifice and Southern Living. Of course she could teach in New Orleans. But she hadn't got a job there yet. She felt that she was sinking into a quagmire of crisis and decay and Southern Living. Ordinarily she was an industrious and functional member of society.

Like any crazed young person she was subject to the varying malaises of the spirit and the soul, which she thought she had cured with her engagement to Monroe. She had been searching for some truth, some duty, which she found in him. When you're twenty-five you wake up every morning and say, What am I searching for? Where is the purpose? What is truth? Eventually you raise the answer to at least one of these questions. She had banished her malaise through the decision to fulfill abstract concepts of duty and obligation. And yet there was something wrong with this scenario. She would relinquish the engagement if he wished. He owed her nothing. She was lucky that he loved her once. Maybe he loved her no longer. She couldn't force him to love her. But she thought she had found her moral purpose, and she had given her word.

It was a dark and stormy night. She batted her eyelashes at it. However, the night did not respond. It had better things to do.

The message light on her telephone throbbed. There was a message from Walter Sullivan. There was no message from Monroe.

She studied the last suave sight in New York, of the angels atop Grand Central. Actually it seemed to resemble the Fiery Pantheon. There the angels raged toward heaven. "The realm of the heroes or persons venerated; memorials of the illustrious; a temple dedicated to all the gods"; thus was the Pantheon defined. The night rained on. She tried batting her eyelashes at it again. Neither Park Avenue nor the night responded to her overtures. As to the angels atop Grand Central—another matter. Angels are often incorrigible flirts. Why? Because they pay you the compliment of flirting with you, and ask nothing in return.

8

Meanwhile the Stewarts attended to the performance of their personal duties and obligations in preparation for their trip. One member of the party had not shown up—Monroe. He was instead replaced by a total stranger—Walter. Mr. Stewart was disturbed. Walter had bemused him in Virginia. But when he told him good-bye there, he truly thought it was the last that he would ever see of him. He hoped it was, because the situation was definitely getting out of hand. Privately Mr. Stewart held the view that to have invited Walter on the European trip was an act of madness. But he kept it to himself. He had a long fuse of toleration.

Cousin Malcolm disappeared for a while. "He's excitable," explained Mr. Stewart. Amnesia was a problem. The Stork Club, Toots Shor, El Morocco, these were his remembered but defunct resorts. He was a man you could listen to tell the same stories every night for fifteen years, and you wouldn't mind. His illegitimate children, his war experiences, the dinner dances he went to in Biloxi, the Southern governors he had known, his ski vacations in Chile. He looked like John Barrymore in his later phases. When he talked about his youth, he got tears in his eyes. He always talked about his youth. He was now seventy-five years old. Exactly how long was his youth,

Grace wondered, because it seemed like his youth ended about five minutes ago. Whenever she saw him at a wedding, say, in New Orleans, he always had to leave early because he had about six more parties to go to.

"The South—it's a destroyed people," he would say. He would make leading remarks. But they never led anywhere.

For fifty years he had lunch with his father every day. Every day for fifty years he visited his mother at five o'clock, the Southerner's hour. His mother at that hour changed into a "housecoat" or "hostess gown," those mysterious and incomprehensible accoutrements of an old-time type of Southerner's life. What did it signify, Grace wondered, to change into a housecoat at five o'clock? That you were home for the rest of the evening ready to receive guests? Was it your drinking costume? Certainly Malcolm had a drink with his mother at that hour every evening. For fifty years. To Grace the incredible ritual and regularity and custom of his life seemed alluring. It was even somewhat similar to Monroe's life.

In some families the young generation are lost souls because their forebears were legends. This was not the case with Mr. Stewart but it was maybe the case with Cousin Malcolm. It was maybe the case with Monroe. He tried to be manly, and you liked him for trying; the effort was noticeable, but you liked him for having some sort of standard he aspired to.

Part of Monroe's family still lived in a plantation on the River Road. His mother's sister married into the DeLords, who owned the plantation called Lord Hall. It was a place at the end of the earth, and then on the green winding levee road, you suddenly came upon the house, which, amid the ruins and the remoteness, gave a ravishing and unlikely glamor. There were always these elderly gents, the DeLords, rickety old guys with dark sunglasses and cigarettes and canes getting out of limousines at parties there. Like you'd see an old-fashioned black limousine drive up and the door would open and a mahogany cane would come to the ground and then some handsome rickety old guy in sunglasses smoking a cigarette would get out standing silhouetted in front of the plantation facing to the levee. Handsome and ravaged and rickety and with the old dark defiant glamor smoking cigarettes. There always seemed to be a number of them. The DeLord men. The irony is that the Colliers married into the DeLords and Grace had always had a thing for the DeLords, going to parties there in her first youth before she was engaged to Monroe and destined to enter the family. Lord Hall always fostered a kind spirit to her. There was the passage of time. Through the years some died, some married, but none had aged, in her vision, because to her the ravaged handsome rickety old society guys in limousines were always the same. Monroe had a thing about the passage of time. The passage of time upset him. Even the passage of time like every night. It was another thing about Monroe she could incessantly romanticize, like his DeLord uncles she had a thing for. She could have been upset by the passage of time since she used to go to parties at Lord Hall at least ten years ago in her favored youth. She didn't see it that way, being so thrilled to be there at any time after New York; the thrill outweighed the regret for the passage of time.

Monroe would drive to Barataria in his black convertible, the same kind that one of those old guys would show up in at the plantation, romantic soul that he was, or surely would have to be, to live such a life, but she failed to recognize that he had never known another. Driving back by Tchoupitoulas to get to the new bridge entrance, past old cobbles of old warehouses with everything quiet and old and deserted and historical and crumbling, and past a new casino with its avenue of palms, across the river, to go fishing. His father used to go to Barataria with the DeLord boys by taking the ferry at the foot of Napoleon Avenue. The fishermen rented out a hotel. The hotel looked like colonial Africa. There was a set of wrought-iron chairs painted white with dashing green umbrellas in a garden where the roses flourish and the tropic sun gives its air of paradise, and then you walked down to the levee, where you came to a lake that reminded you of your youth and past on the Gulf Coast and Mobile Bay for the water was brackish and brown at the banks; it was another completely deserted area at the end of the earth on a pier with a hammock and chair just looking out to this raging lake. Then the next day the fishermen got picked up in a boat to go out through the waterways and swamps and bayous to where they had their camp, from there to fish in the Gulf.

To her it was intensely romantic. Everyone kept saying that no one was as romantic as she or saw things that way, they just did them, they just went fishing. But she could never get over the glamor of her native place. That was the beauty of Monroe. He had never given it up. He never would. He personified it, the romance of their native place.

To Grace, these were his heroic exploits: He went fishing. He drove a car across the Mississippi River Bridge. He hung around with the dashing if decrepit DeLord men. There seemed to be layers of glamor in his mere existence. No doubt if he went to the dry cleaner's, it would be filled with layers of glamor.

But for him to go careening out in those glamorous remote waterways, that was half the glamor of it, its remoteness. His life there was so romantic yet so worldly for he must have understood the world was various and vast yet chosen this remote exotic spot. It must have taken a romantic, a defiant, a loyal spirit to do that.

The DeLords had also married into the DeCourcys, in that case a distant relative of her father's family. So it was really the Colliers, the DeLords, and the DeCourcys who owned Lord Hall, ironically the three families who held significance for her. In short it was all sort of incestuous.

So why hadn't he come? Maybe he was visiting his ailing relatives somewhere. It was stretching it to think that Monroe could get to Istanbul. He could barely get to Baton Rouge.

9

She studied the last suave sight in New York, of the angels atop Grand Central. A policeman patrolled it on a horse from below, the second to last suave sight in New York.

She watched an old movie about W. C. Handy played by Nat "King" Cole. W. C. Handy kept staying in his hometown, Memphis. He kept writing songs of world renown, and poking down Beale Street every night. Once he got to Davenport, Iowa, apparently a jazz outpost of the time. Then he returned home in disgrace to his father. Then he got as far as Cincinnati. Pretty soon he was poking around the Mississippi Delta and made his way to Moorehead, where the Southern crossed the Yellow Dog, as he wrote a song about. Then he was back in Memphis. It reminded her of Monroe.

She kept wishing for a rooted life. Like the street Monroe lived on, where he knew all his neighbors and all their dogs, and they certainly knew him and his dog, considering he devoted his whole life to his dog.

A news program came on. There was a story about a little boy who was a hero for he caught a crook. While reporting the story they showed the neighborhood. It was a modest suburb—but there was something in the green, the lawns, the trees, the sidewalks, something indefinable, that reminded her of the

South. Just when the children turned the corner, the way they rode their bikes, the way the trees looked—it was someplace very close to the most old and familiar and thus enchanted places of her heart. Why do they have those strange accents? she wondered. Yes, they're in an old familiar green place and they're speaking in a certain jocular and strange accent and locution. The pavements glistened. The sky was black. There were palms. She noticed it was sleazy. That was not a criticism. She would not criticize her region. It was an observation. It reminded her of Florida too. The Gulf South. She waited patiently for the dateline at the end of the story but none was given. But finally just at the last minute before they went to the next thing they blew up the item from a local newspaper that the story had come from and yes, it was *The Times-Picayune.*

Then she read about Nabokov's youth in Russia, at a ravishing estate outside of St. Petersburg with old parks and gardens, and upon the Revolution, his sudden departure on a throbbing boat across a hopeless sea, to Constantinople and beyond, consigned to exile, never to see his native land again.

She fell asleep and had the recurrent dream of a crushing azure beauty by the sea and she couldn't tell if it was somewhere in the North or if it was the Alabama coast. In this dream, which was disturbingly recurring to her in New York, she searched piteously for the location of the ravishing place, the pellucid green of the sea, the crushing, saving beauty of it, one place to take refuge in, to decide on, but when it came to remember how to find it, whether it was in the North or South confounded her.

Some people have a recurring dream in life, she knew. This was hers.

In the middle of the night she seemed to see a man standing in the room and to feel the touch of his hand, a luminous figure in a dark room. It was in her hotel room and it must have been around three in the morning. Your worst nightmare: to wake alone in the middle of the night with a strange man standing in your room. The apparition appeared to be wearing a seersucker suit and bow tie and tennis shoes. When this became apparent he seemed somewhat less threatening. His identity could then be perceived. When she saw it was Monroe she felt better. She felt she had an overwhelming love for him. This made her feel better, to have an overwhelming love for someone. He was a connection to the past. He was a connection to that spot of land on earth a person holds most dear. She had an uncomplicated love for him. This made her feel better, to have a simple, uncomplicated love for someone. Of all those who could be dear, he was dearest. Why? She felt remorse. Then he bent down and gave her a thick book with a blue cover. It was a book of etiquette. She opened it and there was a pressed flower inside. When she found it he looked away.

Then he said to her specifically, in a slightly pleading tone of criticism: "Grace, you always love the same few things, you always go back to them, you always cleave to them." He did not mean it as a compliment. He seemed to mean it as a criticism. Perhaps he only meant it as a truth, which he seemed to disdain, he who above all should be considered guilty of it.

For their honeymoon Monroe planned a trip to the Louisiana countryside. For six days they would go to plantations and Southern gardens and the Gulf Coast. "I don't think I could be alone with you for six days in antebellum homes," said Walter when this was described to him. "Southern gardens and plantations—plus you—that would be a little excessive." That was sort of funny. It was crusty. He couldn't swallow all that plantation tour stuff. Monroe wasn't crusty. He could swallow all that plantation tour stuff. Not only could he swallow it, it was mother's milk to him. He came from one, he had lived on one—a plantation. His whole life was a fantastical and exaggerated portrayal of an old South impossible to exist. But it did exist. Its fantasticalness obsessed her.

But that was obviously a demented vision into which she was dementedly descending. And besides, where was he? So in New York as a preliminary but significant gesture of relinquishment she was trying to cancel the reservations for their honeymoon which Monroe had made. This proved to be difficult. The Southerners are sometimes very firm beneath their gentleness. They are known as Iron Magnolias. When she tried to cancel one reservation at a plantation in St. Francisville for three nights the receptionist said she would still be charged. The bridal suite was always booked months in advance. That was the understanding. "I can let you talk to Miss Mary," she added doubtfully. In Southern plantations or businesses the ultimate ruler is always called Miss Mary. She is an Iron Magnolia.

"All right, I'll talk to Miss Mary," Grace said bravely.

"Miss Mary doesn't usually talk until after five," drawled the girl.

"O.K. I'll call after five," Grace said meekly.

So she spent the next two days fruitlessly trying to get through to Miss Mary. That is part of the drill. You psych yourself to deal after five with an ancient alcoholic matriarch sitting at her desk in the plantation after the cocktail hour with an old hurricane lamp and a ceiling fan and then you can never get through to her. So finally Grace said to the receptionist, in her best Southern tone of incredible gentleness, with a tad of a drawl, "I'm canceling these reservations months in advance and I really don't see why we should have to pay for the whole three nights." Silence. Whispering drawls. Static electricity. The hum of ceiling fans, the crackle of ice cubes in Miss Mary's drink.

"So how shall we leave it?" Grace persisted. "Shall we say that I'm willing to pay a small portion of it for good faith but I don't think it's fair for me to pay the whole thing?" Silence. The hiss of hurricane lamps. Night sounds from the plantation. The clink of glasses, the whir of the fan. Slaves perhaps being tortured. Mulattoes perhaps being poured into huge vats of boiling water. "Or are we going to get into some sort of dispute?" she closed with genteel horror. "Oh no," said the girl phlegmatically. Nothing would be more unseemly than a dispute.

For New Year's when she came home from New York for the holiday they always went to the Gulf Coast. Whenever they went to the Gulf Coast at that season it was freezing and pouring rain. Still the coast road was beautiful, a suave old boulevard along the sea.

They stayed at a bed-and-breakfast in Pass Christian. Walter said he dreaded bed-and-breakfasts, when she told him about it later. Knickknacks, curios, a bathroom across the parlor. He said he would take Motel 6 any time over a bed-and-breakfast. He said he dreaded the morning when you had to meet the other guests, sitting down at the dining room table for breakfast and you had to socialize.

One year they had tried to cancel their New Year's reservation on the Gulf Coast but the proprietress of the bed-and-breakfast was another Iron Magnolia. She was gently but firmly aggressive and kept calling Grace all the time even after she had canceled the reservation to check on her intended whereabouts during New Year's.

One night leading up to New Year's she called and said, "Do you want me to rent out the Bluebonnet Room?" Of course the Bluebonnet Room is exactly the name to make the hearts sink of those who dread bed-and-breakfasts.

"Yes, do. I don't think we'll be coming," said Grace.

"But you're not in the Bluebonnet Room. You're in the Rose Room," she said.

"Then why are you asking me about the Bluebonnet Room?" Grace asked innocently.

The proprietress launched into a lengthy and incomprehensible explanation which Grace had to ask her to repeat several times because it was so incomprehensible. It had something to do with asbestos and a bathroom on the other side of the parlor. Finally something dawned on Grace. It dawned on her that they would have to go there, and once they got there they would have to socialize with the other guests. It was sort of like being engaged to Monroe. You couldn't get out of it. There was something inexorable about it, like the advance of Sherman's army to the sea.

When they got there it turned out that the proprietress had gently but inexorably misrepresented many things. She said the room had a view of the Gulf. It had a view of McDonald's. She said it was a lovely room with all the conveniences. It didn't have a bathroom so you had to go through the parlor to get to one. You also had to share it with the Bluebonnet Room. They were building a bathroom in the Rose Room but it would be finished next week. Meanwhile they had just tried to dry the asbestos from the construction work, and maybe Grace should leave the windows open.

"Do you have a cold drink?" Grace asked meekly.

"Do you want Coke?"

"Yes."

"We don't have Coke."

A great general always knows when to retreat. Grace retreated.

They met the other guest the next morning at breakfast. The other guest was a professional calibrator. What's that? Grace asked. It's someone who takes measurements to make sure that there are sixty seconds in a minute and sixty minutes in an hour. You mean you sit somewhere in the middle of the earth and make sure that a minute is a minute and a second is a second? Grace asked. Not exactly, he laughed, but he could not really explain what use his measurements had. He said he also measured pressure in tires. But where do you do this, Grace asked, all over the world at once or just in one gas station in Biloxi? He couldn't quite explain. Monroe suggested later it must have something to do with the military, and they drove home in a blinding rain the next day along the suave old boulevard she adored.

10

Walter paid a call.

"I'm not sure I could be in Louisiana at the same time as you," said Walter. "It would be too claustrophobic. All those Southern gardens and plantations and drives along the Gulf Coast. Have you considered Philadelphia?"

"I did live in New York, you know."

"So you admit it."

"As you know, I lived in the North for many years. I'm not just a sheltered Southern matron."

"You're not technically a matron, you know," Walter observed. "You keep living in some future time period. You're not taking the present into account. If you're so matronly and so Southern, what are you doing here?"

"I may be Southern but I've seen the world. I've lived in the North. It's just that right now I don't live anywhere because I'm traveling. And I'm about to remove to this demented scope of Southern Living and plantations and Southern gardens."

A demented silence ensued.

"Do you see what I'm saying?" she asked.

"Oh, it's far too obscure, I can't figure it out."

An interesting silence ensued.

"You're saying you have doubts. Why don't you face up to them? Why don't you think about them?" said Walter.

"I'm trying to follow, adhere to, a course I've laid out for myself. I believed in it. Maybe it was a dream. It may be insane to live in a dream but it's madness to live without one." She stopped. "And if I lose it I will be in a Nameless Hour."

"A what?"

"A Nameless Hour—it's where you have no one to turn to."

So now there was a Nameless Hour. He could never get her little rubrics straight. They were too nutty.

"If I lose Monroe I would take the Nameless Hour, believing it, like solitude, to be the truest constant. Do you see what I'm saying?"

"So you're saying you would become a misanthrope."

"Sort of."

"How can you be a misanthrope when you're constantly doting on everyone?"

"I'm trying to tell you about my ideals. If I lose him I'm not going to be able to just run to someone else. Do you see what I'm saying?"

"Maybe some day I can come to understand it," said the hapless Walter, and departed, while she studied the angels atop Grand Central who guarded his receding figure.

11

When she lived in New York she was surrounded by weeping winos, drug dealers, people who have been nonviolent for a whole year, the functionally insane, and the tubercular. The severely and chronically mentally disturbed. She knew the exact terms because they were always putting flyers under her door about it. They built a place for crazy people on her block. It had ornate hand-operated elevators, potted palms, a doorman, restored elegance. It kind of made her wish she was crazy so she could live there.

As she frequently lay awake at three in the morning hearing the screams of the functionally insane, she listened to "America's favorite radio psychologist" for hours on end. It was amazing that she was America's favorite radio psychologist, because she was always screaming at her patients and making them feel bad. They would call in and say, "Oh, Doctor, I love your show, and I'm so nervous, I finally got through to you, I've been waiting for hours, I—"

"Sharon, you're not telling me what your question is."

"Well, I've been married for eight years, and I'm thirty-four years old, my husband is thirty-five, we haven't had sex for three years, and I—"

"What's your question, Sharon?"

"Well, I love him but he's not interested in sex and I—"

"Sharon, you're still not telling me what your question is."

"I'm very depressed, and I've stopped eating, and I—"

"Sharon, I can't help you if you don't tell me what's wrong."

Apparently you had to ask it in the exact form of a question before she could proceed, like a game show on TV. The only people she was nice to were depressed young men who had guns. She always asked depressed young single men if they had guns. Then when they said yes she said gently, Brian, I think you should give the gun to a friend.

You had to have a gun to get through to this woman.

Everyone was always telling her these horrible problems—they thought their son was having sex with animals, their husband left them for their young secretary after fifty-one years of marriage, they hadn't left the house in weeks—and the psychologist just kept getting more and more annoyed, heaving grandiose sighs of irritation and asking them what their question was.

Degraded forms of psychology such as radio psychologists and self-help books were a bit of a hobby with Grace. Due to her acquaintance with both amateur and professional psychology, she often came into a room full of people, say at a party, and would have everyone talking about their innermost, hideously intimate personal problems within the first five minutes, then go to the bar to get some hors d'oeuvres, leaving everyone holding the bag with no idea what to say to each other. She herself suffered from bouts of self-loathing, perhaps stemming from an exaggerated concept of honor. Members of the Fiery Pantheon, for example, would never fall from grace. Still she herself wanted only to be paid some mind, which her custom of effacing herself often made unlikely. She wasn't personally vain. She thought herself to be very fossilized and drab, with a repressed Victorian demeanor.

Everyone kept telling her to get brighter clothes. Maybe it would help her sexuality. Where she came from, it was the custom for women to decorate themselves and be knockouts. You were supposed to bring suitcases full of clothes and agonize over what to wear.

A salesgirl tried to help her. But the old obstacle cropped up. The salesgirl kept getting more and more shocked by the customer's admonitions to be drab.

"This is a bit too plain," said the salesgirl.

"That's just the thing. I'm a Plain Jane," said the self-effacing customer.

"Now, that's too big, you need a smaller size," said the salesgirl.

"Oh no, it's just right, we need to cover up as much as possible," said Grace.

"But why? You should show your shape."

"No, you see that's not suitable for my drab, matronly persona."

The salesgirl looked at her wide-eyed.

It was a strange sensation to hear this beautiful young girl saying I'm so drab and matronly. It was as if she were an actress preparing for a role in which she had to be drab and matronly.

Walter had reflected it seemed to have to do with her being engaged. As if that were her conception of marriage, that you must become a drab figure devoted to hapless self-sacrifice. In fact he had never seen her behave in another way. "But it was the vague air of shambles . . . the unself-conscious carriage, that appointed her an instant citizen of Paradise" in Walter's view.

As she walked home among the crowds on Broadway she began to snap. Why can't they be Southerners, dressed in resort wear at Hilton Head Island; why can't they be cheery robust Southerners devoted to comfort, prosperity, the golf course, the green, at pleasant resorts on the Georgia coast, or Florida, in the uncrowded South, devoted to pleasure and gardens and humid resorts, wearing pink shirts and green pants, enjoying life in a more simple way, the environs and atmosphere less neurotic but instead peaceful and with a certain undefinable gaiety, brought on by the mixture of beauty and peace, the madcap palms and ancient oaks? Yes, why can't they be Southerners, Walter thought across town, sitting at a bar in Times Square with his head in his hands, why can't they be self-effacing and softhearted and mistakenly think themselves drab? Why can't they be decorous and elegant and kind?

“Jane, you’re encouraging that boy,” said Mr. Stewart to his wife, in their hotel room in New York.

“DeCourcy, how can you say that?” she responded. Mr. Stewart carried his grandmother’s maiden name as his somewhat startling given name.

“You’ll find you’ve caused quite a bit of trouble on this matter,” said Mr. Stewart.

“Not at all. The boy needs help. We’re helping him. He’s disintegrating. I’m trying to pick up the pieces and paste him back together, don’t you see?”

“Nonsense, Jane. Sheer nonsense. And you know it.”

“No I don’t know it. Look at Sally.”

“What about her?”

This was their son Peter’s wife, whom Mrs. Stewart believed to be disintegrating. But then, Mrs. Stewart believed that each one of her sons’ marriages was disintegrating. Her own marriage had been established long ago, and saved at a crucial moment from imploding. Now it was her job to prevent everyone else’s marriage from decay.

“What’s wrong with Sally?”

“You know as well as I do.”

Each of the wives of Mrs. Stewart’s sons was in need of psychiatric treatment. They provided striking examples of insanity. Peter’s wife did not know how to load the dishwasher correctly, a deep source of grief and agony to Mrs. Stewart, and the source, in her opinion, of the disintegration of his marriage. The rest of her daughters-in-law showed other pointed examples of insanity such as forgetting to take the garbage out.

Those of Grace's brothers and their wives who had been able to get away from their daily activities at work in New Orleans to join the family in Virginia had not stayed long, nor would they accompany the family on its travels. Sons and daughters-in-law were the subject of too much psychiatric analysis and marriage counseling for their liking. You had to be a strong soul to ignore and at the same time appreciate Mrs. Stewart's psychiatric diagnoses. Not everyone was up to it. Some were. Her husband was. And so was Grace, although she would not have credited herself with being so stalwart.

"You'll find that Monroe will not be pleased by this turn of events," said Mr. Stewart.

"What turn of events?" asked his wife.

"Now, you know as well as I do, Jane. What is he supposed to think when he gets here and finds this young man drooling over Grace?"

"Drooling over her, DeCourcy?"

"I'm not going to gloss it over."

"But Grace is engaged to be married.

"Exactly."

"She would never falsify that."

"But don't you see the trouble that could come? You can't tell me that you don't see the trouble that could come."

Now, many people in New Orleans had many problems, including many members of the Collier family, but Monroe Collier, the betrothed of her only daughter, Mrs. Stewart had chosen to adore, and to introduce into a chamber of idolatry in her heart previously reserved for no one, since she idolized no one. Her gaze on humanity was far too clear for that.

Thus Mrs. Stewart was determined to dredge Walter upward from the spiral of doom to which he customarily was pointed, in her view. Mr. Stewart saw this crisis taking shape in his wife's mind. He watched it reach a peak over the week in Virginia. As for his own position, regarding Walter, it began to decline. He began to feel concern where formerly he had felt all bemusement. Formerly he had been amused by Walter. Now he felt more darkly.

"This trip is shaping up as a Disaster with a capital D," muttered Mr. Stewart.

13

Mrs. Stewart thought it over. Disaster with a capital D. Actually, the idea invigorated her. Disaster, pathology, breakdowns, signs of mental turmoil. Psychological visions dawned. As she now came to think of it, she had seen Walter gulping down vodka tonics in a disturbed manner in the hotel lobby after dinner. Now, here was some pathology to study. But she did not find, in her analysis, that there was a danger to Grace.

"As you should know by now, DeCourcy, I am nobody's fool," she began in the opening argument of her rebuttal case. "We don't have to be so formal all the time," Mrs. Stewart argued. "If Walter wants to go to Europe, he can join us over there. Your movements are so guarded, DeCourcy. Your manner is so formal."

"Well, one's manner should be formal. You can't be jerking all over the place," said Mr. Stewart.

"Lest society be rent asunder," said Mrs. Stewart, looking at her husband closely.

The conversation seemed to lose steam at this point.

But she felt that she had reached a dramatic conclusion. Having reached this dramatic conclusion she approached the door, and Mrs. Stewart approached a door in a way that showed that it demanded to be opened. In another time, Mr. Stewart would have held the door, and she would have swept out of the room. Her sweeping-out-of-rooms days were now over.

So she tossed out a parting remark. "Sally is in stagnation. And Frances has gone bananas."

Mr. Stewart digested this to the best of his ability. Maybe he should give it some thought. Then he pondered the more immediate problem, using more of practicality than psychology.

If his wife wanted to behave like a team of Viennese psychiatrists, Mr. Stewart was not so sure that it was such a hot idea. In point of fact he had resolved to make inquiries, as he put it, about Walter.

Mr. Stewart was assured that there would be trouble of some kind between Walter and Monroe. It was not that he preferred one or the other. He had always liked Monroe well enough, given the circumstances, the circumstances being that he was in a duel with him. Walter he had kept a sharp eye peeled on from the beginning and he had not disliked the boy. He had gotten sort of a kick out of Walter.

But he would have to make inquiries.

Thus decided, he glared off into the distance for a while, and then retired.

14

When Mr. Stewart went to New York, it was as if he had just wandered in from the 1940s. He spent his time meandering down Madison Avenue searching for tailors and hatters from the 1940s, trying to get obscure items of clothing long since discontinued. Occasionally he would meet up with some like-minded old gent from the 1940s who had been forced to move his premises to a hole in the wall somewhere. There they would repine for the old days, and the passing of narrow lapels.

He had a phobia of cash machines, although he was curiously obsessed with them. He liked to smoke cigars and had a phobia of all the places nowadays that wouldn't let him smoke cigars. In the 1940s he could smoke cigars in elevators, haberdashers, Brooks Brothers, not to mention restaurants and hotel lobbies.

If there was one thing that Mr. Stewart had a phobia of beyond all other things, it was the concept of having a Social Security number. Countless clerks, bureaucrats, insurance agents, and tax officials had been driven slowly and meticulously insane by Mr. Stewart's refusal to give out his Social Security number. Just ask yourself, how many times in a week does someone ask for your Social Security number? Then ask yourself, what would happen if each time it was asked for in the routine manner, you replied that it was your personal business, it was none of their business, and what right did they have to demand it?

Even old friends and acquaintances with whom he had kindly relationships spent numberless hours tearing their hair out trying to extract from Mr. Stewart his Social Security number for routine insurance forms.

Thus Mr. Stewart had a good bit of trouble in New York trying to renew his passport without revealing his Social Security number, but being a lawyer, he ultimately succeeded, and was also able to procure Sea Island pajamas from a bygone tailor who had been forced to remove his premises to a small stand in an upper floor of Brooks Brothers.

* * *

After dinner, Mr. Stewart retired to his desk for study. Why? Because he had other fish to fry than entertaining guests. He had to conduct his various studies, be they of new things in California, or old things in ancient Greek, or how to evade the worldwide mania for identification numbers detrimental to the individual and his privacy.

He had a curious correspondence with various obscure scholars, theologians, and others. A born-again Christian of his acquaintance had written to tell him that there would be a rending of evil on June 9. There wasn't. She had also predicted that the world would end in October. It hadn't.

In her latest correspondence she protested that the local high school football team should not wear the colors red and black because they are Satanic. And they shouldn't let their mascot be a bulldog because that is the offspring of men and dogs. For some reason Mr. Stewart found born-again Christians very bemusing. He liked to analyze and attempt to prove or disprove their beliefs, depending on the evidence available. Born-again Christians or religious maniacs of any kind he felt a sort of bond with. He also liked crazed young people.

He was enamored of something called the Severn Bore. It was some sort of tidal wave. The Severn Bore appeared with demonic irregularity in the Cotswolds region of England. Smaller bores came in autumn and spring, but the Great Bore came only intermittently, as various scholars informed Mr. Stewart when he wrote to inquire.

Mr. and Mrs. Stewart had actually witnessed the Severn Bore. Mrs. Stewart was dubious. It was supposed to be a tidal wave, but what it really amounted to was a mound of debris containing lightbulbs, wire hangers, and other forms of garbage floating quickly down the river. The banks of the river were lined with British eccentrics in lawn chairs with binoculars and picnic hampers also waiting to view the Bore. They gathered there at the appointed hour for the expected arrival of the Bore. Bore lore was exchanged. A motorboat was launched to ride the surge. One man exploded in anger before the Bore arrived and drove suddenly away. He could not endure the wait. Tensions apparently ran high. Another man kept taking equipment out of his trunk, batteries with test tubes in which he would pour water from the Bore. There was a mother and son duo who lived near the Bore and came to see it *very* often. They were the receptacles of an amazing amount of Bore lore. They looked shrunken. They had no sense of love of life. Until the Bore arrived—and then they came alive.

Flotsam begins to shift its direction when the Bore arrives. Excitement mounts. Experts virtually foam at the mouth. Then a small surge of debris comes floating past. Earnest Bore buffs stick around for hours afterward to observe the direction of the flow reverse itself. Others drift off, bemused.

You had to be a fan of anticlimactic experiences to appreciate the Bore, concluded Mrs. Stewart.

At lunch in the hotel dining room while awaiting the viewing of the Bore, Mr. Stewart lit up a big cigar. Nobody frowned. He then walked into the elevator and went upstairs. There was no sign abjuring NO SMOKING IN ELEVATOR—in fact there was an ashtray in the elevator.

In Zurich every summer he picked up his Havana cigars, and went for the periodic checkup of his grandfather's watch, which he wore on a ribbon in his trousers pocket. He made a studious tour of Europe calmly taking notes on points of interest such as canal aqueducts, Cistercian abbeys, exchange rates, dynastic porphyry tombs, foreign invective, Merovingian ruins, tympanums, topiary, and traffic jams. Only he knew what some of these things were.

His companions often complained that he was obsessed with the obscure, but he gently explained that any inquisitive tourist traveling in England would be obsessed with tree girths, just as any tourist in France would be obsessed with Merovingian baptistries, or in Italy with water chains, or in Bavaria with church stuccators. The simple truth was that he must follow his star, and life is not worthwhile unless you follow yours. His star led him to take his family on a gorgeous ocean liner every summer to Europe to see the world. You could not fault his star.

At home, a head of white hair belonging to Mr. Stewart could be seen in a black convertible driving down St. Charles Avenue every evening exactly at six-thirty after work, with opera blaring to the oaks.

In his own crazed youth, if it could be called crazed, a garden party had been held at the time of Mr. Stewart's tenth wedding anniversary in 1954. The men wore white tie and eccentric safari helmets under green-and-white-striped tents. The women wore white gloves. They carried umbrellas for the shade. There was an orchestra among the palms.

Many exciting developments occurred in their lives at that time. When the baby-sitter, a glamorous black girl named Tweet, went out on dates, actual members of the New Orleans Saints (football team) came to pick her up, inciting in Grace's brothers a state of nervous paralysis brought on by the pureness of ecstasy. The mayor came to take out another one of their baby-sitters, also a glamorous black girl, on dates. King, the butler, leaned on his broom in the kitchen and sang Nat "King" Cole songs. He was a deacon in church. His singing reduced entire congregations to tears. The gardener called Mrs. Stewart on the telephone and told her he was in love with her. Grace's brother became a Communist. He was picked up by the police in high school for playing pinball at the airport at three in the morning. He was a hero the next day at school. Then he was forced to go to dancing school, wearing bow ties. His cronies sneaked out at night and drove across the football field over and over until it was destroyed—either in protest against dancing school or in favor of communism. The place was crawling with crazed young people who rode around in beat-up convertible Volkswagens without their shirts on because of the heat. Every morning the temperature would start out at eighty degrees, and get hotter through the course of the day. Nor did it cool off at evening or night. It just kept getting hotter. Grace grew up and became the belle of the ball, despite her attempts to be drab.

In the ordered society of New Orleans, she was a wild bohemian compared with those around her. At her age others drove station wagons, had three children, were married to lawyers, and lived in a beautiful house on the park. They stumbled, hugely pregnant, out of station wagons with three toddlers in the backseat, wearing their hair pushed back in wide headbands. Grace was your standard, garden-variety crazed young person and held this position for longer than most. She would not have admitted it. But in truth she never thought that she would really join those multitudes bound by marriage and children. She had spent her youth being transfixed by the palms, then going dementedly to cafés in the Quarter late at night, in hopes to spy her heroes. You knew someone for years, ten years, then suddenly, one day, you were standing in some overladen green park in New Orleans, you saw them at a distance from the bandstand, and suddenly you were seized with love for them—you said to yourself: How could I not have known it before—there is the man I love.

15

The man she loved was an old-time New Orleans man. Monroe was an archetypal Southerner. He wore a certain kind of clothes, baggy khakis and a starched white shirt. You know the type. Vice president of the Bank of the South. Insurance broker. Commodities trader. He would work in his father's insurance business. Or he would work for his father's shipping line. He was still in love with New Orleans after all these years. He was still in love with the South. He made his surroundings elegant by his love for them.

Monroe's father owned a small tugboat and barge company that operated on the Mississippi River. This was equally as romantic in Grace's fevered imagination as being an insurance broker. Yet Monroe had made the impossibly bold move of leaving his father's office. He had made the impossibly bold move of leaving New Orleans—yes, for Mobile, for Tuscaloosa, for Birmingham until somebody stopped him. Then he had come home. Yes, he had worked in his father's shipping office at one time. But then he had made the impossibly bold move of leaving his father's business for journalism.

One day in the future Monroe's father would take to ailing, and Monroe would be called on to leave his job at *The Times-Picayune* and take the helm of the family business. This was almost unbearably romantic, although it would not prove to be romantic for Monroe, who did not have an aptitude for business, and who would run the business into the ground, and take to ailing. But the business would be saved by a series of uncles—the DeLord men. Yes, the impossibly romantic DeLord men.

Grace could be a part of it all. She could be chatelaine of Lord Hall, receiving the romantic and decaying DeLord men staggering out of limousines silhouetted at the levee, the DeLord men smoking cigarettes at the office, talking into car phones on the way to the plantation . . . Hey, wait a minute. The DeLord men were running everything. The DeLord men were running Monroe.

If the DeLord men were running Monroe, it was still

romantic. You could not deny it was quaint. The DeLord men would run him while he put on white tie and tails to go to a ball, and maintain their place in society.

Monroe went to lunch and dinner at a dozen watering holes in New Orleans where at each he was considered a regular. He had a zippy sports car. He was always late. He had no routine. Then he worked at the *Picayune.*

When he worked at his father's office, he had the opportunity to travel. He had the opportunity to wear shorts and go visit his ailing relatives in the middle of the week if he felt like it. And he felt like it a lot. He was touchingly attached to his relatives. Like many Southerners. Like Grace herself.

In New Orleans you would have seen him standing lost in thought on a corner of St. Charles Avenue, in the glittering night, under the arcade of oaks, wearing white tie and tails. She pined for men in white tie and tails.

After living in Tuscaloosa, Alabama, Monroe wanted to live in Birmingham. Mobile, Tuscaloosa, Birmingham—Alabama was the source of all knowledge. He wanted to show Grace Birmingham. So it was there that they had met one Friday in late winter, she flying in from New York, as they often met up in the South.

There were nuns on the plane to Birmingham. God was with them. It was certainly the South. Everything was more pleasant and spring-like and the people good-humored and robust, the women laden with paint, the men abstracted and pleasant. The man at the first-class lounge in the Atlanta airport where she caught her connecting flight let her in although she didn't have a first-class ticket. "Are you having a bad day?" he asked. "Not really," she said. "Well, go on in, anyway!" he cried. The men on the plane to Birmingham were robust and blond-haired and genteel with vast expressions of cheer.

Grace got there a day early in order to experience Birmingham. She walked out and the weather though chilly was sunny and clear. It was sort of deserted. Every once in a while, on the downtown streets, you would see these incredibly handsome and genteel men—bankers, lawyers, Birmingham scions of society—and you would think in amazement: How can they be so noble, when the world is vast and various, as to stay here and defend the land of their forebears? How can they be so faithful, when she, for instance, couldn't? Then you'd see a young one, like Monroe, in his khaki pants and pink shirt, and would think it even more: How can you be so noble, accepting your lot, your sphere, and not yearning to move out of it?

Grace kept trying to figure out Birmingham and she couldn't figure it out. Every newsstand downtown had books about the Civil War, prominently thrust between *The New York Times* and *Wall Street Journal.* Society scions populated the streets. It was hilly, it seemed Northern in many ways, no leaves yet on the trees.

A distant acquaintance whom she looked up took her to a cocktail party. People in Birmingham had a quality that many Southerners have: They had this world-weary, worldly-wise air as if they had just been standing at the edge of a yawning abyss, looking down into a yawning vortex of ruin, and had seen it all—as if they were possessed of the most tragic knowledge the world could know. It was as if the Civil War were transpiring in their very hearts, for they had some inner knowledge of destruction. It didn't matter if it was your hairdresser or a society matron—they would have that air about them. If you got your hair cut in Birmingham you would get the best haircut known to man, because the hairdresser would be world-weary and jaundiced and had seen it all—right there in Birmingham—and was basically the source of all knowledge.

The party was at the country club. It was typical for Birmingham: a dark Anglo-Saxon Tudor manor. For some reason that was their theme: Jolly Old England. In New Orleans you got things done in a fake plantation style or a fake French

Riviera style, but in Birmingham the theme was strictly the Anglo-Saxon Tudor castle, plunked down in the South.

Birmingham seemed truly an anomaly. The people had the personality of New Orleans, with their mad drawls and world-weary knowledge, their bemusing hopelessness; but Birmingham is a postbellum town—unlike New Orleans or Charleston or Savannah. It is a gutsy-looking industrial town overlooked by suburban hills.

So the country club was typical. You went in and immediately felt a certain fresh robust air of prosperity and comfort, but the styles didn't mix—the Tudor beams, then suddenly a fake wrought-iron grill and Dixieland banjos to stand for the Old South, then the Jolly Old England red coats of the band.

She got hooked up with ladies who had mad drawls and were obsessed with church controversies. They were at the hairdresser, the tearoom, drawling at the shops. The Southerners were happy in the New South—as in Atlanta and all purlieus of the New South the people were happy and robust and prosperous. Grace was an outsider in being the only Southerner in Birmingham who wasn't ecstatic. But actually she was starting to be ecstatic after being there for half a day. After being there for three days they had to peel her off the sidewalk to get her to leave.

It was an incredibly small world, Birmingham. Birmingham was the type of town where you kept running into people you knew even though you didn't know anyone there and had never been there before in your life. But she kept running into them at tea shops and parties.

Monroe arrived and took her to truly one of the most fantastical places she had ever seen. It was called The Club. The neighborhood reminded her of New Orleans, because it was so dilapidated. You drove up a dilapidated mountain and came to this 1950s old-time nightclub. The place was vast. It was a fantastical old-time supper club with a suave swing band and immense underpopulated rooms and vistas. There were spellbinding views of the glittering hills.

It reminded her of Los Angeles. In Los Angeles the hills are always glittering, for some reason. Wild horses had to drag her to Los Angeles, where once she had to go, but then when she got there they had to peel her off Sunset Boulevard to get her to leave.

It seemed that every time she left a place, wild horses had to drag her away. When she moved from New Orleans to New York, for instance, basically she grabbed on to the bedstead and wild horses were harnessed to her and she held on for dear life while they dragged her away.

These same wild horses dragged her at one time to Los Angeles, which kept trying to be Florida and kept missing. It looked like Miami. Palm trees and flat boulevards and white buildings and the sea. But it did not have the bemusing hopelessness of the tropics. She couldn't understand its soul.

If you're from New Orleans then Florida is in your blood and you understand it. You understand its soul. No matter how tacky and bleak it may seem it doesn't depress you because you understand its soul. It is a green old frivolous place with no pretensions to anything else. That is its soul. But that was not the soul of Los Angeles.

The Pacific Ocean was too big. The hotel was glitzy and new and this gave her anxiety. It was a shining new pink marble hotel on the vast Pacific, which was pitiless and barbaric. Everything was too vast in California. They had these vast barbaric boulevards. Sure they had palm trees and art deco in Santa Monica. It kept trying to be Florida, but in Florida you would be watching the elderly shuffle through crumbling art deco courts in Miami, which would give it humanity. It would be seedy and hopeless and depressing, which would also give it humanity. Also in Florida you have humidity, which people don't like. Southerners don't like it either, but at least it's in their blood so they understand it. It's atmospheric. It's romantic. Where California is more bland. Bland and sleazy is a bad combination. Sleazy and hopeless is better. So she moved to Hollywood. She moved to Sunset Boulevard, to a crumbling château inhabited by demented old stars. The clerk was a Filipino houseboy. No one was ever there. The gardens, which were partly in a European court with vaulted colonnades and green chairs, were always beautiful and deserted. It had the air of being down on its luck that Hollywood is known for. Broken-down wrecks with broken dreams. She loved it.

There was an alcoholic girl with a dog buying Scotch at the store. People lived in pleasing bungalows with little lawns and palms, but behind these pleasing bungalows was some sad sordid tale—the blinds were always drawn, they had ten cats and chain-smoked all day, they never went out, except to buy Scotch at the store with their dog. But she loved that. It was a first cousin of what she loved in Monroe. If all he did was chain-smoke with the blinds drawn and then go to the store to get Scotch with his dog, she probably would have loved him even more. But what he did was pretty close.

His forebears were legends, the DeLord men. He tried to uphold their standard, as he devoted himself to his ailing relatives such as the DeLord men themselves when they were too sick with diseases brought on by their vices to go to the parties where Monroe represented them. While he unflinchingly did what they said, upholding the family, as according to their dictates he defined the scope of their society.

The DeLord men were arbiters of that society, elevated to the very pinnacle of its civilization. Why? What distinguished them? Their presence denoted an antique stratosphere of social sanction.

In point of fact they were really just regular guys, regular Southern guys, and it would be difficult to say exactly what it was about them that had catapulted them to the very pinnacle of society. It may have been that they entertained a lot. They gave a lot of parties. In this way they indicated their interest in society. But their social position was inherited. If they had moved to New Orleans from Ohio they would not have been able to get into society by giving a lot of parties. But they had originated in New Orleans, after coming over from France. They had been in the same location for six or seven generations, and their residence in Louisiana began on a plantation, at a time when even the city of New Orleans consisted of but two or three vast plantations later cut down and subdivided repeatedly to incorporate a regular city.

When you knew Monroe you knew that your fathers or uncles were best friends, that your grandfathers had been best friends, and so on back through generations. This was an ornate old society, indescribably solid, and to Grace it was endlessly fascinating, this very solidity.

On New Year's Day the DeLord men went to the Sugar Bowl wearing seersucker suits for it was eighty-five degrees in the shade. They were these dapper tropical creatures which only New Orleans could breed. The DeLord men gave a party for Grace. They all came in their seersucker suits and dark sunglasses and white bucks, polite and debonair and gallant. She admired them because they would always cheerfully perform their duties in life, not only cheerfully but always with gaiety and grace. In the North she had grown used to angst. Everyone had angst in the North and talked about it all the time. But if the DeLord men had angst they would do anything to hide their pain, and never show it, usually by going to more and more parties, and drinking more and more cocktails. They were truly debonair.

So it happened that on lower Park Avenue in the summer evening a white-suited Southerner stood beside what was once a car. He seemed to be lost. A dog peered dolefully from what was once the backseat of the car.

He was holding a bunch of peonies. She hadn't seen

peonies since she was in Alabama. She pined for Alabama. He just stood there as if lost in thought.

She perceived who it was, Monroe.

They kissed. She was shocked.

The man she loved stood in the dashing twilight. He did not notice that the twilight was dashing. It was not his way to notice things like that. That observation was left to those who beheld him in such surprise.

She could not help staring at his car. You couldn't really describe it as a car.

"What happened to your car?"

"It exploded in Virginia. I was visiting a sickly aunt . . ."

She went into a reverie.

His dog peered dolefully from the backseat.

"I can't stay," he said. "I only came to pay a call," as if he had just driven over from Calhoun Street. "I'm driving down to Alabama to visit Miss Camille. She's ailing."

Grace could not help but go into a reverie. Miss Camille would be a variation on Miss Mary, the basic ruler of the South, who runs the plantation, or runs the family, or runs the business, or runs the inn, but she doesn't come into the office until five. You can't talk to her till after five. She runs the show, but she can't get it together to start doing business until after five? What does she do until five?

Grace was in her reverie. She couldn't seem to snap out of it.

"You can't drive to Alabama in that car," she finally came out with. "It's exploded."

"Oh, it'll be all right."

"How long are you staying?"

"I'm leaving now. I just came by to say hi."

"You drove all the way to New York in an exploded car just to say hi?"

"Gracie, you know how Miss Camille is. Especially when she's ailing."

He was as destroyed as his car. He was as destroyed as the South. He couldn't cope. But she loved it that he couldn't cope. That he was so destroyed. On the other hand his car could explode and he could still manage to wear a white suit. He could still manage to be delightful. He didn't know he couldn't cope. He wasn't aware of it. Only she was.

"I know, I know, but you'll spend the night, at least?"

He kissed her. "I think that can be arranged."

"We're leaving Sunday for the trip. You can't make it?"

"Gracie, I've got a lot of ailing relatives right now."

It was always touching to her that he felt he had to look after his relatives. He felt he had to steer the ship. They were all so destroyed. After all Aunt Lord was out of traction, but was still in the hospital. Cousin King returned from a convention in Charleston and feeling overwhelmed spent ten days under an oxygen tent. Uncle Ferdinand was seen wandering around Virginia and seemed mentally in fair shape but very feeble in walking. He was working on a history of the DeLord family, incoherent in spots, but he was a great comfort to Miss Camille.

"I'll try to join you over there," he said vaguely. He kissed her again sweetly. She loved him. "Now where are we going to put Miss Maggie?"

Miss Maggie was his dog.

Miss Mary, Miss Camille, and Miss Maggie formed a holy trinity in her reveries that evening. When she called at her father's office or other establishments in the South she too was Miss Grace. It was sweet to be Miss Grace. It was sweeter after all than to be "Hey you" in New York. But she had been "Hey you" in a society in chaos for so long that to be mistress of Lord Hall, demented chatelaine of the crumbling plantation on the River Road drinking whiskey sours with devastatingly handsome decaying society gents getting out of limousines at the levee, seemed of course as if a very dream. A very sweet dream, but spending the night with Monroe gave her the degenerate desire to stagger down to cafés and go out dancing to all hours. Possibly this was not the desired effect of love.

But why? When she thirsted for him so she felt the night with him was not enough and only gave her a sad desire for the world. Sad because she did not want the world. She wanted the South, and him.

Was it all an apparition, her demented bond of honor to him, representing some loyalty to the South, her demented insistence on keeping her word to him and cherishing her ideal of him?

He left the next morning to tend to his decaying relatives.

16

Walter paid another call.

"I've been psychologically analyzed by your mother and now I feel better."

"What's her diagnosis?"

"I'm filled with rage."

"What are you enraged about?"

"We haven't gotten that far yet."

Honor dictated that she tell him of her visitor. But she froze. She was like a batter who steps up to the plate with the bases loaded. "It's odd the way you know me is neither here nor there," she began, "because I used to be a solitary glamor girl, and am about to be a matron, but am in some weird in-between phase, like some sort of vegetable."

"Don't worry. I'm a vegetarian," offered Walter.

Then she started rambling about the Fiery Pantheon. There was also this Nameless Hour. What is it? Walter wanted to know. It's when there is no one to turn to, not your husband, for you don't have one, but even if you did have one, nor your friends, nor anyone. You mean like right before you die? said Walter. But she said no, millions of other times. And when are these times? asked Walter. Usually toward midnight, she said, or around two in the morning.

"Some people call that bedtime," said Walter.

"Tell me more about this Hour of Desolation of yours," said Walter.

"It's not an Hour of Desolation. It's a Nameless Hour."

"O.K. O.K. What is it?"

"There comes an hour no one will answer, no one will be responsible. You are alone, especially if you're meek."

"Shrinking violet, eh?"

"Exactly."

"I'm not sure that guy in Virginia feels that way."

"What guy in Virginia?"

"That guy who goes around speaking in a monotone saying the same thing over and over and he looks like he's about eighty years old."

He tried to be gruff, but when she was near, his brain began to crowd with nightingales and angels, palm trees, old empires, and praised estates. It was becoming very crowded in his brain. Proximity to the Fiery Pantheon perhaps caused you to smolder dementedly. Proximity without entrance—it caused an exquisite agony. If you could get into the Fiery Pantheon, so far as he could tell, you would lead the life of Riley. All your troubles would be over. You would have this girl going around adoring you all the time, and worshiping the ground you walked on. Your every move would be adored.

"Look, maybe we should cut through all this," he said.

"Cut through all what?"

"Cut through all the niceties and formalities that people seem to feel are necessary."

"Necessary for what?"

"Maybe I should kiss you now," he said, smolderingly.

She responded in gossamer peals of laughter, which was not exactly what he had in mind.

Then he took her to see *Swan Lake*. *Swan Lake* was sort of for little girls, he decided. There was in fact a little girl sitting next to them. She was crumpled into the shape of a pretzel with her head mashed against the seat, sleeping. Walter pointed her out, saying that her demeanor represented his own reaction to *Swan Lake*. The swans were O.K. The swans when they first came out, like the old waltz that accompanied them, represented some classic knowledge, like when you heard a line of Shakespeare for the first time, yet you realized that it had been ringing in your ears since the day you were born.

An entourage moved down the aisle from time to time which contained at its center a former opera star who received a standing ovation every time she got up. And she got up a lot. She got up at each intermission several times and walked up and down the aisle with her entourage. Each time she did so she brought down the house. The crowd threw roses, yelled out adoring epithets in Italian, clapped insanely, stamped their feet, and exhibited many other signs of adoration. Even if she stirred during the performance, as if maybe she was thinking about getting up, the audience swooned over the balcony yelling out superlatives in Italian, stopping the show. The crazed opera fans were to Grace the third to last suave sight in New York, after the angels atop Grand Central, and the policeman on a horse. Then there was the falling swan.

There was a wooden swan meant to roll across the set. Except the swan got stuck in the middle of the stage behind a tree and then broke out awkwardly going in the wrong direction. Also, Prince Siegfried sort of fell down after one of his jumps.

Finally it was over and they returned to the humid night. Grace was ecstatic. Her reaction to *Swan Lake* was certainly the opposite of his. She adored it. She was on cloud nine. Life was a Gay Rondelet.

"A what?"

"A Gay Rondelet."

"Is that a gift shop?"

"It's the opposite of the Whirlpool of Doom."

"Oh, great, so now we're in a Vortex of Doom."

"We're not in a Vortex of Doom. We're in a Whirlpool of Doom."

"Well when are we going to get out of it?"

"That's just the point of it being a whirlpool. It's sucking us in."

She noticed he had a way of stretching his hands out, when they met, in a curious sidewise motion as if to guide her to her seat.

Walter walked her back to her hotel, and attempted to kiss her good night. He failed. But Walter had a plan, and reasoned that it was not yet time to put it in effect.

"Back to the salt mines," he said.

He walked toward the angels atop Grand Central, and returned to the sirens of Bellevue, which described a Whirlpool of Doom reverberating through his neighborhood.

17

"I'm wearing a blue satin cocktail dress studded with rhinestones," said a girl attired with hideous opulence coming up to

Grace and Mrs. Stewart sitting in the lobby of their hotel. There was a fashion show going on.

"Grace, if you could just wear a *finished outfit* when you're with Monroe," said Mrs. Stewart. "You ought to wear a *finished outfit* when you teach, Grace," she said. "Volume, Grace. Volume," she added, studying her hair.

"Volume?"

"Your hair, Grace. Your hair should have *volume*."

"O.K. O.K.," said Grace.

"Your hair has reached a new low, Grace," observed Mrs. Stewart. Mrs. Stewart subjected her daughter's hair to a dark and prolonged study. Her hair needed conditioner, observed Mrs. Stewart with the same penetrating urgency it would be appropriate to apply to a strategic arms conference in a world war. If only she would use a volumizer, Mrs. Stewart noted with the gravity it would be appropriate to attribute to a major advancement in the canons of philosophy. Close scrutiny was given to her very unsatisfactory clothes. Mrs. Stewart felt that her daughter dressed like a Chinese opium addict.

"You know, Mother, with some people, shopping elates them. Or getting new clothes, new hair, it elates them," said Grace. "I'm not one of those people. My outer appearance does not elate me."

"I've got news for you," said Mrs. Stewart. "*Elate* is not a transitive verb."

An interesting silence ensued. She studied her daughter's face.

"Grace, is it on or is it off?"

"It's on."

"Grace, you should be *radiant*. You're engaged to be married. You're not *radiant*."

"Thanks a lot."

A new tack was struck.

"Grace, I'm not going to pry into your personal life anymore. Nothing could actually interest me less than your personal life or psychological problems. Your personal life is just not something that can hold my interest," she went on for some time, "but I could tell by your tone when we left Virginia after you saw Monroe that you seemed unsatisfied with your visit with him."

"I'm unavailable for comment."

"Grace, I'd like to make a very provocative statement," announced Mrs. Stewart.

"Yes?"

"Let me attempt to explain something to you."

"O.K. Go ahead. Attempt."

"There's a certain person who I think is very fond of you who has been spending a lot of time with you whose initials are W. S."

"I thought you think he's crazy."

"I think he's deeply flawed, and I think some of his views are darkly inaccurate, but he's growing on me."

"I happen to be engaged to be married."

"And after your engagement was announced Sky McCloud sagged to his knees and hasn't gotten up since."

"So?"

"Men all over town had to recover."

"You speak in hyperbole, Mother dear."

"And now Walter is going to pieces."

"I disagree."

"Grace, you're *extinguishing* him."

"I don't have anything to do with him."

"That's just it. It's *extinguishing* him."

"I told you before, he's a hypochondriac. Haven't you noticed that he has a fatal disease every time we see him?"

"That's what I've been trying to *tell* you all. He's *somatizing*. He's in latency."

"Latency of what?"

"Put it this way. He's not living up to his potential for human happiness."

"Why does everyone have to be so happy all the time?"

"Grace, if I die on this trip—"

"But, Mother dear, you're not going to die."

She drew herself up like an old general. "I am in my decline," she announced.

"You don't seem so declining to me."

"But if I die, I assume Walter will come to the funeral, and maybe then you will understand how he feels about you."

"Really now, Mother, we're going to be thrown together a lot on the trip. I don't have to go to your funeral in order to see him."

But she talked of death, and matchmaking after her death. She had recently taken a fall in New Orleans and fractured her hip. The ambulance came and she was lying on the stretcher, imperious and ironclad as ever in the moment of her frailty. From the stretcher she observed that Peter's wife was in stagnation and should read more books. She should also learn to load the dishwasher correctly. But first she should read some Spinoza. When Mr. Stewart came to the hospital later, Grace recalled, having heard of the fall, Mrs. Stewart got a stricken look when she saw her husband, and finally crumbled. "I'm so sorry, DeCourcy," she said, and she cried, and Mr. Stewart had a stricken look also. Then she added that Peter's wife should consider therapy.

She was dressed as ever to the nines, on admittance to the hospital, and had refused to sit in the wheelchair, had refused assistance when it was offered, and had started lecturing the doctors on medical procedures which they had, according to her, learned incorrectly in medical school. At night she would ring the bell in her room and lecture the doctor who appeared about what he had learned incorrectly in medical school, notifying him of her own advanced degree in clinical psychology from Radcliffe.

"Several people have died since I've been here," she informed him. "And one woman was transferred. She's now dying in a nursing home somewhere. Mrs. Bysart had retina surgery yesterday so now it's just down to me and Mrs. Lupe."

"Have you let your friends know you're here?" asked Grace.

"According to Frances the entire town is surging with the news."

Her mood changed and sometimes she cried. "You see when I was younger I had vanity," she told her daughter.

She told the doctor she had had a "cognitive disassociative episode" during the night. She was constantly diagnosing herself and everyone else in sight.

"Frances has conceived the idea that she should give a series of buffet dinners," she told Grace fiercely. There was always her curious mixture of intellect and domestic detail, both related with equal fervor.

For the first twenty years of her marriage she had kept a record, in a leather book, of all the dinner parties she gave, with a space for each entry describing the menu, the seating, the centerpiece, etc., ending with a space for Remarks. Here Mrs. Stewart would comment on the party as a whole, usually with some withering summation. "Dinner extraordinarily good. Conversation extraordinarily excruciating."

It must be said that when Grace viewed her mother in her frailty, yet lecturing the doctors about their incorrect diagnoses, the overwhelming feeling that passed over Grace was a blinding admiration for her mother.

Previously she had felt oppressed by her mother. Her mother was constantly telling her that she, Grace, and all her acquaintances and members of her family and everyone else on the globe had pathological problems and needed emergency therapy. It was not the most relaxing atmosphere in which to live. But now Grace was struck with a twilight sanction for her mother, and reveled in her psychiatric theories.

* * *

Mrs. Stewart was not intrinsically a Southern matron. Mr. Stewart had brought her from her native Massachusetts to New Orleans, which it had taken her exactly thirty years to adjust to. Thus she was an outsider, and this explained her ability to penetrate in observation the society surrounding her: the South.

When she first came to New Orleans she could not help but notice that at the cocktail hour the women changed into oriental housecoats, everyone drank heavily, they got in towering arguments about genealogy and who married who in 1910 and in general turned into a Tennessee Williams play—as Mrs. Stewart looked on incongruously with her tweed skirts and knee socks and high ideals from the North.

It was a defining moment in her married life.

When Mr. Stewart had proposed marriage, Mrs. Stewart said, All right, but I'll have to administer a Rorschach test. She then made him look at a bunch of inkblots and determined that he was normal.

At the time, she was still deeply involved in her studies in psychology at Radcliffe; nothing could take her away from them. Except, as it happened, Mr. Stewart. She left a year short of gaining an advanced degree in clinical psychology to go to New Orleans to get married. Still, nothing could take her away from her beloved psychology. In New Orleans she held various jobs attached to local mental hospitals and research institutions.

By the time of the present period of her life she had become quite frail due to osteoporosis and she had retired from her work. It may be that her retirement from her work caused her to direct her energies toward family members, social acquaintances, total strangers, and generally chance subjects such as Walter. A certain excess and undirected energy in her chosen field still occupied the central portion of her heart, although she had officially retired. Such as would be the case in anyone truly called to a vocation.

In the marriage of Mr. and Mrs. Stewart, two opposing and mutually irritating trains of thought and philosophies of life constantly were at war. In a way their marriage was a long combat, to which they were dedicated. It was a form of irritation that was not unconstructive. Each was necessary to the other. In the ordinary course of life Mr. Stewart found his wife's dark search for pathology amusing, but more, that it had a base of truth. No world of honor, Mr. Stewart knew, such as he and his father had adhered to, could completely exist. And so she dazzled him with her dark knowledge.

Currently the tables seemed to be turned. He saw it all. This Walter character was coming on to construct a doom for Grace. What were his intentions? Were they honorable? Mr. Stewart did not know. Usually it was his wife who perceived abnormality and doom. Now she looked the other way. Why?

18

Mr. and Mrs. Stewart had met on a transatlantic liner. It was a small ship on the open sea in 1939. War loomed. People did strange things. They wept after one small cocktail. They danced incessantly. They fell in love, they wrote billets-doux, they whispered little nothings, they met at odd hours in the bar and talked endlessly, or remained silent for embarrassing periods.

All this Mr. and Mrs. Stewart had done, when, at the respective ages of twenty-five and twenty-two, they had met on the transatlantic crossing.

Mrs. Stewart was going to Europe for the first time in her life, to Paris, before returning to Radcliffe to pursue her advanced degree in clinical psychology. On the ship she administered various psychological tests on Mr. Stewart, and was satisfied with his relative normality.

Mr. Stewart was amused. He had no use for psychology. Neither had he any use for it forty-five years later. She was a beautiful girl with glamorous blond hair and fierce interests. He might not be one to advertise his feelings, although on the boat people did things that were inconceivable to them when in view of the land, exhibiting long adoring silences and suicidal rages. Mr. Stewart was no exception. There was something in her glamorous blond hair and fierce interests that had pierced his heart.

When they parted Mr. Stewart sent postcards on from Egypt. "Today we saw a diametrical tomb in Memphis. DeCourcy." "We visited the oldest church in Babylon. Also a Babylonian prison. DeCourcy." There was no emotion in his notes. She wondered that his feelings for her must have changed. But on his return, he stopped in Cambridge and, at her apartment, got down on one knee and told her that he could not live without her.

She was uncertain. She asked for time to think it over. He went into a visible decline.

Her relatives came to New Orleans to meet his relatives. They went to dinner with his great-aunts. She was concerned by their grandeur and their abnormality. Everything about them was anachronistic. Even his name, DeCourcy, was anachronistic. She told her mother she could not go through with it. Her mother looked at Mr. Stewart's celebrated father, she looked at the sumptuous appointments of the Stewart family home. She took her daughter aside and fiercely whispered, "You're going through with it."

The war intervened in their courtship. Mr. Stewart was sent to Africa to work in decoding and intelligence. He wore dusty khakis and no shirt. Small black children followed him around and brought him straw hats and cigarettes and photographs of naked women. His colleagues were other young men in no shirts and khaki trousers. He was subsequently in the Pacific, altogether serving for two years.

His letters from New Guinea and North Africa had been as dry as his notes from Egypt. "We studied an advance in cryptography today. The weather is intolerably hot. We were given insufficient rations. DeCourcy." He did not know how to express his feelings, though all the feeling was there. But the war came on to elevate their courtship, and he associated all the tragedy, heroism, and futility of the world with his love for her.

He was awarded the Silver Star for gallantry in North Africa. Intelligence work had not in Mr. Stewart's case involved situations of danger, except on one occasion. On that occasion he had intercepted and decoded an enemy message which he had delivered personally to General Montgomery, the British field commander, calmly walking through minefields at night. He sustained no injuries. He did not view his behavior as brave. It was like walking from the office to the courthouse to deliver a brief to the clerk. It was as dry a matter to him as the law would prove in life to most others, though it did not prove so to him. The law to him was fabulously exciting; the war was a dry matter. Something out of the ordinary had come across his desk, of which he perceived the importance, and he simply took the most direct course of action. In that moment, as he walked across the desert in the night, he thought of his father. In his life, his father was the idol whom he always doubted he would be able to live up to.

It was expected that on his return, he would take up the gauntlet thrown down by his father. He was given a hero's welcome. But it did not at first pan out. He spent his time with Cousin Malcolm drinking cocktails and weaving toward the pittosporum in Bermuda shorts. He even went to the Blue Room. He was in some sort of decline. But their ways soon diverged—his and Cousin Malcolm's. Malcom went on a ski vacation in Chile that never ended, and Mr. Stewart took his place at the bar. But something was still lacking for him—the future Mrs. Stewart, whose absence had been the cause of his decline. His intentions were very fixed. They could not be altered. Once Mr. Stewart gave his heart, or pursued a line of thought, that was it. It could not be altered.

A singular parade of relatives made their way to the future Mrs. Stewart's door. One by one they came in to enlist themselves to plead the cause of Mr. Stewart. His own father, the great man, came, and the future Mrs. Stewart was charmed. One of the great man's claims to fame was that while serving on a committee to evaluate Prohibition in 1930 for the President, Stewart was the only member of the commission, with his penchant for dissent, to conclude that Prohibition was completely useless and should be repealed at once. Perhaps it only added to his charm that the sole foe of Prohibition on the commission was a man from New Orleans who was said to be fond of his cocktails.

The Radcliffe graduate student was persuaded to become the future Mrs. Stewart, and abandon her studies in the North. She removed to New Orleans, where she stood in a vast receiving line at her stiffly formal wedding. Entire civilizations could have flowered in the time that she stood in her receiving line, receiving countless aged relatives and retainers of the Stewarts, many in wheelchairs. All of them had seen one another, and had seen the young couple, every day previous, and yet they stood for hours in the stiffly formal receiving line as if it were the eighteenth century. By the time she received the last person standing in the line, the entire reception was over. The band had left, the food was gone, and a lone black woman of ample proportions swept the hall.

Mr. and Mrs. Stewart repaired to an undisclosed location—actually a hotel in the French Quarter. Exhaustion was profound, as it always will be after huge, vast, formal weddings. But Mr. Stewart got down on his knee again and told her that he loved her. That night he told her that he loved her many times, and each time, she felt that she was in a dream, and she could not bring herself to believe his words. It was too much a dream, a war hero, his love for her, his fantastically extensive family; and she felt a sorrow. The next day they flew to an undisclosed location—actually the Italian lakes, motoring from Milan to the Villa d'Este at Lake Como—and so their long life together began.

It wasn't that she didn't love him. She had never met so honorable a man. But she who was such an expert on psychology could find but turmoil in her own soul.

The many years passed until Mr. Stewart and his wife grew frail, and never did the turmoil in her own soul cease. Nor did she ever determine truly what was going on in his.

When they returned from their honeymoon in 1946 his father gave him some investments that had originally been made by the previous generation. His father made suggestions as to how they should be handled, some portion to be invested in an institutional fund in New York with a quaint white-haired gent from U.S. Trust who would take him out to lunch at the Brook Club once a year, the other portion to be held in New Orleans at the local brokerage house. Or, he suggested, his son might want to look after the investments to make changes in the portfolio himself. Some might be tempted by this to go on a ski vacation in Chile that would never end, like Cousin Malcolm. Mr. Stewart, by contrast, listened calmly to his father's advice and then put all the stock certificates in the name of his future descendants quaintly in a bank deposit box in New Orleans, where they moldered for half a century. "Investments—that's not my line," he said. "I practice law."

19

"Is the Walter Sullivan situation under control?" screamed a Wall Street big cheese in the halls of Merrill Lynch.

"We're sending him to Nassau to meet with the head of the Bolivian utilities about privatization at the Latin American desk—two nights," screamed back Walter's boss.

"Good. Then he'll be in Milan later this month for the privatization of the Italian utilities."

They kept madly sending him to travel. It was as if he were James Bond, which he found quite satisfactory, although he was frequently tired.

"What's happening with the Walter Sullivan situation now?" screamed the head of Merrill Lynch's bond department—another link in the chain of inexplicable imbroglios that Walter seemed to cause on Wall Street.

The second screamer was a hearty fellow from Chicago. He invited Walter to have champagne in his hotel room for a series of farewell parties being held in Walter's honor—for the sabbatical and the Italian desk in London. Parties awaited Walter often. Farewell—Welcome Back—So Long—whatever the occasion might be.

In truth Walter felt somewhat disoriented. He was frequently exhausted by his pace at work, the imbroglios he seemed to cause at the office, the series of Farewell and Welcome Back parties instigated in his honor. But he kept that to himself. He was a soldier in a war that never ends.

It was one reason why he liked Grace's angst. He himself didn't have time for angst. Or maybe he wasn't constituted for angst. But he liked angst. Grace had a lot of it.

He did not have much time to ponder it further for he was called away.

He paid Grace another visit before he left to tell her of his trip. He said he would be gone only for one night in Nassau. Then he would see her again. He discussed with her his plans.

It turned out she doted on Nassau. It reminded her of New Orleans. "Does anything *not* remind you of New Orleans?" asked Walter. But it was the tropics and she was ineluctably drawn to them, she raved on. The way the light was, the peacocks, the bygone glamor. Not to say the palms.

She asked Walter if he liked it.

"I'm not as sold on palm trees as you are," said Walter.

She went on unfazed to dote on it some more. It had an air or memory of black tie and the twenties. Green-shuttered dormer windows of defunct tropic mansions in astounding ruined gardens. They were once casinos, nightclubs, private clubs. Their abandoned gaiety still haunted the place.

It is more breathtaking flying in to Nassau than to Barbados or Jamaica for some reason. The sea is gin clear, as they say, or turquoise and pellucid pale green. On this occasion Walter stayed at Greycliff, where the head of the Bolivian utilities met him for dinner. He was a lonesome, unpretentious man. There was an astounding ruin down the street. Walter noted its strange enticement. It had been the British Victoria Hotel, emblem of the British Empire in the West Indian colonies.

They walked out as they smoked their cigars. Then Walter

retired and read *The Wall Street Journal,* stocks and bonds, being an old-fashioned man, in his undershirt smoking cigars. He watched the basketball championships—Carolina was playing. Sports, stocks, bonds, just an old-fashioned man.

It was certainly very pleasant. Not too much can go wrong under a palm tree. Walter supposed he doted on the palm trees for a while. Maybe he would start doting on everything. What did she *not* dote on? he wondered.

But there he was in Nassau, like James Bond, looking out from his balcony, smoking a Havana cigar. James Bond had done a job in Nassau, had fallen in love with the place, and kept a house there, which he lived in for some months of the year. Maybe one month or two. So there he was in Nassau like James Bond, crusty, solitary, dangerous. Well, maybe not dangerous.

His business done, his work accomplished, he prepared to return to New York.

Packed in his suitcase was again the tuxedo, in case the need should arise.

20

Grace had to look at the picture. She was engaged to be married, she had met a crazed young person in Virginia who seemed to be, as she now saw, maybe less crazed than she herself and who was following her around the world, and she had just met a young man named Cotton Baxter, who lived in the hotel where she was staying in New York. He seemed to be a very strange person. For generations his family had lived in hotels. Cotton received maid service twice a day, a fresh bathrobe in cellophane every morning, and chocolate mints every night at his bedside. Men brought up chairs when he needed extra chairs. Secretaries were available on the fourth floor. Everything was delivered. He never went to a grocery store.

Cotton had clerked for a Supreme Court Justice. Grace asked him what you do after clerking for a Supreme Court Justice. Don't you go out and try to find yourself and agonize over everything after you clerk for a Supreme Court Justice? she asked Cotton. Not necessarily, he said. You join a law firm, you become an assistant district attorney, a federal judge, or an investment banker. So I guess you don't go out and buy a Minnie Pearl fried chicken franchise, mused Grace.

"I want to see more of you," said Cotton. He invited her to a party he was having that night in his hotel room. It is true that she had batted her eyelashes at him madly. She noticed it as if observing a third person. In some horror she saw herself sashaying across the hall and batting her eyelashes at him as he returned to his room.

Walter had just returned from Nassau. She continually tried to bring Monroe into the conversation when Walter paid a call so as to remind him. Not to torture him. She felt it was the honorable way.

"Maybe Monroe isn't going to light a hundred candles when I get home at night but that doesn't mean he doesn't love me," she said when Walter returned from Nassau.

A cigar-smoking silence ensued.

"Monroe lived in the North once too," she added. He had gone to Princeton. The claim to fame of his college career was introducing grits to the menu there. The DeLord men had all gone to Princeton. "You see, the South was always with him. That is an ideal we share."

"Oh, I forgot. Grits are an important ideal for humanity."

"I know you love to deride me. Maybe it is a demented picture of the South I portray. I know you haven't met Monroe on his own terms rather than on mine."

He knew these things to be true. He didn't romanticize things as she did. He didn't live in one place and think unrelentingly of another. He didn't incessantly contrast where he began to where he was now. It was true that the two places were disparate, the North and the South. But he found beauty in both. He did not pine for the South and dislike the North. He liked the North. He noticed. He liked. He did not repine. He did not have angst. That of course was why he liked her. She provided all that for him.

But somehow this picture didn't square with her stern sense of honor. The scenario was not shaping up as it was meant to be. She must tell him of the recent visit of Monroe. She was building up to it. Or was it kinder not to tell him? She would be behaving like a crazed young person herself, what with all her plans laid, if she dallied with Walter now. It was not something she could do.

For what purpose was her sheer and sole acquaintance with honor if not to prevent such an act? Honor would forbid her from breaking the bond of her word. Love is an emotion. Honor is an action. Thus would she adhere.

21

A deranged cousin of Cotton Baxter's ensnared Grace into conversation, psychoanalyzing her. He said she was a mother type. Then he said she was a father type. Every human profession was represented at Cotton's party in his hotel room. Lawyers, novelists, investment bankers, real estate brokers, journalists, screenwriters, comedians, and two girls in fishnet bustiers and leopard-skin Capri pants.

Walter took a certain dislike to Cotton. "Who has a name like Cotton? What is he, a mothball?"

She cast him a doom-laden glance.

The hotel was very sumptuous, and crawling with butlers, for some reason, dressed in livery and wearing safari helmets, creating a tropical atmosphere. Some of the young men had long hair and bows on their shoes. There was one boy with his hair slicked back who looked as if he had just stepped out of a Luchino Visconti movie of *Death in Venice.* Grace observed that the party appeared to be predominately comprised of Crazed Young People.

"Repeat after me, Grace. 'I am not a senior citizen. I am not a senior citizen,'" said Walter.

"You're living in some future time period," he went on.

"I'm just trying to be ready when it comes. I'm just trying to adapt."

Cotton was making eyes at her across the room.

"Considering that you bill yourself as an international expert on marriage and honor even though you're not married yet, maybe you shouldn't be taking this mothball guy so quickly into your acquaintance," said Walter. "By the way, has he been elevated to the Fiery Pantheon yet?" said Walter. "Or is he consigned to the Enshrinement of Doom?"

"You seem to have gotten up on the wrong side of the bed this morning," she remarked.

"Maybe I got up on the wrong side of the Fiery Pantheon."

"Speaking of which, I heard from Monroe very recently."

"And was he enshrined, or doomed?"

As no answer was forthcoming he went on, "And where is he now?"

"He had to run off to Alabama to visit an ailing relative."

"We both know what that means."

"We do—?"

"He should be demoted to the Slightly Tepid Pantheon," said Walter. Then the series of butlers with safari helmets ushered them down to the first floor, where there were armchairs and couches and a vast array of drinks.

Grace was seated next to Walter at the dinner that followed. On her other side was Cotton. Within ten minutes of dessert Grace had revealed to Cotton her entire life story, innermost personal problems, marital status, and psychological profile. Walter listened in dismay. He attempted to make his departure. "I have a personal thing," he said.

"A personal thing?"

But Walter fumbled with his tie and grew silent. He rose and brusquely thanked the host. "I'll leave you with Cottonhead," he said under his breath to Grace. However he just stood around with his hands in his pockets and showed no signs of departing.

There were some investment bankers from Merrill Lynch. You would hear a snatch of conversation—"I'm on the fixed income side." To Grace this proved to be romantic. Few perhaps would find romance in the fixed income side. But it was New York and Wall Street and the young men of the world.

There was one handsome devil—the fixed income guy—with dark sunglasses and a suit and tie sitting languidly surrounded by some fellow bankers.

"Do you know him?" she asked Walter. To her he was picturesque.

"Yes, I know him," Walter said.

"What's he like?"

"You know how some people are tormented and they don't fit in? He's not one of them," said Walter matter-of-factly.

They were the glamorous young men who fixed the income

of the world at Wall Street who fit in and hung out with Cotton Baxter at hotel parties and then took the train to Westchester with the newspaper folded under their arm.

"What *is* the fixed income side?" said Grace.

"It deals in debt instruments," said Walter.

"That doesn't really clear it up for me," said Grace.

"He sells bonds," said Walter.

Apparently that only made it more romantic. Few would find romance in selling bonds. Walter, for one, found no romance in selling bonds. She was at it again. Romanticizing everything.

If bond salesmen could find a place in the Fiery Pantheon, then what was the Fiery Pantheon coming to? he wondered.

"It takes three things to run a successful business," said Cotton's deranged cousin, buttonholing Grace. "A dreamer, an entrepreneur, and a son of a bitch. I'm the son of a bitch," he said.

Cotton's deranged cousin was ensconced in a couch. He looked to be about forty-five, robust, ruddy, a regular guy.

"You look lost," he said.

"I don't know," said Grace.

Later he made a beeline for her.

"I like you," he said.

She accepted the confidence in silence.

Grace wandered over to the next room. Cotton's deranged cousin had given her his card. He followed her in.

"I think I'm in love with you," he said. He appeared to be drinking heavily. "You're a very sensual woman. You're a mother type."

"Actually I'm terrified of having children."

"Oh. Well, there are too many people in the world already. There are too many people in this room."

Grace said that she was engaged to be married.

"I'm threatened by you," he said.

"How's that?" said Grace.

"I gave you my card. Would you write to me? Or would that threaten you?"

"Maybe I'll drop you a line."

"Your fiancé is probably just a kid. You threaten him. I write poetry," he said. Eventually he started falling over in his chair. "I'll bet he doesn't appreciate you."

"Well, as a matter of fact he hasn't really shown up for several appointments I had with him lately . . ."

"Your husband is just a kid. He's just a kid!" said the man.

"What am I, Methuselah?" said Grace.

"You're ageless, you're timeless," said the man. "I would like to have sex with you," he suddenly came out with. Actually he came out with it several times. It was the crowning achievement of his series of startling admissions. Then he sort of fell over in his chair.

"I'm very Victorian," said Grace, apparently unfazed.

She strolled away in a reverie.

Cotton's deranged cousin was in the elevator choking on his drink, supported by his business associates. They were practically carrying him out. "*Grace,*" he screamed. Grace and Walter watched him from the door. He kept screaming her name as he walked down Park Avenue, supported by his colleagues, toward the angels atop Grand Central.

"*Grace,*" screamed the man on Park Avenue to the night, as they stood under the awning at the hotel.

"What was that all about?" said Walter.

"I'm a very sensual woman," said Grace. "I'm a mother type."

"*Grace,*" the man could still be heard to call as he stumbled down Park Avenue.

She went back to her table and began to shovel hors d'oeuvres down her throat.

Walter wondered, would he find Cotton Baxter and his deranged cousin in Istanbul when he joined the Stewarts? What exactly would he find there? he was beginning to wonder.

Lately his veneer had crumbled. Ordinarily he had a suave and sardonic veneer, generally oriented toward making trouble of some kind. Lately it had crumbled. He would have to get a grip on himself. He was accustomed to trouble, crisis, and turmoil, and was not accustomed to being cast as the normal one. He himself was in crisis, reevaluating his position at Merrill Lynch and his future. But what had become of his crazed young person mode now? Grace seemed to be taking it over.

Unexpectedly he saw a vision of himself hanging around forlornly at the hotel bar with Cotton Baxter and his deranged cousin, having lengthy discussions into their drinks. She had the type of unexpected beauty of the librarian who takes off her glasses and undoes her hair—Why, Miss Jones, you're beautiful.

Walter took her by the elbow, determining to see her to her door. He would soon see her in a different setting. Maybe she would settle down.

He saw her to her door, and for his trouble, was rewarded with a firm handshake. He would have to get a grip on himself. He walked toward the angels atop Grand Central, and got a cab in the great suave night.

She returned to her room and started cleaning it up. She arranged things obsessively into rows.

She was planning to call on the judge she had clerked for before she left town. Shyness frequently propelled her to reclusion but be bold, she thought, or else be barred from traffic with the great. So she forced herself to call him.

The judge was not sorry to hear from Grace when she passed through New York. When she had clerked for him, at first the judge did not give Grace much of the time of day. But a slow respect for her dawned on him. He came to value her opinions and he came to hold her dear.

To her the judge was well known before she ever met him. He was a legend. She was painfully aware at all times of this, sometimes finding it difficult even to be near him, for it was so awe-striking and nerve-racking. His shrine in the Fiery Pantheon was even more shining than that of her father, if possible. Yet even amid all this, or perhaps because of all this, the judge's feeling for her dawned on him. He had taken a liking to her.

After all if you were in the Fiery Pantheon you had this girl adoring you all the time, wringing her hands in admiration of you, going around worshiping the ground you walked on. The judge told her once that he had never seen anyone actually wring their hands before, until he saw her do it.

The judge was an extremely handsome man of seventy. He had an athlete's grace, at seventy, an upright posture, and a stern demeanor. Normally Grace was cowering in general awe of him.

On this occasion, it was a Saturday morning, and he was wearing a black sweater that seemed to heighten the effect of his very white hair and his old blue eyes. She met him in his chambers. He had some crisp angelic Mozart playing on the radio. It seemed very like him, though she had never before heard him play music of any kind in his chambers. But the crisp angelic Mozart violins seemed to define him. He took her hand and held it and then directed her to the couch at the side of his desk. He began to pace about the floor with his hands behind his back, as he did when preparing an opinion.

She sat in silence drinking him in, and reveling in his white-haired but only slightly decrepit grace.

The judge had an element of pity in his heart for Grace. He felt she was a tortured soul. He perceived her curious innocence. Not everyone might perceive it because she was often surrounded by old flames lying in demented heaps. He saw through that. He saw a young woman near to thirty who seemed waiflike and bereft in some way. He had been very glad to hear that she was getting married. He himself, a fond patriarch, who had long ago lost his wife, had many grandchildren who reveled in his radius. There were many who lived to be near him.

"It distresses me to see you doubt yourself," he said. There was a sweetness in his concern, yet a masterfulness and no-nonsense brevity about it.

"It displeased me."

He had the mastery of a God-like figure who would make you cower in fear even though his concern for you was sweet.

"Overall I am pleased with you."

He struck her as very romantic. He was the most romantic man she had ever known and would ever know. These young men could not compare with him. He was a heartthrob. He was the heartthrob of the world.

He was a much older man, a very masterful man, who spoke in commands. Stand aside. Sit down. Come here. Speak of yourself. I am pleased with you.

He had advised her many times, and had worked closely with her for a year. He paced the floor. They talked of other things. He spoke of his retirement, his return to private individuality, his decision to decline a Supreme Court appointment, so similar to that of her own grandfather. But he knew what he meant to say.

"You know, Grace, that I am attracted to you?" said suddenly the handsome, dashing, and romantic judge, the slightly decrepit last hero of the world.

Shock permeated every fiber of her being.

No doubt he knew it would be that way.

He looked at her gently and yet also sternly. Shock that would be lasting, a deep and lasting shock, was all she felt as she sat dumbstruck.

He came and sat down beside her. She was virtually holding her breath. "Can I kiss you now?" he said sternly.

She couldn't really follow what he said, as he talked some more. She was too shocked. It was too wild a prospect for reality that the foremost legendary member of the Fiery Pantheon felt this inclination for her. That she received this compliment from the gods. He actually bent across and kissed her. To this she could not respond.

He seemed to know that this was how it would be. No doubt that was why he ever thought to behave in such a manner with her. He hated corruption. That was why it had been his vocation to be a judge. His act had no bearing on his towering integrity. It increased his towering integrity, that he loved. Perhaps one of the last things that a man learns is to understand innocence when he sees it. He saw it in her. He was safe with her. On her side she saw life in him. Such life as she thought she lacked. She thought she was fossilized and drab. Yet life was such a thing that the god you revered suddenly kissed you one fine day. She couldn't really grasp it still.

He stood around and talked to her and paced the floor, and angelic Mozart played. He looked at her with his piercing blue eyes and passed her the gauntlet. I expect great things from you, he said.

He met his maker later that year. For this she was prepared because he had reached the age where every time she saw him she wondered if it would be the last. It was. When he walked the earth, the earth was populated by vast heroes, who actually called you up or wrote to you once in a while. You actually worked with them, you talked to them, and you could call yourself their friend. The world had gigantic heroes knocking around in it, and you actually knew them, and after, it wasn't the same.

The honor of knowing him, much less of being made a pass at by him, ennobled her dauntless existence. Anything her dauntless existence held from there would be downhill.

The world was less heroic when he left it, the book of life was written in a smaller print, for she had met her hero, as in his noble solicitude he looked outward instead of in, and bothered with an insignificant girl. You would think he would bother about world wars and philosophy and the Supreme Court. But after a legendary career, he wasn't interested in the Supreme Court anymore. He was interested in helping an insignificant girl.

Two things he said were striking. "Your heart's not in the law," he said. Then speaking of her personal life he said, "You should find some character from the South who lives in New York, who may seem strange, but you need someone different, who will put up with you, who knows your foibles, who even makes them into jokes, who may seem unlikely to you; say he works on Wall Street and—like you—does an excellent job even if his heart's not in it. It is that standard of honor which distinguishes you. Some day you will find your vocation. That is what I wish for you."

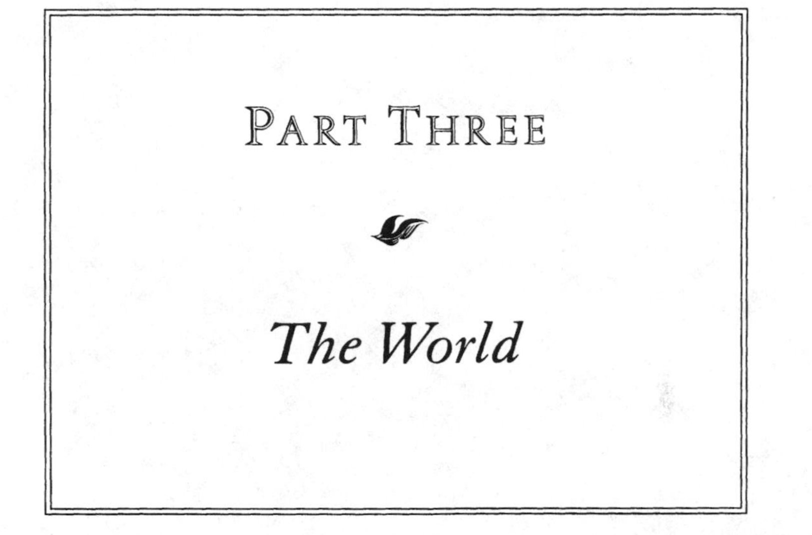

Part Three

The World

1

He walked through Kensington Gardens to Belgravia. The embassy was closed. The embassy was always closed.

The Algerian Embassy was in a part of town that reminded Walter of New Orleans, but also of remote colonial outposts, Egypt, Africa. A lot of London sometimes conjured that to him—the old Empire. Fallen empires obsessed him. He planned to visit many of their fallen seats in the course of his complicated itinerary. His hotel had a black wrought-iron railing with gold gilt posts and potted palms and what looked like bougainvillea growing through the gates. It seemed almost tropical in certain moments, with the gaiety of some of the old architecture and the summer shrubbery. Then he walked to Mayfair. Grace would have said that Curzon Street was glamorous. A light rain fell. She would have said that the sky was a rinsed cobalt gray or twilight. Everything was a rinsed cobalt twilight to her. Everyone wore white tie and tails. Or at least that was what she noticed. She saw what she wanted to see. It rained every day, and was quite chilly all the time. In truth there was always a row of men in black tie in a taxicab in Grosvenor Square. A black Rolls-Royce gliding up in the twilight.

It was Walter's hope to go into Algeria when the ship he was to meet stopped in North Africa. If successful in obtaining the special visa for Algeria, he would fly to Istanbul to join the boat, and when it came to port, he would take the Trans-Maghreb Express from Tunis.

As a crazed young person suffering from various identity crises pertaining to his prospective job as a European investment banker at the international department of Merrill Lynch in London, Walter had as usual come to some firm and radical decisions about his life. He had decided that his relationship with Grace must end, which he was planning to put into action by rushing to her side in Istanbul. Alternatively, he was planning to end their relationship by inviting her to escape to Algeria.

One thing was certain. His plans to end their relationship did not seem realistic.

He returned to the Algerian consulate by the underground, which was experiencing a gas leak, resulting in a long delay. He was instructed to leave his passport at the embassy, and to return the next day at three.

He arrived at the Algerian Embassy the next day at 3:05, expecting to collect his passport. The consul was in his street clothes and complained bitterly that he had been waiting since three. The consul then demanded a receipt. This was the first mention made of such a document. Walter left, passportless.

The next day he noticed that his drab nemesis, the Algerian consul, had been summarily replaced by a nubile young Numidian secretary. This at least looked promising. However, she dismissed him from the embassy with a brisk directive that visa collection was at nine-thirty only.

He went back to his hotel and sprawled limply on the bed, staring at the ceiling.

Walter saw an exhibit at the Victoria and Albert Museum about the current Queen. It was sanitized. But the sovereigns aren't supposed to have a personality. When they become monarchs they have to be colorless. The best part was at the beginning describing her ascendance to the throne at the age of twenty-six, a faint speech, scratchy 1940s music. He sat in the garden of the museum, some palms here and there reminding him of Grace, and of the old Empire, elements of the tropical and the exotic where they do not intrinsically belong. Palms in London—it was incongruous, like Schubert playing blithely on the Nile when Walter was in Egypt.

He passed by the Algerian Embassy and was rudely rebuffed.

Then he took an architectural walking tour led by Richard, an ex-actor, whose career highlight was having Noël Coward describe one of his auditions as "frightfully bad." The tour, entitled "Aristocratic London," consisted of walking aimlessly through Belgravia and listening to Richard describe his fruitless attempts to get various careers off the ground (acting, interior design, restaurateur, etc.).

"This is where my aunt stayed. That was my first flat. You didn't see me, but I was an extra in *Upstairs Downstairs,* which filmed here at this spot. My scene was cut."

Later Richard degenerated into recanting violent confrontations between himself and members of the British service industry (waiters, conductors, etc.). But Walter later took a page out of Richard's book and summoned the Algerian consul to a duel.

Walter insisted on scrutinizing the public on its attitude toward the British monarchs. He incessantly quizzed the serving maids and hotel proprietors on this point. Engaging his stiff-necked landlord in conversation, Walter suggested that he spoke with an Irish lilt. The proprietor revealed that he was from Scotland. Walter asked him if he missed his native land. He didn't. Walter must have been under the influence of Grace for he then began to rhapsodize on how agonizing it must be for the fellow to be separated from his beloved Scotland. He asked him again if it was agonizing. It wasn't. He asked him if he agonized over the demise of the British Empire. He asked him if he agonized about the British monarchs.

"Agony does not loom large, I'm afraid," he said.

Agony loomed large with Algeria, however.

More troubles at the embassy.

* * *

Walter had declared war on Algeria. More troubles—daily—at the embassy. Every day he went there and was turned away. He came at 3:05 instead of three and was turned away. He came without a receipt never before mentioned and was turned away. Finally he went on the last morning possible before he was determined to leave the continent of Europe. A tormented group of fellow supplicants were also waiting.

The Algerian secretary said, "Collections from two to three only."

A cruel joke. Walter had been told to come at nine-thirty.

Finally a British gent piped up and said, "This is getting to be a bit of a joke," in his prissy English way (but polite of course compared with an American), and the secretary said, "It's not a bit of a joke," in the same prissy, polite sort of mode. She curtly informed him, "Collection is from two to three."

"This is getting to be a bit of a joke, isn't it?" persisted the British gent. All the supplicants were crowded around the consul's secretary. All others in the small gathering had also been similarly bamboozled.

"No, it's not a bit of a joke. Collections are from two to three." The supplicants were grumbling.

Walter went up to the secretary and said solemnly, "I'd like to ask you just one question."

He stepped over to the side. She followed. He tried to look smoldering. He gazed at her dangerously. "Are all the women in Algeria as beautiful as you?" he said.

She paused.

"Step this way," she said. Then she took his passport receipt and walked into an office. A few moments later she returned with his visa.

A sort of uproar ensued among the supplicants. "We are also here for our visas," they said.

"Collection is from two to three," she said.

"What about him?" they said, pointing to Walter.

"He is a special case."

"I am a special case also," said the British gent.

"I'm sorry. Collection is from two to three."

The British chap looked furtive. He shifted uncomfortably in his shoes.

He cleared his throat. "You are a very beautiful woman," he attempted.

She paused.

"Very . . . attractive," he trailed off. He coughed.

She gazed at him appraisingly.

"Your facial features are very . . . beautiful," he continued desperately.

But it was in vain. He was arrested for sexual harassment later that day.

Obviously he hadn't taken the seminar.

2

Walter had come to further firm and radical decisions about his life. He had decided to decline the offer at the Italian desk and leave London, which he was putting into effect by arranging to take an apartment in Hampstead for six months, and going to work every day.

He had a lengthy visit from his prospective landlord, Sonya, who said she was an antiquarian bookseller. Whenever you ask a British person what they do they say they are an antiquarian bookseller. Walter asked her where her shop was. She said she worked at home. Whenever you ask them where their shop is they say they work at home. He showed her his edition of Gibbon's *Decline and Fall of the Roman Empire,* which inspired crazed laughter.

Also British people drink a lot. Everyone goes to pubs all day long and has three-hour lunches drinking beer, and then staggers back to the office and then goes to more pubs after work.

In the yellow pages under pest control they tell you how to get birds of prey out of your apartment. What Walter wanted to know was, how do you get birds of prey *into* your apartment? And what are birds of prey anyway? Vultures? Hawks? Bald eagles? And what are they doing in your apartment? The last time he was in Britain he had gone to some country house where they had a whole exhibit of birds of prey, so maybe birds of prey loom large in Britain.

Why was he reading the yellow pages? He saw Grace reading them in New York so he thought he would give them a whirl.

He turned on the radio. Erudite scholars on the radio discussed Beethoven's Ninth for about six hours before they played it.

He turned on the TV. The weatherman said the forecast was "distinctly unsettled." That certainly covered it. The weatherman took one wry, despairing look at the entirety of Scotland, Ireland, and England, and then in a phlegmatic drawl simply applied to it the all-purpose description mentioned.

Then there was a documentary on TV about a woman who suffered from the compulsion to wash her hands every five minutes and the tragic effect on her family.

Due to illness (a vast intestinal-digestive ailment), he could not take the hardy walk along the Thames that he had planned for the next day. He struggled through a business meeting at the Italian desk with Lorenzo. Then he got a train to Eton. At Eton he staggered into a chemist and confided his complaint. The chemist brought out Pepto-Bismol, which

Walter commented was awfully mild, so then the chemist brought out a bottle of morphine instead. In Britain you can get strong narcotics over the counter. So Walter did, and feeling better, soldiered on.

Grace was nutty on the subject of ancient seats of learning, so he thought he would give one a whirl. Whether or not due to the morphine he was swigging liberally, Eton made the desired impression.

In the chapel there were many plaques of old Etonians who were killed in wars, with their ages listed when they died—age twenty, or twenty-three. As in Oxford he had seen a plaque at Christ Church with a long list of men who had given their lives in World War II with the inscription: "These men were the glory of their times. There be that of them." At the entrance to the school yard there was a list of boys who died in the Great War: "Awake remembrance of these valiant men. Renew their feats."

At the Museum of Eton Life they showed a film about the school today. The boys literally wear white tie and tails to school every day. That's literally their uniform. They play Mozart in orchestras and are grilled by their masters.

Windsor was a bit marred by the crowds. Shopkeepers called out lists to each other: Queen Anne—Beheaded? Beheaded. Queen Charlotte—Entombed? Entombed.

Walter staggered back to Eton and procured as a memento for Grace small gold earrings from the 1930s. Some boy's mother's, no doubt. He almost felt like some boy's father there, hearing of them killed in wars at twenty-one, seeing them in their white tie and tails straggling off to class among the ancient spires. Crazed youth for them was spent in fighting wars at twenty-one, and in a hero's grave by Walter's age.

He was an American, he was young, he had not fought in wars, he hadn't seen the collapse of an empire. But one thing he knew from his studies. If there was a decline, there would be a fall. He wanted to be in the vicinity of it.

Back in town the huge megapolis seemed slightly sleazy like Times Square in New York but almost more sleazy in a certain unexpected way because it was once so grand, as the ancient spires described the vastness of the world and the insignificance of your place in it.

Then he noticed Richard, the ex-actor, conducting his architectural tour based on the events of his acting career. Richard, for one, was coolly unconvinced of the insignificance of his place in the world, ancient spires or not.

3

Forty souls once occupied the Italian desk of Merrill Lynch in London, dapper Milanese with Florentine tailors and British Jaguars. But now it had dwindled down to two, one man from New York, and Lorenzo, a volatile chain-smoking Sicilian.

No one knew how to deal with Lorenzo. Everyone was afraid to deal with Lorenzo. Normally Lorenzo insisted on having lunch with everyone at the Italian desk every day, and later in the afternoon, taking them all out again for coffee. He screamed, he raved, he ranted, but he considered the Italian desk to be a family, of which he was at the head, and he expected devotion, which was not altogether forthcoming, considering that there had once been forty employees and thirty-nine of them had left.

Lorenzo had been brought in from Milan by Merrill Lynch for his supposed deep and broad connections throughout Italian industry. In fact, Lorenzo knew no one in Italy. Actually he knew one person—his father-in-law. His father-in-law owned the leather furniture company that Walter had taken public at the Italian desk in the previous year. The extent of Lorenzo's deep and broad connections in Italian industry thereafter seemed dubious.

There was a worldwide recession, and deals at the Italian desk were few and far between. In London there had been terrorist bombings in the financial district. Many further unfavorable circumstances were caused by the Italian bank scandals. You had to be careful about whom you worked with in Milan. You might have lunch with them one day, and they might be in jail the next.

The Italian government was going bankrupt. To stave off bankruptcy the Italian government was selling off everything it owned. Basically Italy was having a Going-Out-of-Business sale. They were selling the utilities, the telephone company, the national brewery. They were even selling the post office.

Merrill Lynch was trying to get a piece of all this business. Walter would be relied on for his expertise in executing and managing transactions of all types. Lorenzo would supposedly bring in the business, and Walter would get the deals done.

The Italian Prime Minister was going haywire. Describing himself as "totally calm," he proceeded to swear on the heads of his children that all was pure as snow in his administration and to smash a reporter into a fence.

Lorenzo was becoming desperate. He was now making frequent business trips to Palermo. It was noted in New York that his huge expense account seemed to be predominately associated with Sicily. Apparently as a result, the government privatization business started coming Merrill Lynch's way. But Lorenzo seemed oppressed, frantic, melancholy, and agitated. While answering a call in Lorenzo's office and absentmindedly opening his top desk drawer, Walter noticed that it contained a cigar cutter, a pistol, and a stiletto. Walter found a dead fish wrapped in newspaper at his desk. A thug appeared in the men's room.

In his previous stint at the Italian desk Walter and Lorenzo went to Milan at least twice a month. There Walter was forced to have a ceaseless round of drinks at the Principe di Savoia each night with Lorenzo. Walter put in a request for an apartment in Milan, so he wouldn't have to constantly have drinks with Lorenzo at the hotel. But now Lorenzo was spending his time in Palermo rather than Milan.

Walter did not like the look of things.

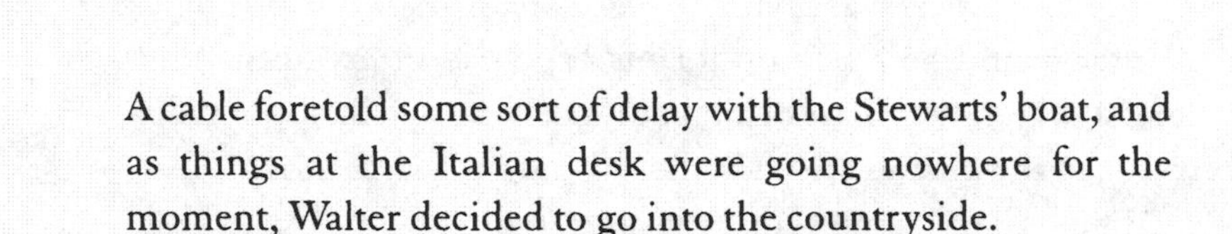

A cable foretold some sort of delay with the Stewarts' boat, and as things at the Italian desk were going nowhere for the moment, Walter decided to go into the countryside.

He drove first to the Cotswolds, of which the most impressive were the Slaughters, as distinguished from the Swells. Walter wondered if people in Upper Swell lorded it over people in Lower Swell. He took a walk from Upper Swell to Seething. The name of the town accurately described his condition. He walked along a green canal through some green meadows with sheep and low stone walls and several great stone houses.

He planned to visit Blenheim Palace. Woodstock, the manor town in which the palace was located, was pleasant. It didn't do any less for Walter than a Cotswold; whatever a Cotswold really was, Walter wasn't that crazy about it. Certain places haunted Walter, but the Cotswolds were not one of them. He didn't really know what they were. Like all people who specialize, Walter's knowledge was limited to his specialty, and had certain gaps in other areas, such as the Cotswolds, angst, and romanticizing the South.

The situation of the palace seen from the gates at the edge of the city through the park, designed by Capability Brown, was marred by a trillion cars and tourist buses. Winston Churchill had been born in the palace. There was Winston Churchill's obituary for his uncle Sunderland, Duke of Marlborough, about how the British had to cope with losing their Empire and with the aristocracy being relieved of their privileges and political duties. The world the duke had been born into was not the same as the one that he had left. Walter had a liking for the man who had presided over its demise.

Walter then went down to Kent. He stayed the night at Canterbury in a hotel run by two maniacs who were the type that if you asked them one question they would not stop talking for the next six hours. But Walter liked that kind of person. Everywhere Walter went the hotelkeepers were loquacious, decrying his image of British reserve. Maybe it was something in Walter that drove them to start snapping.

He liked to get them started on the twilight of the British Empire. It didn't matter if it was a twenty-year-old punk rocker with nails pierced through his eyelids, or a disgusted eighty-year-old gent in Tunbridge Wells, you could get them without too much trouble to ramble on about the twilight of the British Empire.

The next morning Walter called the Italian desk to check his messages and received a demented fax from Lorenzo saying that he had been apprehended by the London police based on information from the Italian authorities pertaining to the bank scandals in Milan. In addition, two Italian clients that Merrill Lynch had recently raised money for on the New York

Stock Exchange under Lorenzo's direction were now under investigation by the Securities and Exchange Commission. There was a message from Mr. Keeney, the one poor soul from New York who remained at the Italian desk under Lorenzo's jurisdiction, who called a business meeting for that afternoon in Richmond.

Walter seethed, but did not have time to repine. He was a soldier in a war that never ends.

5

The weather was distinctly unsettled. A freezing rain began to fall. Walter made his way to the hotel at Richmond, which was situated in Nightingale Lane, directly overlooking the kingly Thames and valley.

When he got to the hotel and met Mr. Keeney he was shocked to see his boss from New York there, the tough customer. Odd as it may or may not seem, Walter was unaccustomed to failure. Now he had a pang. But he knew that he could not be blamed. Of course it had nothing to do with him; it had everything to do with Lorenzo. It was the end of Lorenzo. New York had other plans.

Mr. Keeney was an analyst, a meek and mild-mannered man who did research. He was not suitable to take over the Italian desk. His boss asked Walter if he would. Walter thought it over. His exploits were interesting but he felt it was actually better to be in jail than to wake up with a horse's head on your pillow. He would be left in the midst of multibillion-dollar privatizations that would represent some of the largest transactions in human history. He would be left in the midst of a crumbling government and business associates who left animal parts wrapped in newspaper on your doorstep.

"Let me tell you how we're viewing you," said the boss. "We love you. We've talked to Merrill. We've talked to Lynch. We've interviewed you, we love you."

He passed him a cigar. Walter was dubious. It was not really what you would call a safe, pleasing assignment. But he thought it over and accepted, though demanded to conclude his sabbatical, which still had a month to run its course. He would go to Istanbul and try to work his magic on the possessor of his heart. He must still find the entrance to the Fiery Pantheon. Then he would rescue the international fortunes of the firm of Merrill Lynch.

The temperature plummeted to forty degrees. They rolled back in to town at 9 P.M. having been trapped for hours in a London crawl. The boss insisted on taking Walter out to dinner at a restaurant in Mayfair as a celebration of his rather vast promotion. There were a lot of decadent-looking people there. Some of them turned out to be American, actually the most decadent-looking ones. Anyone starting their dinner at 10 P.M. in this sumptuous Mayfair address with a red visage and unscrewed tie askew and hair flying everywhere in freezing and raining weather would have to be decadent.

They discussed his compensation. On a previous occasion when his boss had dared to give Walter a puny bonus in consideration of the grueling hours he put in, Walter had quickly threatened to quit, entertaining other offers, and cowed negotiations had ensued. Now his boss knew better. So they reached a mutual agreement. Yet some had thought him still to be a person who was just glad he had a job, glad to work hard, and would bear anything; some still thought he was just the same hardworking kid. Now instead they saw him become a man. Who at twenty-five would be the linchpin in the international investment bank of Merrill Lynch.

Their agreement reached, cigars smoked, and telegrams of congratulation sent from Wall Street deities, he finally retired to his room.

He turned on the TV. There was a James Bond movie on. He knew there would be.

There is a great moment when you see, however distant, the goal of your wanderings. One thousand years of the Byzantines and five hundred years of the Ottomans, plus a strategic location, brought stability and prosperity to Constantinople, the seat of empire until 1922. When the last Ottoman sultan fled Constantinople, in the Roaring Twenties, it had been the greatest city in the world for sixteen centuries, holding this position longer than has ever yet been done.

The last Ottoman sultan fled Constantinople in 1922, taking refuge with the British government. He was driven away from the palace at Yildiz in pouring rain to a British battleship waiting in the Bosphorus. Accompanied by his doctor, his bandleader, a secretary, and his only son—a small boy—the last Ottoman sultan departed history leaning on his cane and went into exile in Malta.

Naturally he would bring his bandleader, mused Grace. If you're the last sultan about to go into exile in Malta, you need your bandleader. Empires might decline and fall, but if you're a sultan you need a bandleader. Have bandleader, will travel.

Grace had seen a photograph of him in *Sultans in Splendor,* a book she had procured on the subject. In the photograph of his arrival at the port in Malta with his entourage, his doctor bears a world-weary philosophical smile, his bandleader seems quite genial, and his chauffeur in a snappy starched collar and bow tie convivially shakes hands with some other fellows in bow ties and fezzes. The little son appears excited, and the sultan himself totters valiantly ahead on his cane—in all comprising a strangely jaunty party.

The Ottoman Empire gave her a sense of well-being. Barbaric oriental influences and sultans gave her a sense of well-being.

She noted that in the 1920s some members of the sultan's harem and his eunuchs were still living as squatters in Topkapi Palace, having no place else to go, or any understanding even of the city, for they were sequestered there under the sultans. The palaces were vast, and they were not allowed outside their walls.

Toward the end of the Ottoman Empire the sultan was becoming overexcited. The palace was seething with intrigues. The sultan developed a passion for parrots and white hens with black heads. He went out in a phaeton while boys with palm fronds led the way. He was rowed along the ravishing green-blue Bosphorus surrounded by slave boys in green turbans and eunuchs in scarlet fezzes, as his band played the imperial anthem.

Much of the world was ruled from his glittering domain. The Ottoman Empire extended as in the days of Rome to North Africa, where the Egyptian khedives, the Tunisian beys, and the Moroccan sultans looked to the Ottoman sultan for authority. Cairo was seething with parties. Glittering European hotels were opened such as Shepheard's in Cairo and the

Winter Palace in Luxor. European influences came into the sultan's world, for his own world was doomed. The British Empire was overpowering it.

By the late nineteenth century the Ottoman Empire had become known as the Sick Old Man of Europe. The last sultan certainly looked like one, judging from his photograph in *Sultans in Splendor.* "He was what the last of a dynasty might be expected to be like, a tentative and skeptical elderly man who always appeared as if he was about to announce a disaster." Inseparable from his bandleader, he left the world stage in 1922.

Here was the collapse of an empire to tell of, what once had been the greatest empire the world had ever known. Even amid the mad traffic was also the quality of decline, hopeless, dark, once a great empire, but now not. A place whose day is past. Such gloomy gaiety, the air of quietude somehow even in the rush, and faded grandeur. Such a place had truly seen it all, had seen something very great, and had regarded it with unmoved elegance, as it now regarded its decline.

Former Ottoman mansions were now in the utmost decay. Laden on their bygone splendor was the grime of centuries, and an accompanying attitude of humility and resignation. It reminded Grace of New Orleans. The truly exotic thing was how everything had gone to seed, and was not lamented. Calm indifference to decay and chaos reigned.

The night before she left New York she had a dream that Istanbul was the city across the street from where she had grown up. In the dream she had grown up in a quiet green ancient and exotic town, like New Orleans, but across from her sloping street—which had stone walls and green trees and quietude—was Istanbul, the great city, and she always knew that one day she would cross to there.

7

Walter's Turkish Airlines flight to Istanbul featured a computerized movie screen that provided a map charting the flight's progress as it flew east. Also reported on the screen were time zones, temperatures, frequencies, and speed. A staggering amount of technical information was fed to the passengers, along with a staggering amount of strong Turkish coffee. The constant computerized maps and information on the movie screen gave Walter a certain technical confidence—although if they had crashed they would have shown the computerized plane falling from the route, the altitude dropping, frequencies careening, etc. But they just kept having computerized technical information and strong Turkish coffee preventing that air of defeat from attempted luxuries unsuccessfully masking misery and exhaustion at five in the morning customary on international flights.

There was a rather menacing creaking sound behind his left shoulder. Every fifteen minutes a computerized siren went off, rather like that of a European ambulance. The creaking stopped; then there was swaying. Walter preferred the swaying to the creaking. The man sitting next to him gave him a broad smile. There was a great air of anticipation and excitement, going to old Istanbul, and Walter and all his fellow passengers felt it.

As usual Walter sat next to a lunatic on the plane. Approximately two hours before they landed Walter made the mistake of asking the lunatic next to him if he liked the action thriller movie that Turkish Airlines had shown on the flight. The fellow apparently interpreted Walter's question as a request to have each line of the screenplay dramatically facsimilated including various explosions and gun reports, which he vigorously re-created. He finished his ecstatic account of *Alien Soldier* as the plane arrived on the tarmac in Istanbul.

Walter strolled off the plane and proceeded to the smoke-choked terminal. (The no-smoking craze has not hit Istanbul.) He took a cab to his hotel. It was an evening of incomparable loveliness. The weather was warm. It was the tropic zone.

Walter's taxi driver proceeded to the Dolmabahçe Palace of the Sultans, and pulled in to the gate. Apparently he was lost, or had mistaken Walter for the sultan. The language barrier did not help. Walter only knew two Turkish phrases, both of which he repeated incessantly, and in which he proved to be mistaken. However he was able to overcome the problem and they then proceeded to his hotel, the Pera Palas, which had rows of rosewood tables with plain white tablecloths in grand Edwardian salons with plain wood floors and long deserted corridors—faded, empty, and completely elegant.

The situation of Constantinople on the Bosphorus divides it between Europe and Asia. A sort of Levantine resignation marked the European quarter.

The Pera Palas was upkept in some semblance of the luxury in which it had originally been built as the terminating point for the Orient Express, the resort of abdicated kings and sultans. It was the Levant, when Europeans married into oriental families, drawn to Constantinople by the prestige of the sultans and the Ottoman Empire. Now, however, no one was about, no glittering entourage, and an air of intense quietude, humility, and resignation seemed to pervade the place.

There were forty-five-foot ceilings, vast public rooms, huge empty dining rooms, salons. The floors were made of porphyry and marble. Ornate iron chandeliers, Turkish rugs, rosewood chairs, and writing tables occupied long corridors.

There were bare bulbs in rows above the iron Beaux Arts overhang at the entrance, and potted palms. The elevator was an ornate wrought-iron cage, hand-operated. In the emptiness and desertion, and the threadbare quality, one felt a place that has had its day.

Walter had, for some reason, expected Istanbul to be a sleek European cosmopolis like Vienna—but of course it is not. It had that moment, but it passed.

That passed when the sultan departed with his bandleader; it passed across the Bosphorus, across the thin line of ravishing blue to the Orient.

Walter was experiencing a "mild inner relapse" of the "column of flame." He lay on his bed with *The Decay of the Mongol Empire* and attempted to recuperate.

He had a message from the Stewarts to go down and meet the boat. The boat was set to sail in two days.

Walter's room in the hotel was not as seedy as he would have expected in a place that was so fading. There was a balcony on to the Golden Horn. The room had old-fashioned armoires and appointments. There were long pale green corridors with Turkish runners on the upper floors—everywhere deserted. Walter then passed out.

Receiving another message from the Stewarts about his whereabouts and welfare, he roused himself. The Turkish flight from London had not left Walter unscathed. A Turkish flight from London is the perfect place for a bona fide Column of Flame to reappear, and so it had. He went downstairs to the café and had some Turkish coffee, to revive himself. There was old opera playing. It was Caruso. There was a truth about the place, and thus a profound comfort. He could not deny—for he was under the influence of Grace—its resemblance to New Orleans.

He strolled out into the night.

* * *

As Walter walked past the Galata Bridge he was transfixed by a scene of arresting beauty. It was only this. Ferries and ships were sailing madly past in chaos, under the blanket of pollution that you come to love in Istanbul, the very smell, rank and gutty, the thick blue air, and smoke, over a mad rush of ferries sailing at the port, and battered ornate vehicles madly crossing at the bridge, the domes and mosques and minarets hanging in the air, vastly settled in the hills, the prayer to Allah going up, in a weird tuneless toneless singing through the town, the ferries madly crossing, the ships madly setting sail, the crush of old ships steaming out, the Bosphorus a ravishing shade of blue. It quieted Walter, this frenzy. Like the prayer to Allah, with its dark beauty. He imagined himself to be on one of the ferries steaming out into the night, having his glass of tea on deck, leaving the mad dark city behind, looking to the oriental sea.

From the bridge he looked across to a mosque settled vastly at the port, laden with the grime of centuries, attaching to a labyrinth of domes and minarets and weird iron corridors, leading to the Egyptian spice bazaar.

Along the Bosphorus, its ravishing shade of green-blue, there were dark markets and fish stalls. The ferries continued to sail madly out. Farther up he saw the Istanbul Stock Exchange, and across from this, some cruise ships were docked, with blue wood chairs and tables on the deck. He inquired for the boat he was to meet, and it was pointed out. He approached with a sudden misgiving. What was he doing here? But his mind was filled with forlorn hopes, death or glory charges, and last stands. So he ceased to flinch.

8

It may be that the Lord will raise thee to a praised estate. This was the aim of the whirling dervishes, numerous in the Ottoman Empire. In an effort to conquer pride the whirling dervishes developed a practice called *malamat*, which means reproach, censure, blame. The practitioner cultivates the habit of self-reproach, as well as actively avoiding the praise of others.

When the call to Allah goes up through the night it is an instruction to prayer, sometimes equated with self-examination, from midnight until dawn. And some part of the night awake for it, a largesse for thee. It may be that the Lord will raise thee to a praised estate.

Grace was sitting on a blue wood chair on deck with blame and censure honoring her heart, listening to the prayer to Allah go up in the night. She would bear blame and censure, if there was any to bear; she deserved reproach. These ecstatic ruminations did not prevent her from batting her eyelashes at the Bosphorus once or twice.

She had made her customary effort to be drab. It did not prevent her from flirting with the Sea of Marmara. Walter noticed that she was wearing the same dress that had caused Cotton's deranged cousin to go stumbling down Park Avenue screaming her name.

But it was not for him that she had made the enticing attempt to be drab. It was a general thing with her. It must have had the same effect on certain others, at least ordinarily Monroe, not to mention Cotton Baxter and his deranged cousin, her demented old flames in Virginia, and numerous sundry others, Walter reasoned, since to her old and new flames collected as moths around the fire.

After the feeling of depression caused by Monroe's failure to show up, she was left with disillusion. But she was not disillusioned with the Fiery Pantheon. Members of the Fiery Pantheon would never fall from grace. The one thing she had confidence in was honor. Honor prevented her from placing blame on any other than herself. Honor prevented her from doing a lot of things. But it did not prevent her from shedding tears.

A strange thing happened when she saw Walter come on board. You knew someone for some amount of time but suddenly, one day, you were standing in some overladen green park in New Orleans, you saw him at a distance from the bandstand, or you were at Lord Hall and he was silhouetted at the levee, and suddenly you were seized with love for him—you said to yourself: How could I not have known it before—there is the man I love.

This was how it was when Walter came aboard the boat. It wasn't New Orleans in a green park at the bandstand. It was beneath the weight of the uncaring centuries at the far side of the world. But it was a curious thing.

It is always remarkable when someone sees your soul to a better degree than you see it yourself. You could count the people who see your soul on one hand. Others might know you but they would forget; their knowledge of you was like a weak and undisciplined thing. But that wasn't so with him. He didn't forget. It stuck in his mind. But why? Others might labor to be beautiful, and spend hours fortifying their appearance, and searching for the latest style. It was too much saddle and not enough horse, thought Walter. She was always so waiflike and bereft of domesticity or a regulated life—when you come down to it more of a crazed youth than he. Maybe that interested him. He had seen a kindred soul. The Fiery Pantheon was little different in the end than forlorn hopes, death or glory charges, and last stands.

He had seen it long ago. She only saw it now. But she was stricken with it. Suddenly she had identified him. There was the man she loved.

As a result, she proceeded dementedly to behave as if the opposite were true.

9

Walter had procured for Grace and at the dock bestowed her with a somewhat odd and poignant item: a wrist corsage. He thanked Mr. Stewart for his friendship and the friendship of his family, talking at the dock.

"Take care of my daughter," said Mr. Stewart gruffly, "while you're here," he could not forbear from saying. "That's how you repay me."

Mr. Stewart was the type of man who wore a tie at all times when traveling, even though he was supposed to be on vacation. He didn't always wear a suit, he might wear old khaki trousers and a sports jacket, but he would always wear a tie.

Walter was not wearing a tie when he came on the boat that evening, but he wore a tie thereafter.

His long black hair seemed to have grown longer, giving him a slightly frenzied though sort of Continental appearance. He kept running into people he knew. In the Levantine ghetto he ran into people he knew. On a remote aspect of Elephantine Island in Aswan he ran into people he knew. In the Egyptian Museum at Cairo he ran into people he knew.

When he brought out his wallet to purchase Turkish aperitifs Grace noted it was filled with worldwide currency—rubles, deutsche marks, dollars, pounds—making him seem more Continental. Wherever he went it was as if he had been born there. He could have been born on a Turkish boat. He could have been born on Wall Street. He seemed accustomed to his setting no matter what it might be. He was the type of man who would fly to Cairo, Istanbul, Shanghai, procure a car, and calmly drive into the heart of the vast cities of the world as if he had been born there.

But whether work had made him cosmopolitan or worldly in that way, or whether his might have always been a worldly presence, Grace could not discern. Monroe's was a presence confined to its point of origin, its native place; she could not tell what he would be like in such an alien environment for she had never seen him in one. He was of a place, that was what she loved in him.

Walter bestowed gifts on the women in the party. For Mrs. Stewart there was the silk scarf he had procured for her in New York. For Grace the earrings he had got at Eton.

He seemed to have a lot of ailments. He discovered that there was a British narcotic containing codeine on sale aboard the ship, with which he treated his consumption, while knocking back several glasses of a Turkish aperitif resembling absinthe. Codeine and absinthe may seem like a singularly nauseous mixture and indeed produced cavernous silences accompanied by glazed stares.

Mrs. Stewart attempted to probe Walter on the subject of his family. She succeeded only in eliciting from him a muttered phrase or two. The word "smothering" was muttered.

"They're very warm," he said. "I mean they're very cold." Then he lapsed into a paralyzed silence.

"He's still somatizing," Mrs. Stewart pointed out.

"Maybe we're smothering him," put in Mr. Stewart.

"That's *his* family," whispered Grace.

Walter actually seemed to Grace quite robust. He didn't actually look sick. He never actually looked sick.

The passengers were slowly coming on board in preparation of sailing in two days. Mrs. Stewart analyzed them as they boarded, carrying their clothes on hangers and bearing alcoholic beverages. In Istanbul the passengers were meant to sleep on board while the boat was docked in port.

The boat was extremely small, taking it in consideration against your ordinary cruise ship. Walter was tactfully staying at a hotel. Meanwhile he spent the evening on board with the Stewarts.

An orchestra performed Strauss waltzes and Django Reinhardt jazz duets. The passengers included many Turks, it turned out. The men had fine white suits, cigars, and the air among their families of tradition and paternity. The women were immaculately coiffed and groomed, struggling across the deck in their high heels and genteel finery. It seemed an old and upper-crust society, the white-haired gents with their cigars, and their air of responsibility. There were also some glamorous crazed young people, in baggy linen suits.

There was some dignity in the Istanbul society people, an old order, the men burdened with responsibility, behaving handsomely.

At night the Bosphorus became entrancingly illuminated. Grace expressed the opinion that it was the most beautiful river she had ever seen. Walter said that it was not a river, it was a strait. There was something thrilling and refreshing and ravishing and sweet about it, Grace observed. It was a ravishing shade of blue. On their side was Europe, and on the other, Asia. Beyond was the Black Sea, and Russia.

At dinner were more cultivated Turks whose refinement

and gentility touched her heart. She expressed the opinion that it was like New Orleans. Each party had a patriarch, to whom the most honor was due. The prayer to Allah went up in the night. The boat was uncrowded, save for the elegant few.

Waiters in white jackets served orchid juice from silver trays. Lotions and potations were produced. Plates of plums were brought.

There was something slightly barbaric about the Bosphorus. There was something slightly barbaric about the boat. There was ever the mad crush at the port, the ferries madly sailing out, the prayer to Allah singing through the sky.

Walter prepared to leave for his hotel. He said good night to Mr. Stewart, and they shook hands. Mrs. Stewart had previously retired. He went to say good night to Grace. Should he kiss her on the cheek, perhaps? Walter felt uncertainty and indecision covering his heart.

He wasn't sure about this crazy Grace. But after all she had a right to her crazy illusions. It may be insane to live in a dream but it's madness to live without one. That's how you had to look at the Fiery Pantheon.

"Do they have this Hour of Desolation of yours in Istanbul?" he ventured.

"It's not an Hour of Desolation. It's a Nameless Hour."

"O.K. O.K. What is it? I forgot. I don't get it."

"It's sort of a Black Hole."

"And you're in it now?"

"You come to a point in your life where if you behave in a certain way, with a rigid rule of conduct, according to the standards of the Fiery Pantheon, then you can live with yourself with some serenity, and dispense with the Vortex of Doom, Netherworld of Torture, Wild Brooding Agony, etc. Of course then you miss your Wild Brooding Agony, as you notice life is a bit drab without it."

"So you're in more of a Gray Hole."
"I almost miss my Netherworld of Torture."
"So we're back in the Vortex of Doom."
"But you see it's actually gotten more drab than all that. Though I've always been drab."
"I'm not sure that guy screaming your name on Park Avenue thinks you're so drab," he said.
He kept trying to be gruff, but again the nightingales and praised estates, palm trees, and old empires were crowding in his brain. It was becoming very crowded in his brain.
Then she asked, "If we're ever in New York again at the same time, could you take me down to Wall Street and show me around?"
"Are you going to romanticize it? Are you going to put bond salesmen in the Fiery Pantheon?" he asked gruffly.
And yet of course he did not know the name of Wall Street had become romantic only because he worked there. He conquered there.
So he said good night, and left the boat. A steward from the ship walked with him to the bridge to get a cab. The great city passed by his side, and marked him with its beauty.

10

"Jane, you persist in encouraging this boy," said Mr. Stewart to his wife, in their stateroom on the ship.
"It's a bit late in the day to think of that, DeCourcy," she said succinctly.

Mr. Stewart felt that his wife's so-called interest in the young man as a psychiatric case was becoming disingenuous. It was plain that she now brazenly pursued matchmaking. He did not like the idea of procuring beaux for Grace. Not that she needed help. Her old flames already lay in demented heaps around the world, so far as Mr. Stewart could determine.

"So you admit it."

"I admit that he's come halfway around the world."

Mr. Stewart stopped to think of it.

"Rather sporting of him," he commented.

❧

Mrs. Stewart observed her fellow passengers, looking for signs of alcoholism, pathology, and mental illness, all of which were in ample supply. Psychological visions yawned. It was not that she wanted to make trouble, though it is also true that her mind was like a vast searchlight seeking for trouble. She claimed to be sublimely unconcerned about the conflict with Monroe, finding in her daughter a single-hearted innocence that she recognized as being very similar to her husband's. But Mrs. Stewart had certain ideas, versed as she was in decay.

"You're not in touch with your feelings, DeCourcy," she said.

"Good. I don't want to be in touch with my feelings."

Mrs. Stewart felt that one should show anger. Mr. Stewart felt that one should be civil.

"I don't happen to enjoy having crockery thrown at me," he explained.

Mrs. Stewart drew herself up like an old general. She spoke majestically. "I am in my decline. There's not much left of me. I am enjoying what is left of my life, and I don't happen to enjoy being unappreciated."

He looked at her slowly. It was true that she was increasingly frail. Her posture was twisted into a proportion of pain. He tried not to feel in order to preserve his own equanimity. He was captain of a large ship, the vast panoramic members of his household. It was necessary to sustain control and steer the ship.

Mr. Stewart may or may not have agreed with his wife about his sons and daughters-in-law and their psychiatric needs. In any case his sons had never cost him as much emotion as had Grace. It was the love of his daughter, and his charter membership in the Fiery Pantheon—which though he may have kidded her about, he may have cherished in his heart.

Mr. Stewart had made inquiries about Walter. His father was a retired professor. His "people were respectable" as Mr. Stewart would have called it. They were not in the "demimonde." Only Mr. Stewart of course would speak in such antiquated parlances. They were not "disreputable." In his world you traveled with aged relatives and steamer trunks and were not in the "demimonde."

Inquiries may be too strong a word. He simply asked his old friend Collier in New Orleans if he knew Walter's family. Collier knew everyone. The matter ended there. They talked it over privately. It was a bit sticky because Collier was the uncle of Monroe.

But he had made his inquiries and was satisfied.

He found a few checkered spots in the career of Walter, but most people growing up in a town like New Orleans have checkered spots, it being a wild town full of alcoholics, casinos, strippers, and having three sons of his own, Mr. Stewart could not be shocked at the career of Walter.

His own children had been driving him crazy for many, many years. He was certainly inured. His sons had been in trouble at their schools, they had taken drugs, they had become Communists, they had stayed out till four in the morning at nightclubs, they had proposed to one girl and then married another, they made bad investments, they did not bring their children up correctly, they were too reclusive, or they stayed out too late. Of course it all came to worse pinnacles when they were younger. Raising a daughter, though it had its rewards, was a hair-raising occupation. This had been especially true fifteen years previous. An adolescent girl is not in possession of her faculties. Young people. They're nuts, he concluded.

And in all his children's attitude to him, there was mixed with love a definite element of fear, for Mr. Stewart was very stern, and things were black and white to him.

Whereas in Northern families when the scions go astray, the father simply lets them go, turning away in disgust. It could hardly have been more different with the Southern patriarch, such as Mr. Stewart. It was not in his concept of honor to leave an outstanding debt. He would pay his children's debts. He would look their troubles in the face. The Southern patriarch took responsibility. Such close families frequently exist in the South, sometimes, it is true, verging over to the abnormal. You will sometimes see there a forty-five-year-old man still living with his parents. You will see a man living in the house his father was born in, perhaps oppressed by the shadow that his father casts.

"I appreciate you, Jane," said Mr. Stewart to his wife.

"What's left of me," she corrected.

He knew his wife of forty years well. He could not imagine life without that slim blonde creature, her turmoil and her wit.

He could not forbear from thinking of that other trip upon a boat in 1939.

"We're getting too old for these trips, DeCourcy," said his wife. "And you're right: I would say this trip is in some jeopardy," she formally announced. He could tell that this idea exhilarated her. "It may be my last, you know." She said this with a certain gaiety. She was quite fearless.

Her fearlessness consoled him. But Mr. Stewart had his own refuge from the world. There would not have been a Fiery Pantheon if he had not set the standard. Even Grace perceived that there were those who had to doubt and question it in order for it to exist. Someone had to question it. Mrs. Stewart and Walter were alike in that they questioned it. In a way they were more worldly than Grace and Mr. Stewart. But Mr. Stewart was incorruptible, and meeting with this rarity in the world had caused his daughter to construct the Fiery Pantheon and hold it as a standard. If you held to the standard it was easier to live with yourself, if possibly a bit drab. But it was not drab to Mr. Stewart. The head of white hair belonging to Mr. Stewart could be seen in a black convertible, the preferred car for dashing old men in New Orleans, like the DeLords, and perhaps prematurely, Monroe, driving down the Avenue every evening exactly at six-thirty under the sweltering oaks, with opera blaring to the trees. There was an atmosphere to the thing. There was his dream of honor. That was his refuge from the world.

11

Walter slowly strolled into the lobby of his hotel. He noted that there were gilt palm trees on the gold tiers of the chandeliers. He procured a cigar, and strolled around the public rooms. A belly dancer had just come on in the dining room. Pianist dazed with boredom. This belly dancer had been coming on for the past twenty years, Walter could tell. An elderly Turkish gent seated at the rear seemed quite intrigued, though. Nor was Walter strictly unenthused. He stayed until the show was over. The column of flame had momentarily dispersed, and he felt a strange crazed energy despite his jet lag. When the belly dancer finished, he retired to his room, and took up *The Decay of the Mongol Empire.*

A sumptuous breakfast was served in the dining room of Walter's hotel. There were windows to the Golden Horn, white tablecloths, and old rosewood chairs.

Walter had a new series of ailments. Aching bones, specifically lower back.

He was reading an article in the *Tribune* about eccentrics, trying to find out if he qualified.

The traits identifying an eccentric in the article were these:

1. Indifference toward professional success.
2. Combativeness with colleagues.
3. Unfashionable clothes, mismatched socks, uncombed hair, and a distracted air.

He looked at his clothes. He was wearing a suit and tie, for Mr. Stewart's benefit. Whether it was fashionable, he didn't know. The eccentric in the article wore loud Hawaiian shirts with striped ties.

4. Research into "happy, obsessive preoccupations."

Walter was clutching *The Decay of the Mongol Empire* on his lap.

At the end of the article an example was given of someone judged to "have potential" in the eccentric line. He had quit his job because he didn't want to be a "slave to monopolistic fourth-rate opportunists."

"I'm doing something different," he said. He was standing outside a bank selling outlandish buttons and photographs of the Loch Ness monster.

Walter went out to the Turkish baths. It involved lying naked on a slab in a steam room. A man came and poured buckets of scalding water over him. Another man came and twisted his limbs into excruciating contortions that were incredibly painful while saying "Good massage?" and then asked him to crouch naked and poured more pots of scalding water on him. After he was scalded, another attendant came with a huge pail of hot water and beat him with ropes. Finally he came out. Actually they wheeled him out. He was basically in the shape of a doughnut. The porter hurried up to wrap a turban on his head. An old gent fetched him tea and cigarettes. As he departed the masseuse came up to him and said, "Tips?" so he paid, then the water carrier came up to him saying, "Tips, tips," so he again complied, then the washroom attendant came up saying, "Tips?" Then the ticket taker said the same, and the porter, and the gent with cigarettes, and then a man he had never seen before came up to him and said, "Tips." He was cleaned out.

There were old arcades among the embassies, baroque angels on the vaulted ceilings, a profusion of wires crossing everywhere, barbershops, cigar stores. A man carried a fox to the furrier, holding it lengthwise straight in front of him by the head.

Walter saw a man leading a bear on a leash down Embassy Row. The bear was wearing a ring in his nose. A lone tourist leaped out and gave chase with her camera, but no one else seemed to find it extraordinary.

After walking back to his hotel at 1 P.M. Walter passed out upstairs. The prayer to Allah at two-thirty woke him up, and he proceeded to the dining room. There was a wedding taking place in the reception hall. Walter was incessantly surrounded by weddings and engagements.

There was strange chanting through the afternoon, strange Islamic chants and prayers to Allah carried through the air all over town, singing through the town. This had always seemed to Walter comforting. A holy city.

As if endorsed by God, he proceeded out. Walter had a date with Grace.

❦

At an old restaurant from the Belle Époque on the Bosphorus, which was a shade of ravishing pale blue-green, Walter waited for his date. He strategized, contemplating the battlefield. He was wearing his seersucker suit, which luckily he had happened to bring, since it satisfied Mr. Stewart's dictates of formality. He seemed to be slightly feverish. He appeared to be devising something. He tested his cough. Suddenly he coughed his most revolting cough, as if to horrify the onlookers. He had chosen wrongly in his audience, however. The few Turks sitting leisurely around the place had seen it all, and Walter was not interesting from the viewpoint of the uncaring centuries. In fact there were few places where an American roused less remark than here. Walter did not merit a raised eyebrow.

There was an old Edwardian splendor—long galleries and a single dining room with plain wood floors, white tablecloths, and windows with blue awnings to the Bosphorus. It had the sheerest elegance. Uncrowded, faded, threadbare, but once very grand.

Grandeur. Frequented by no one. On the Bosphorus. This is what Grace loved.

His date showed up. They had lunch. From across the table she studied Walter's face. She struggled with herself. Momentarily she batted her eyelashes at him. But at the Topkapi Palace of the Sultans, she walked through the Door of Repentance.

There was still time, Walter thought. That was only the beginning of the date. He took her to a neighborhood of Istanbul resembling Budapest or Prague, amid some smart shops and cafés that were very little different from New York. The café habitués were more fashionable, however, than they would be in New York—more like those in Rome or Paris. Proprietors walked out of their establishments through ancient courts and talked into cellular phones. This was an area of antique shops, and as a result, Walter required the assistance of a spatula to remove Grace from the premises.

But the date was still not over. He peeled her off the antiques district and brought her to the viceroy of Egypt's summer palace on the Bosphorus. It was on the Asian side. You go out of Istanbul past the Dolmabahçe Palace shimmering on the strait and cross to Asia.

The viceroy's palace was now a hotel. There was a sloping walk beside the Bosphorus. There was something slightly barbaric about the Bosphorus. There was something slightly barbaric about the hotel. Along the walk were oriental lampposts painted white with filigree, overhung by the branches of gigantic elms.

Grace kept saying everything was barbaric.

A movie was being shot. It seemed to be an art film. The people wore strange costumes and lounged about the circular reception hall. Everyone smoked cigarettes. Camera equipment choked the upper halls.

There was a stone balcony overlooking what Grace perceived as a barbaric rose garden.

There seemed to be a wedding taking place that night at the palace that reminded her of New Orleans.

"Is it by any chance barbaric?" said Walter.

For her the world had certain themes. She was always raving about palm trees and white-haired gents and men wearing white tie and tails. Not to mention barbaric rose gardens.

"I take it they wear white tie and tails in the Fiery Pantheon," said Walter.

She saw what she wanted to see. She saw a world of white-haired gents encloaked in honor and white tie and tails.

The Bosphorus became lit up entrancingly with lights. There was one thing she couldn't understand. There seemed to be two brides, but one was the real bride, and the other was some sort of shadow of her for some other purpose as in some inexplicable Turkish custom. One bride was seen coming in and going out of the palace on tiptoe holding her skirts and someone else holding her train, as if she were a china doll—while the other bride dined alone at a bride's supper on the terrace, after everyone had gone home, as several men stood by, and the orchestra serenaded her. One place was elaborately set.

"I know, I know, it's barbaric," said Walter.

But it seemed significant, the real bride and the shadow bride, a mirror image of a touchy situation like her own, as if one bride were marrying Monroe, and the other was still deciding what exactly to do but going through the motions in a shadow exercise.

On the Bosphorus there were a few other nice outside cafés and the boat station of wrought iron painted dark green. To kid her Walter said he saw a man there in white tie and tails. He said even the fish were wearing white tie and tails.

❧

The date was still not over. Finally he took her to see the whirling dervishes, her dream.

For it may be that the Lord will raise thee to a praised estate. It was Grace's aim to attend the Whirling Dervish Convention in Konya on July 17. It was actually a festival but she called it a convention. On that day the dervishes dance in the Sports Palace. But she was unable to negotiate the trip to the remote and obscure W.D. Convention and had to acquiesce to the level of just going to the W.D. museum in Istanbul. There they arrived to be stunned by the information that the dervishes were dancing then. Stunned because they are elusive, for only the graced to see.

They wore black robes over starched white tunics and long wide skirts tied at the vest with one thin sash, and tall tan hats or turbans. They shuffled slowly round and round a circle bowing to the master. It was boring. Then suddenly just as her eyes were about to glaze over there was a loud clap and one by one they started whirling, first with their arms wrapped around their chests, then faster in a graceful motion they released their arms and flew them up toward God, whirling madly, using one foot as a pivot. It went on for an hour or so and the feat was that they didn't fall from vertigo. They whirled around so fast that each became almost invisible.

While whirling they are in a praised estate, conducting a form of prayer, literally trying to be closer to God.

The date was over but the ecstasy was not.

Grace had met a rabbi on the boat whom she was consulting on some points of guidance, for she was in a moral quandary. This Walter character kept showing her the world in a fantastic manner; she was grateful; it was ecstatic; she needed guidance. The rabbi was from Budapest. He was interested in ecstatic religions. He had been to a whirling dervish convention. He rambled up and down the deck chain-smoking French cigarettes. There was something mysterious about him but he had vitality and inspired your confidence. Grace attempted to ask him a number of theological questions.

"I'm not in charge of heaven. I don't know," said the eccentric rabbi, in his thick Hungarian accent.

The information that he did give out was equally eccentric."Who am I?" he said. "I am just a little lower than the angels. Who are you? Just a little more low than lower than the angels. But we couldn't exist without each other. Do you comprehend it?

"We are schmoozing," he chuckled in his Hungarian accent.

This rabbi was eighty-nine years old and had seventeen brothers and sisters in Budapest. He had escaped from Budapest in 1939, leaving a wife and infant whom at the time he did not know that he would never see again.

Of this he told an elliptical story. "Napoleon said to his soldiers, 'Tomorrow we face the worst enemy we have ever done.'

"'But, General, we already conquered the world.'

"'The enemy within.'"

Once the rabbi was late to officiate for a wedding. He felt remorse at his rudeness and after performing the ceremony made a formal apology to the assembled company. "There is a story among the sages," he said, "that if the rabbi is late to the wedding, it is a good omen for the bride and groom." This white lie he delivered in his sonorous Hungarian accent, to the thrall of the crowd. That was what Grace liked about the man—his crazy aphorisms, which tested your credulity but inspired your hope. He was not bound by convention. She liked his daring because she believed in his piety.

But when he took his departure for the evening, he stretched out his arms to embrace her. He kissed her on the cheek. He continued to hold her close. His mouth moved dangerously close to hers. She disentangled herself and fled. A desperate Walter, who had loitered at the boat, viewed it from a corner of the deck. Not only was she surrounded by demented old flames, but she had just been made a pass at by a rabbi.

The curious thing was that although she was an incorrigible flirt, she mostly flirted with inanimate objects, such as the Bosphorus, the Sea of Marmara, or the angels atop Grand Central. Those who felt moved to succumb to her charms were precisely those with whom she would not dare to flirt. This of course caused them to become demented with desire. In this case, in a man of the cloth, it was going a bit far. In this case it lowered him in her esteem. He was craven. She could not seek further counsel from him. She would flirt with a city, she would flirt with an orchestra, she would flirt with an empire, but not with a rabbi.

So she ventured to a mosque with marble courts and columns laden with the grime of centuries, watching one man bend and bow and kiss the ground to Allah.

13

Walter walked through old Stamboul. He bought cigars, called his broker, and read the baseball scores. He indulged in some teeth-gnashing as he walked along Embassy Row. What was there to do with this crazy Grace?

Of the embassies, the Russian was the grandest, an Italianate stucco palace painted a gay dark red, with palm trees. He walked into one of the secret passages off the Grand Rue de Pera. There was a fur store with a stuffed mink in a screaming position in the window. (The kindness-to-animals craze had not hit Istanbul.)

He saw a herd of turkeys walking down a street, poor souls, being herded toward some restaurant, the destination of their doom.

He stopped at a dive that reminded him, being influenced by the possessor of his heart, of New Orleans—plain fresh food in unprepossessing dives, everyone smoking cigarettes and drinking coffee. He contemplated how the no-smoking craze had not hit Istanbul. Istanbul was sort of like New York in the forties, everyone smoking cigarettes, old architecture, sort of suave (even with a herd of turkeys walking down the street), old-time, beautiful, like New York once must have been. Apparently other health hazards were not observed in Turkey, either; everyone was promiscuous, they smoked, they drank absinthe all the time, etc. This information Walter had learned from his Turkish friend Onya Zonat.

Walter kept running into people he knew. At the Winter Palace in Luxor, Egypt, he ran into people he knew. On a hydrofoil to Africa he ran into people he knew.

Walter had run into someone he knew on the Stewarts' boat. Apparently she was visiting friends. She was not meant to take the cruise. Walter had arranged for her to join the Stewart party on the boat at dinner. She too was engaged to be married, he learned. She would bring her fiancé to dinner to meet Walter. Walter was surrounded by engaged girls everywhere he went. Onya might have been a Turkish counterpart to Grace, except that she did not attempt to be drab. She was a glamour girl.

That evening on the boat the Stewarts sat on deck in blue wood chairs and awaited Walter's guest. Instead of bringing Orhan (her fiancé), Onya brought a suitcase—the engagement was off, they had fought, could she stay with Walter, or on the boat—in short, trauma, drama, and crisis were incessantly enacted as per usual.

Despite this shocking news those present all had dinner on the boat. Mrs. Stewart was revivified at the new upheaval and its psychological ramifications, and by the end of dinner the entire restaurant was doing a conga line on the dance floor, led by the supposedly heartbroken Turkish girl.

Who was this girl? Grace wanted to know. First she is supposed to bring her fiancé to dinner. Then she comes along the dock carrying a suitcase, apparently planning to move in with Walter. Crushed by trauma, the next thing she is leading a conga line on the dance floor.

No one had found it extraordinary that Walter had a friend in Istanbul, or that he would bring a guest to dinner. In fact Mr. Stewart, on first hearing, felt relieved. Before he even knew that this girl was engaged or disengaged, he had the feeling that maybe Walter had found some other girl to drool over.

The theme of the rest of the evening was Orhan, Onya's fiancé, named for an Ottoman conqueror, and apparently a misanthrope. He, like Monroe, was the perpetually absent character of a play who is always spoken of and analyzed ceaselessly. What would Orhan think of this? What would Orhan think of that? Orhan likes this. Orhan likes that. Orhan detests that. If Orhan doesn't get five naps throughout the day he goes to pieces. He likes to take five naps throughout the day. He hates to go out. He likes to stay on the farm. It was hauntingly similar to the original nonappearance of Monroe in Virginia.

However his ultimate appearance did live up to the buildup.

The next day Onya picked up Grace and Walter and brought them out an hour's distance from the city, where they met the misanthrope.

You had to take a boat to get there. They took a ferry from the Dolmabahçe Palace to an island in the Sea of Marmara that had a sort of haywire gaiety, with palms and Ottoman summer palaces on the ravishing green sea. There was a long blue awning at the dock in an arcade lined by old-fashioned wrought-iron light standards on the barbaric pure green sea, next to a crumbling Maltese ferry building. Six cheetering

Arab women in black silk veils and galabiyas got off the boat and followed after their sheiks. On the drive by horse-drawn carriage, the only mode of transport on the island, the winding roads were thick with palms beside gay mansions, roses, peonies, hydrangeas, bougainvilleas, palmettos, and a tangle of overgrown gardens in the pitiless sun. It was a little barbaric, a little haywire, the ravishing green sea, the grandiose houses that were once the resorts of the Ottoman princes. Orhan was one of their descendants. High society. It was a sort of mirror image of Monroe.

The misanthrope was very lugubrious. He said little. They had a drink and he preserved a misanthropic silence. Finally he spoke in a thick, lugubrious voice.

"Would you like to see me butcher a geese?" he said darkly.

Grace declined this opportunity and Orhan and Walter repaired to the barn.

After the goose was butchered Orhan said to Walter, "It is better if it is marinated in its own blood." He spoke in a thick Turkish accent that sounded Transylvanian.

These were the only words he uttered until after dinner, when he said, "There will be bats in the night. Maybe beetles. Yesterday I saw a huge beetle on the bed. This big." (He showed a fist.) "I had to burn it."

Onya invited Grace and Walter to stay the night. Orhan described a series of horrors awaiting them in the guest rooms. He bedeviled them with ghost stories of the region. The sultan had had the forest burned to massacre the Janissaries. Their burned bodies had been found on the property. Maybe some had survived or were ghosts. But watch out for the bats, he emphasized. Possibly snakes. Grace's hair was standing higher and higher on end throughout the day.

In fact Orhan had made it all up just to torture them—befitting, at any rate, his reputation as a misanthrope.

* * *

Onya's attitude toward Orhan seemed to be a little iffy. But anyone's attitude to Orhan would be a little iffy. First she would say she wanted to delay the wedding. Then they would get in a fight and she would say she was incensed because Orhan had said he wanted to delay the wedding. "But you *wanted* to delay the wedding," Grace tried to gently remind her. Then she would make other similar contradictory statements. Grace was left with a very iffy idea of whether Onya and Orhan would actually be wed. Similar to the way it was going for Grace and Monroe.

Repelled from the farm by the misanthropic Orhan, Grace returned to the boat, where Walter dropped her off, and brooded in the great suave night.

14

Onya started bringing Grace and Walter to visit all her relatives. The men were nutty misanthropes similar to Orhan, who kept puttering around making little incomprehensible comments, and the women were gracious and normal.

Grace kept wondering why the mad parade of Onya's relatives would show them such elaborate hospitality, but that was the spirit of the place. It was genteel. It was the oddest mixture of the barbaric and the genteel. At the homes of Onya's relatives potations would be brought, the wives would sit and talk in perfect English, and the husbands would putter around in the garden or keep away in their studies making fleeting and eccentric appearances.

One of the nutty misanthropes who seemed to compose Istanbul society was Onya's uncle, also named Orhan. Turkish men all seemed to be named for Ottoman conquerors, of whom there had been after all a limited number, so that all Turkish men had the same name. They were either named Orhan, Suleiman, Mehmet, Hassan—or Genghis, for the Mongolian hordes.

Orhan was not what you would call the life of the party. Neither was the other Orhan.

Walter asked him about the village of Konya, where the whirling dervishes began.

"What's the point of whirling?" asked Grace.

"What's the point of living?" said Orhan.

Walter shifted the conversation to the Roman ruins of Antalya.

"You can see that anywhere," said Orhan. "Don't waste your time."

Judging that business would be a topic more interesting to him, Walter asked about the economy.

"It is terrible. Not as bad as yours, though."

Walter asked whether he thought it would improve, especially with all the opportunity in Eastern Europe and Asian Russia.

"No. It is the natural course of all economies to decline."

Walter quizzed him about the Muslim religion. Did he ever go to the mosque? he asked. Of course not, he said. Like all Turks the family was Muslim but being of the ruling class, they did not perform traditional Islamic observances and seemed not to like them. Who is the ruling class? Grace asked. Orhan is the ruling class, replied his relatives. He certainly ruled those present during these tyrannical exchanges.

Yes, he was a Crusty Old Bastard. She knew the type. Terse and crisp yet somehow enigmatic, mild, who set your heart at rest because you felt that you had met with him before.

Grace persisted in attempting to ask Orhan a number of theological questions.

She asked him if he believed that God was actually real.

"How do I know that you're real? How do I know that I'm real?" he said.

Grace asked him about the Dolmabahçe Palace.

"Yes," he said. "Do you like it?" His eyes shone.

"Oh yes."

"You like that?" His eyes glittered.

"Yes, I love it."

"You love it?" smiling sweetly, egging her on.

"Yes."

"It is a phony."

He exulted.

The crusty white-haired misanthropic Orhan and his wife lived on the Bosphorus just north of Istanbul. Grace asked if it was considered a suburb of Istanbul but this was scornfully denied.

The mad parade of many relatives were staying at Mr. and Mrs. Orhan's apartment, including the maid, the grandmother, two crazed young people who came from America for the holidays and hadn't been seen since, Onya, her mother, her uncle, his wife, and the gardener.

Hassan, the uncle, looked as if he just leaped off an elephant in India in the British Empire. A small man with a large waxed handlebar mustache and leering grin, he himself looked like the sultan.

The grandmother was an elderly nodding smiling sweet pleasant woman prevented from participating in all and any conversation from having no English. Then every once in a while she would call someone up and start screaming in Turkish into a cellular telephone, making a striking contrast in her personality.

Hassan told an elaborate story about how Russian women go down to the dock at Eminönü (foot of Galata Bridge) and sell their wares and then they sell themselves. They first did this after the Revolution and now they were doing it again.

Onya had just come from a confrontation with her erstwhile fiancé, the younger misanthropic Orhan. Everyone awaited the result. One by one they all went off to whispering conferences about the turbulent engagement.

Then Hassan came pacing back and said scornfully, "He is weak. It is psychological," in disgust. So Grace assumed the outcome was not so great.

Their situation was a mirror image of her own. It was very odd. They were the Turkish counterparts of New Orleans society and the turbulent affairs of its crazed youth.

A conversation ensued about the Orient being threatened by the Occident and the fall of the Ottoman Empire. Grace went into a reverie, enraptured by their barbaric glamor. Then she finally suggested, "Don't you sort of wish you had a sultan?"

They all stared silently. "How do you feel without a sultan?" Grace persisted.

There was a photograph in *Sultans in Splendor* of the granddaughter of the last Ottoman sultan. She had been the gardener's daughter at Topkapi Palace. The Ottoman line was not aristocratic. The sultans married slave girls from the harem, who had been picked up in Nubia. In the photograph she leaned out of a window with a cigarette hanging out of her mouth, dressed in the shapeless housecoat, drab sweater, and kerchief of the observant Muslim woman.

Orhan barked out a few argumentative comments, then put on his pajamas and went to sleep.

Later he reappeared in his pajamas and Grace asked him about the descendants of the sultans and Ottoman aristocracy and whether there were any. He responded with unutterable scorn and disdain. He said he thought the grandson of the last khedive of Egypt was kicking around somewhere, he was eighty years old and Orhan hoped that he was happy; this deteriorated into a shrug of disgust.

Walter asked him about Pierre Loti and his interesting association with the town.

"Ah, you find that interesting?" His eyes shone. "He only came here to die."

Walter was suitably tyrannized, and then retreated. A great general always knows when to retreat.

Repelled from the family home by the misanthropic elder Orhan, Walter returned Grace to her boat.

15

On the boat small boys and old men in white jackets came rushing up to offer drinks of orchid juice on silver trays. Beside the port were vats of spices, octopus, and orchids. Various members of the service community from other establishments in town were always coming on the boat to offer wares, as if you would need octopus and orchids on your cruise.

There was a certain madcap atmosphere of chaos on the boat, picking up at high noon and at rush hour. Turkish boys directed traffic in the street, succeeding in creating chaos where none was before. Gypsies asked for money at the gangplank.

An ample panorama of life was provided for Mrs. Stewart to observe.

She maintained a post on deck from which she analyzed the passengers, the shoeshine boys, the gypsies, the orchid juice salesmen, and the ship's stewards. They filled her with equal worry, and she was able to diagnose pathology, mental illness, and alcoholism in very many.

Mrs. Stewart also followed the sporting news. Boxing, Spinoza, European referees, all were equally interesting to her. Uncharacteristic sporting interests were strangely at odds with the genteel elderly figure that she cut.

"What is the problem with these European referees? Something's wrong with Jones' eye. Does he have the heart to be a champion? The fury isn't there."

She had picked up the sporting parlance and it was extremely jarring to hear it emanating from her elegant and immaculately groomed person.

Walter agreed that the champ was very philosophical. When the sportscasters talked to the champ after a loss he would say, So I'm fighting bad right now. So big deal. Maybe later I'll fight better.

"Where is the *rage*?" said Mrs. Stewart.

The Republican Convention was taking place in the United States, an event that made Mrs. Stewart "seethe with anger and distaste."

Grace was subjected to a lengthy political discourse by her mother.

"It's an illness, as far as I'm concerned," said Mrs. Stewart.

"What's an illness?" said Grace. "The Republicans?"

"Grace, you're tuning out," said Mrs. Stewart.

Urgings to write to her senators followed.

Then the case of Walter was resumed.

"He's in amazing shape considering that his entire life is falling apart," whispered Mrs. Stewart.

He did seem to have a lot of ailments. Walter was beginning to confuse his ailments with the sites he had visited, both of which were too numerous to catalog. That night he complained that the shrimp shells he had devoured at dinner were caught in his sarcophagus.

"He's gone berserk," said Mrs. Stewart, after Walter had retired.

"Now, now," said her husband.

But Mr. Stewart brought out a small case from his breast pocket containing a notepad. He started taking notes. He appeared to be taking notes on Walter's ailments.

1. allergy to Bosphorus
2. shrimp shells caught in windpipe
3. sinus headache
4. neck crick

He wrote.

Somehow a discussion ensued on Mrs. Stewart's love life in her youth, the time in youth when you admire someone from afar but if he ever chanced to make advances at you, you would flee. Mrs. Stewart said in her youth she was that way.

"Why do you flee although you adore them? What causes that, do you think?" said Grace.

"Neurotic anxiety," said Mrs. Stewart.

"Prudence," said Mr. Stewart.

Thus the two opposing viewpoints of the psychologist and the lawyer.

16

On returning to his hotel Walter had a message to call Onya's aunt at three o'clock. Already the mad parade of her assorted relatives had grown fond of Walter. What was it about Walter that endeared him to these people with such urgency? Walter wondered. Was it that it's always nice to have an extra man around, a bachelor, to squire around some female who was engaged to be married but whose engagement seemed unsteady or unstable or whose fiancé was never there? In truth the answer to this question could not come from Walter. He was not accustomed to analyzing his appeal. He wasn't sure he had any. It was one of his charms.

He sat in the Orient Bar, awaiting information. The mad parade of Onya's relatives was confabulating about where they were to meet.

The doorman looked his part, with a handlebar mustache.

Walter had procured a book describing the hotel; in the introduction a Turkish historian reminisced about the old days there, when he would walk into the Orient Bar and see Atatürk, "the possessor of my heart," he put it.

Walter visited the room preserved as a museum where the possessor of Turkish hearts had stayed. Atatürk was idolized as the hero of the Turks beyond compare. Atatürk was pictured frequently in cafés and restaurants and homes, like JFK. A dashing handsome man in white tie and tails in the pictures, for he was vain of his appearance, and a bachelor all his life, when he died and his successor was a more conventional type, it was said that Turkey had lost her lover, and now must settle down with her husband.

This information Walter had gleaned from *The Fall of the Ottoman Empire.*

The mad parade of Onya's relatives met Walter at his hotel. Included in the party was also a Turk named Genghis. Frequently the men were named Genghis.

The crusty misanthropic white-haired Orhan was also present. The younger misanthropic Orhan appeared to be out of the picture.

The mad parade of Onya's nihilistic relatives repaired to a

hilarious round of cocktails in Beyoglu, the glamor neighborhood of Levantine society near Walter's hotel.

"Where is your girlfriend?" inquired the crusty misanthropic Orhan.

"She's not my girlfriend."

"No?"

"She has a fiancé. He's coming later."

"And where does that leave you? It leaves you out in the cold," he stated bluntly.

A telegram had been received from Monroe. Monroe had signaled his impending arrival, indicating he would arrive at Istanbul before the ship left port.

Walter had been apprised. He indulged in some teeth-gnashing. He contemplated his next move.

Walter had had enough. He had done all he could. He suddenly thought of his father. Walter's father, who had a bad heart, was forced to retire at an early age. Walter had two older brothers who lived in New Orleans and were ne'er-do-wells, at least compared with Walter. On the occasion that the doctor gave these orders to his father Walter chose to come home and evaluate the situation for himself. He sat at his father's bedside and his father said to him, You are a man, and that's why we have always expected more of you. And the way he sat at his father's bedside was exactly the way in which he was a man. He took a sabbatical to come home and sit at his father's bedside, what a good man and what an interesting man would do. Devote himself. To carefully evaluate the situation of the person whom he loved. To study the person whom he loved.

But a good man has a certain reservoir of forbearance and when it runs out, it is quite gone.

It had run out for Grace.

17

Walter announced that he would fly to London. He would begin his duties at the Italian desk at Merrill Lynch's London office.

He apprised the Stewarts of his plans.

"We smothered him, and now he wants to go," said Mr. Stewart. "We're suffocating him," he persisted, with some gaiety. He seemed awfully gay to see him go. He suspected he would be back.

Grace and Walter drove to the airport to pick up Monroe. The two flights came conveniently together—Walter's to London and Monroe's from New York. Walter was at the end of his rope.

The weather had changed. They drove to the airport in a horrible cold black rain. There were no traffic lights on the highway. There were many slow-moving trucks in the driving rain. Several accidents occurred. Turkey was known for traffic accidents, Walter said. The Turks drive recklessly and the roads are steep and poorly lit while lined with steep ditches.

"How do you know all this?" asked Grace.

"It's in the book," he said.

"Which book?"

"*The Turkish Guide to Death.*"

They persevered in the driving rain amid the rank cold steam while minarets of mosques could dimly be perceived among the hills. Heaps of rams to be sacrificed for the holiday were piled on an exit ramp.

They waited in the airport restaurant.

Observant Muslim women wore a sort of fashion uniform: drab pleated skirt coming to the mid-calf, mottled kerchief covering the head, and dowdy winter coat, with arms extended clutching hands of children. A lot of times you see a perfectly natty young man taking in the scene, and suddenly the Observant Muslim Woman in her drab uniform shows up clutching the hands of his children, when you wouldn't have featured him to have a wife of that kind, judging from his sauntering appearance.

Grace dementedly supposed it was a picture of her life to come.

Grace and Walter sat in the airport restaurant waiting for Monroe's flight to come in. Outside the planes were waiting on the tarmac in the driving rain, which they observed.

A new Turkish airline had started up called Sultan Air. SULTAN was written in vast red letters comprising the whole body of the plane. Grace said they must have chandeliers, huge feasts, and jeweled coffee cups aboard the plane, to befit its name.

Monroe's flight then came in.

An inexplicable Bride and Groom in their full regalia—topcoat, tails, elaborate wedding gown, train, veil, and headdress—disembarked among the other passengers. They were dressed completely for the wedding and on arrival at Istanbul walked off into the evening, the bride holding up her train, mincing along the tarmac in her high heels.

❧

The dapper Southerner in the old white suit again made his brief appearance. It was deeply shocking to her to see him there. She did not dream that he could leave his element, cross the ocean, cast himself adrift into the world. She never dreamed he would show up. It made it much worse. There he was, dark-haired, laconic, serious, in a starched white suit from Louisiana. What must it have cost him to come this far. He represented everything she most desired, but she felt an inexorable destiny apart. It seemed as if the beauty of her old home which he represented was but a very dream.

"She transfigured everyone. All the stray bits and pieces of the past, all that is feckless and gray about people, she pulled together into an unmistakable visage of the heroic or the craven, the noble or the ignoble. So strong was her vision that sometimes the person and the past were in fact transfigured by her. They became what she saw them to be." Monroe was sort of the epitome of the destroyed Southerner. He wasn't the Regular Guy. She didn't really know many Regular Guys. They weren't her type. Actually the bankers she had met in New York, colleagues of Walter's, were the most regular guys she had seen. Walter was the only banker she had seen who had a personality. Maybe in the South the bankers had personality—maybe they were destroyed and demented—but of course if so, they wouldn't know it, like Monroe. But Walter was the only man on Wall Street she surmised who had a personality.

"I lost my car," said Monroe.

She was in a reverie.

"Your car? What happened to it?"

"It exploded again in Alabama."

She went into another reverie. They had gone once to a realtor in Point Clear, Alabama, to try to rent a house. But even though they were realtors, they could barely discuss renting a house. After a long discussion of the fine families of Mobile owning houses on the Point, one fellow sitting in the back of the office under a palmetto tree said it was conceivable that Bill might want to rent his house. It's conceivable, he mused.

But even this exclusion from the fine families of Mobile was everything she loved. There was the New South too of course, where realtors would probably not behave in that way. Realtors in Dallas or Atlanta would likely not behave in that way. But in her pocket of the South, the Gulf South, in fact what is known as the Deep South, people who were realtors gossiped in their office on the Point among the azaleas and were taken aback at the concept of renting a house.

Or the realtor might be a variation on Miss Mary, the basic ruler of the South, who runs the plantation, or runs the family, or runs the business, but she doesn't come into the office until after five. You can't talk to her till after five. She runs the show, but she can't get it together to start doing business until after five? What does she do until five?

One can only imagine. But everyone defers to her. No one defies her. She runs the show. Married? Never married? Matriarch? Loner? One doesn't know. Probably some demented sons in the background, grown men, almost elderly in fact, one with a lame leg, darkly smoldering, sort of dashing. Debonair.

Her sons would wish to run the show. But of course Miss Mary runs the show. Ever since they were babies, she ruled them, instead of them ruling her. And it is usually the case with babies that they rule you and you act as their hapless nursemaid at all hours answering their needs. But with Miss Mary—nothing doing—a cigarette hanging out of her mouth at all times, the ruler, running the show.

Maybe Monroe needed someone like that to rule him. He would wear a bow tie, a seersucker suit, dark sunglasses, and white bucks. They would do anything to hide their suffering, and never show it, usually by going to more and more parties, and becoming more and more ornate. She would look for him and he would be in the basement taking labels off a box of fishing tackle. She would ask him if anything was wrong. "I can't take the pace," he would say, and she would find it fond, or deem it as eccentric, for the pace would consist of retreating to the basement to tie flies, going fishing, and having cocktails on the lake.

The strange thing was she loved him. But she was being

drawn inexorably apart. Drawn into the world and leaving what she loved behind. You think it is implied that he was ineffectual. But why? when he had, in his way, gallantry and tenderness and angst. She loved angst. He would take her to the basement with his fishing tackle and talk about his angst for three hours. She would love to hear him talk about his angst for three hours but she was a little scared it would be stultifying. It was not a road that she would even dare to go down now, although she still thought it was fascinating. She loved it that he couldn't cope. That he was so destroyed. She loved it that he couldn't leave his sphere. But he had left his sphere for her. Here he was.

Well, she got it wrong.

The South was defeated, but not destroyed, and the world was waiting.

Before they even got his bags, before they even got a taxi, before they even left the smoke-choked terminal, Grace, who could not contain an untruth, who was incapable of tactful, heartfelt lies, given with a full heart, sure of the generosity of its deceit—said that something was not right.

Not right.

"Is there someone else?" said Monroe.

"Yes."

"Who is it?"

"It's that guy who just got on the plane to London."

It was awkward for Mr. Stewart. Monroe's uncle was his best friend. At least the invitations hadn't actually gone out. That would be a scandal. But of course it wasn't really that that troubled him. He felt sorry for the boy and he wasn't altogether sure that it was the right thing. He was an honorable boy. Mr. Stewart felt a good deal of remorse on his account. The duel was over but another would undoubtedly begin.

The ship sailed out through the Dardanelles and up the Adriatic to what was then the pleasant area of the Dalmatian coast, near Montenegro. Directly on the Adriatic stood a gigantic antique palace lined by huge palms that was built by Diocletian, one of the greatest Roman emperors, as the place of his retreat in his retirement, in the region of his youth.

Some long debilitating discussions regarding Mrs. Stewart's sons' affairs occurred, and how she pried into them and then felt remorse. A postmortem ensued of the affairs of Onya and Orhan.

"He's not right for her," said Mrs. Stewart. She stopped. "Just as Monroe is not right for you."

"I thought you idolized him."

"Grace, as the Designated Family Healer," she began, "I feel it is my duty to tell you this."

"I thought you adored him."

"Yes, I thought I adored him too. But I've been thinking about him a lot. He's a very disturbed person."

"He is?"

"He would have destroyed you."

"He would have destroyed me? How?"

"You're too similar. It's a very disturbed personality."

"Thanks a lot."

"Well, his is even more exaggerated than yours, Grace. When I see you with him it's as if you are saying, 'This is my pain.' "

"It is?"

"Walter on the other hand is one of the most enterprising young men I have met. I think I've cured him."

But Walter did get on the plane to London. And he wasn't seen again.

19

It would later prove that a small ship in the open sea can pitch quite a lot and most of the passengers would prove to be seasick quite a bit of the time. Long after they returned home, Mrs. Stewart said the house was pitching and rolling. One passenger fell off the dock and dislocated his shoulder. The grand piano overturned in the ballroom.

"It's brightening," said an elderly British woman sitting next to Mrs. Stewart on the deck, with the stiff upper lip of her national heritage. Brightening in her parlance meant that the rain was no longer sweeping in vast flat sheets into the crevice on the deck that they were sitting in, but was instead coming down more daintily in buckets.

The passengers grew restive. Some of them went haywire. There had been a two-week delay at Istanbul before the ship set sail. When it did set sail the seas were rough. The ballroom flooded. The Italians organized a protest. A meeting was held on deck.

The leader asked for remarks from the audience. "We don't accept negative tirades," he said.

"Can we make negative tirades at another time?" asked Mrs. Stewart.

As the ship sailed on, people talked about the universe and the stars in their orbits and grew baffled and apocalyptic.

They came into Venice in a storm. It was raining and it was a shock to see such a town as that again. Grace felt a sharp memory associated with it of her father, who in her youth had taken her to a cathedral in the Adriatic lagoon that showed the green of Paradise, the legions of the blessed, and the angels unfurling the starry sky of night to the end of time.

When the boat came into port it stopped for several nights and the passengers would see the sights and sleep on board at night. At Venice Grace took melancholy walks along the Lido beneath a green-and-white-striped awning with a glimpse of the blue Adriatic down the street. It was a place that had seen its day. She preferred such places, whose day is past, which is true of the Venice Lido, generally speaking. Such gloomy gaiety, the unpeopled palaces, no crowds, deserted colonnades, the air of quietude and faded grandeur. There were baroque cafés with green awnings and cane chairs and white tablecloths, and Venetian sailor boys in old-time sailor suits with black ribbons hanging off the back of their caps.

For her it was a melancholy time. She prepared to return to her fate of demented crazed young person working in a law office without the scope of matronly self-sacrifice she had long been planning to adopt, as she had broken her engagement definitely. Maybe the human soul was not constituted for marriage. Didn't he know that the yearnings of her soul were infinite? Maybe when you were married the yearnings of your soul were more fulfilled. But she had no sense of relief from having broken it off.

She had no sense of having escaped a wrong fate. In all her love and longing for her region she felt she would only be called ever far away from it, and the person who represented it. She foresaw she would return to the anonymity of New York, not having the courage to face the South.

The ship sailed on. They didn't see much of Naples because it was only a "pit stop" at night but it was a dark dilapidated port city and reminded her of New Orleans. A lot of people could make a lot of jokes about how many things reminded her of New Orleans. But "let us not curse exile . . . During the night, in desolate fields far from Rome, I would pitch my tent, and my tent was Rome to me."

Sicily was remote and stifling. The obligatory bride and groom went through the mosque and garden of gigantic palms raging in the sun, at the Norman Palace. The usual wedding was about to take place, transforming some deserted colonnade into a bacchanalia.

Talk about crumbling. That is old-time Palermo. Besotted markets, crumbling palaces, also relics of saints in the cathedral and dead people in the catacombs.

The obligatory bride was there again the next day sitting in a white Rolls-Royce with a white satin bow on it, and wandering through the garden being photographed.

Trapani was a quiet town, with a sweltering port, and a ruined Caribbean square with an immense baroque cathedral declining among the palms, a green gilt dome, and a glamor neighborhood of Levantine society. She found the green of Paradise there. Opera singers wandered in the garden. *La Traviata* played in the park. An avenue of gigantic palms led to the seats with white satin curtains somehow between the palms, and black wrought-iron light standards lighting up the night against the green. She looked on in almost disbelief for she had rarely seen a scene so beautiful.

There were guards at the gate in white uniforms and safari helmets. Then the avenue of palms that was so ravishing. As if it were the green of Paradise.

They awaited to embark the boat for Africa.

Mosques and minarets and domes and a ravishing African sea. Tunis had a sweltering heat, but was flat and calm and everyone surrendered to it. There were some modern buildings but they were not offensive as they are in Europe, where they seem a hideous mistake. Everything was flat and hot, the modern buildings white, on a calm unfrenzied sea—like Gulfport, Mississippi.

There was a spa up the mountain road. The doctor was a handsome stout mustached Arab in a shabby white coat. He was like someone you had seen or known before. The place was like something out of your old familiar dreams. A few worn-out-looking Europeans emerged from the baths, the kind you see in North Africa who look like they've gone over the edge.

She had a Tunisian guidebook that displayed a fanciful but tortured grasp of the English language. There were descriptions of accommodations at different hotels. The self-lacerating gardens of the Hotel Splendide. The Exploitation Restaurant of the Hotel Majestic. The Paradise, formerly an ostrich farm converted to a smart hotel, where you may wander in the ambivalent courtyards.

She knew that she would like Tunisia from the first sight she saw on arrival. This was a small boy at the side of the road, flanked by two little girls, presumably his sisters, whose wrists he was sternly clasping, holding them back while he looked both ways down the road for cars. Such gallantry in the little fellow—and she knew that if a country had a little boy like that, she was bound to like it.

They went along the sea to Carthage, where you see elderly seedy-looking white men in galabiyas who look like old colonial gents who have gone over the edge. The lights on the sea came up—the prayer to Allah.

The boat was docked at the African Riviera, the coast at Hammamet, on the green-blue sea of the lotus eaters. Camels were for hire. Wild horses galloped past. The African Riviera was a modest resort. A brochure at one of the hotels said it was "not on the smart side of town." At night they played a sort of game of multilingual bingo which was so overamplified it was as if they were broadcasting to Libya. It involved a jolly fellow constantly reeling off a ceaseless series of numbers given in five languages.

They hired a car with driver to take them to the Roman ruins at Dougga. The setting for the ruins was the middle of nowhere in a situation of insupportable heat. It was a three-hour drive each way. Bleak benighted dust-choked landscapes. But she was happy there. You cannot tell what place will make you happy, where you will find peace.

She asked the guide how they coped with the heat. "Today, for instance, in the heat of noon, you were happy?" she asked.

"Yes, I was happy. I was very happy," he proclaimed. "To us it is supportable because we were born here. It is what makes us happy."

"It sure is hot," she said.

"She thinks it's hot! It's hot but it's hotter than this where I come from," he said.

You really shouldn't go to ruins at high noon in July in Africa, if you can possibly help yourself.

The lights of the city came up as they returned to Tunis, the air stiflingly hot but with the faintest evening breeze. Dinner at the Baghdad. "I'm in the Mood for Love" was playing in the elevator at the Hotel Africa. Arab sheiks, more chants to Allah going up, women in white veils, a pharmacy with snakes in jars displayed as toiletries.

You lose yourself in such a place. In Europe you find the

beautiful but very rarely the strange. In North Africa everything is just so strange that you forget yourself. Also the people don't notice you.

Women with dyed feet. Sheep hanging that have been embalmed. Chickens being slaughtered in the bazaar. Among palms and minarets in the quiet heat—and the prayer to Allah going up.

The boat sailed on to Alexandria. A broken-down, emotionally upset Egyptologist from Boston came to lead the passengers to Cairo.

He said that life was but a short dream to the builders of the Pyramids, and that is why the Pyramids and tombs exist intact and not the palaces. It would not matter to them if they lived in a mud hut, the guide said, because this was not the life that mattered to them. This life we live is not and never was what mattered in the East. Sinai, Israel, the Arab world, and war across the desert. It is all religion there. It always was and still is all religion there.

The weather was clear and dry, though prone to extremes of temperature, hot and cold, throughout the day and night. Grace took a camel with the guide, galloping in the desert off toward Mecca, among the inscrutable Bedouins. When he got to the middle of the desert in the middle of nowhere, the guide stopped the beast and craned around to face her. "You kiss me now," he said. She demurred. He was philosophical. He gave her Camel cigarettes and said that he had been to Cincinnati.

From Cairo they boarded a small boat to take the Nile to Aswan. At night Strauss waltzes played. There were dignified Egyptian travelers from Cairo. Italian pleasure-seekers. The Italians did bawdy pantomimes. A costume ball was held. They wore monocles and fezzes and carried daggers they had got in the bazaar.

Cousin Malcolm reenacted the plots of *The Egyptian,* with Victor Mature, and *The Mummy,* with Boris Karloff.

Banana plantations along the Nile then prompted Malcolm to a sudden discussion of Robert E. Lee's horse, Traveler.

Ocher courts, palm trees, and the tropic zone; small towns on the Nile with crumbling colonial mansions bearing names engraved into the stone such as the Splendide or the Majestic when nothing could be more the opposite, as they exist in unimaginable squalor, left to rot, laden with the grime of other centuries, and populated by inscrutable Arabs. Evidences of the British Empire, Beaux Arts grandiosity amid the dust. It seemed madcap there, for it did not intrinsically belong, and there was a pathos in it, Strauss waltzes playing blithely on the Nile.

The famed Winter Palace Hotel at Luxor was a sprawling rose-limestone palace with long, empty halls and seedy grandeur. It had an elaborate garden with monumental palms and ocher-colored dirt, cane chairs. Completely deserted save for one old man with a fez. The seven-thirty prayer to Allah going up. Full moon.

They stopped at a sweltering town on the Nile whose like she never saw before or expected to see again. Besotted nineteenth-century colonial palaces, decrepit horse-drawn carriages, Arabic music, Muslim chants. The streets were of dirt lined by eucalyptus trees toward the main square, a circle of date palms and sweet olive. Green shutters, Corinthian columns, and balustrades on balconies of besotted villas and defunct hotels.

They returned to Cairo. Smoldering Babylonian prison. Smoldering medieval bazaar. Chickens being slaughtered by a woman who would bite their heads off and pull their feet off before they were even dead, next to a man being shaved by his barber in a spice emporium.

Grace went to the Cairo Tower with one of her many Arab admirers (their guide) and looked at last upon the dust of Africa, and so she bade adieu to Cairo, never to see it again.

* * *

The boat sailed to Marseilles. It took at least two days to adjust from Africa. You love a place, and then on leaving, regret it for some time. The same happened leaving Istanbul. The regret there lasted longer. Throughout Italy. Italy, however, she was reevaluating. But the pleasures of France could hardly be more different. Gentle, refined, civilized, delicate; the temperate climate; even the ruins there seemed delicate and refined compared with Africa or Italy and those sweltering Mediterranean environs of the Roman Empire. A Southern empire; odd.

She had not remembered the Europeans congregating to gape at their own country. As tourists—similar to what you find in New Orleans in the French Quarter. She had recollected the old country to be at one with its people and the people were a part of it and would not go to gape at it. But maybe they did and she had been too young to notice. There was a France she remembered in her heart, twenty years ago, when her father brought her as a girl. An iron gate ran all along a park, the posts in gilt, the floor of the park in sand, it seemed, rather than in grass, and there was the dappled air, caused by the overhang of green leaves from the plane trees. In the vista of the park there was a château or palace, from which the sand paths emanated, lined by topiary and flower beds, no doubt the work of Lenôtre. It was the most captivating sight. She wondered if this France was gone. And then at Nîmes they turned a corner and suddenly drove past it.

At the cathedral in Villers-Cotterêts they ran into a woman from New York who was searching for misericords in the church. These are the incredibly esoteric and sometimes off-color engravings that are found underneath certain pews in medieval churches that this woman had been insanely devoting her life to. Pornographic choir stalls might be a more apt description. She pointed out some misericords in the church. She described one she had recently discovered in Spain, picturing a derriere with eyeglasses on it. "Hindsight!" commented Mr. Stewart. Ever since she lost her husband twenty years ago, she had been madly searching Europe for misericords, cataloging them, collating them, collecting them, all to no avail, as she could not get the grant she had been trying to get for twenty years to study misericords since no one was interested in misericords—except her.

"They go to Notre Dame and Chartres and look at the stained-glass windows, they don't even *look* at the misericords!" she said in outrage.

Then she told them about the other misericord scholars (Grace asked her if there were any) and she said oh yes and they all had the gayest time when they got together. Mr. Stewart suggested they might soon begin to covet one another's material and have feuds. She was the kind of person who liked being teased about her foibles—she knew, secretly, that they were many. She knew secretly that they were madmen—misericord scholars.

They raced toward Paris through the green French forests, presaging fall, Vaux-le-Vicomte and Ermenonville, Chantilly on its green canal, and the ravishing park of Fontainebleau, gilt gates encircling the châteaux in the green French forests.

From Roissy Charles de Gaulle they flew to London before going home.

While her family rested before the transatlantic flight she went to Oxford to recapture her past. She was exalted to approach the dreaming spires, where she hoped to meet not only them but herself of twenty years ago, that girl taken by her father to see the world and so struck by the ancient spires.

She walked first to Christ Church, hoping to meet herself there—where twenty years ago she had first asked herself what men walked there and rambled through the lanes, in centuries long past, and raised some tears to find herself of twenty years ago and to find the selfsame spot she stood in then, as awestruck now as she was then. She abandoned her map and wandered through the dreaming spires without a guide. Some weren't open, others were barred to visitors—you weren't really supposed to go into the colleges alone and unannounced. But be bold, she thought, or else be barred from finding the unchallenged beauty of the world.

She was procrastinating almost calling Walter, who was now in London. She felt that he was somewhat in a rage, and she did not want to meet him in that mood. She knew that she had caused his anger and she felt wary of continuing to play a sort of Scarlett O'Hara role she seemed to realize that she had a penchant for. She was skating on thin ice. Better to discard that mode. She had tantalized him. Monroe's life she had hurt. Better to do penance. It wasn't only that. She knew that Walter's reservoir might have run out of forbearance for her. She would have to find someone, if possible, just as the judge said, who would put up with her.

So they drove to Heathrow in a cold pouring rain but she was not sorry to fly back to her country, even to New York, which seemed tropical by comparison, still in the eighties, breezy, with everyone screaming at one another but in a friendly way deep down.

In New York during the layover Mr. Stewart wandered down Madison Avenue searching for the following defunct items: challis ties, Herzfeld undershirts, white bucks with nap, white kid gloves, kettlecloth, patch pockets, narrow lapels. "It sounds like you're being outfitted for the British Empire," said Grace.

One of her brothers and his son came to meet the matriarch and patriarch in New York and fly back with them to New Orleans. The little son said he had written a novel and read it out loud in a thickly exaggerated Southern accent for dramatic effects. It contained six chapters (he was six years old), with each chapter revolving around traumatic events in the life of his dog, and each chapter ending with the same refrain, "And then life went on as before"—rendered in the heavy Southern accent giving an atmosphere of *Tobacco Road.*

20

And then life went on as before. The Nameless Hour was a good thing to have. It made you self-sufficient. She returned to her teaching job at Columbia and a society in chaos, lacking gentility, and a position in society, Hey you, that was in striking contrast to that she occupied in New Orleans, where she was exalted to the very pinnacle of civilization.

She returned at times to glimpse the life she would not lead. Some were exiles for politics, revolution, war; it was not meant to be dramatized by world events for her. But she was still an exile. The love affair was with the place. The place you were born in held the revelation of a mystery not given elsewhere to answer. Why do you ever leave your home, which holds the answer to your particular truth? To go out into the world. Then you get stuck out in the world and can't get back.

In New Orleans she stayed at hotels. She stayed at the Pontchartrain, she stayed in the French Quarter, she stayed at the faceless Hilton Hotel downtown. But even a faceless Hilton Hotel, if it was downtown in New Orleans, could hold the answer to the mystery. The mystery lurked somewhere among the hulking tourists eating oysters at the sad café done up as a fake plantation.

Sometimes in New York she hung out at hotels and that was to experience exile and anonymity. In New Orleans a hotel room was different. You knew there was something tragic and sleazy and pitiful out there, but it still held the answer to the mystery.

And what would Grace have been, she wondered, had she stayed there? In her visions she met the person whom she would have been. This person lurked at every corner. This person had frosted hair, wore Lily Pulitzer dresses, and had many children. She was able to make rémoulade sauce. She was able to entertain elaborately and give a small dance for five thousand. Men who went hunting would drop off teal ducks at her house on Sunday night as a courtly present. This person saw the man she loved in the park at the bandstand while an orchestra played. She danced under palm trees. She was surrounded by unsung heroes and nameless lurking sorrows. She would live in the house that her grandfather had been born in and meet his memory at every corner. She would joke around with the decrepit but dashing DeLord men. She would be able to see her beloved father every day of her life. She would be able to trace the mystery, to break the code, to understand, to name the nameless lurking sorrows. She would go to Florida and revel in its bemusing hopelessness, that old glamor, the humanity, of the tropics.

She would be run ragged by Miss Mary, as she would no doubt have come across one frequently—perhaps be employed by one, or find her in the proprietor of the neighborhood restaurant or dry cleaner, her lame demented dashing sons forming a shadowy background, duly reporting to her while somehow seeming to keep their dignity, the lame leg dragging up the stairs, the bow ties, Miss Mary's cigarette hanging out of her mouth, the whir of the ceiling fan.

But it was the intolerable love of a place she carried with her, and if she lacked the courage to face the South, she carried the South with her where she went. Until she went so far that she could not get back even in her visions.

"At the city's heart lie the pattern and the hard core and these I can never make my own, they are too far outside my range." So she stood outside the land of her forebears, somehow barred and looking in as if she were the outsider rather than the native. Monroe had made the impossible gesture, for him, of going out west to California and had not been heard from since. She was left with the weight set squarely on her shoulders of sending the scion of the fabulous DeLord empire away from his duties, which he had formerly so quaintly performed. But it was not a total disaster. He would one day return, and take them up again. He was faithful to them. They were what she most desired and was most fascinated by. Something had driven her out.

It takes a strong soul to appreciate the bemusing hopelessness of an oppressive tropic climate, an oppressive gentility, and an oppressively constant proximity to the place of your earliest residence, the place of your childhood and youth and memory. It was why she so admired the Miss Marys and the Monroes of the world. They didn't buckle under it. But then maybe it didn't oppress them. No doubt they didn't look at it that way. There was a growing danger in her visions. Walter had suggested in Istanbul last year she should always make sure her visions were not obsolete or overly grandiose, like civilizations that are vanquished, empires that fall, so she would not become a brittle pathetic facade amid a crumbling ruin—like Shelley's *Ozymandias,* which she had seen in Egypt. This idea haunted her. She was in danger of living it.

Walter felt he ran that risk too, before he left her in Istanbul last year. He bore his burden with grace, up until then, but you could see the shadows around his eyes. And if you had seen him in London at that moment you would have seen that his burdens had not yet departed.

She thought of him. It was too bad she had never run across him in New York during the years they both lived there. Nothing would have induced her to call him. She must do penance for having tantalized him.

A year had passed since she had seen him last. But he was always with her. She imagined him to be with her in some hotel room in New Orleans on the edge of town, looking at the oil rigs and shrimp trawlers on the lake. On one such occasion she received an unusual visitor.

21

Walter was on a plane from New York to New Orleans. He had just taken the most expensive vacation in the history of the Mediterranean. War was declared before he left. From the Italian desk he had delivered an ultimatum to his boss in New York: 1) He demanded that they hire twelve extra people for his office. These would be crazed young people like himself who stay up until four in the morning doing investment analyses with due diligence. 2) He needed another reevaluation period, the ultimate reevaluation period. He wanted to piece things together.

"We have only one virginity to lose. And where we have lost it there our hearts will be." He felt that he had lost his heart to Istanbul so one day a year later when he realized this, he went back, and down the coast of the green Aegean to the blue Mediterranean and the Greek Islands. He tried to piece things together. Greece declared war on Turkey. He had to leave. He was ejected from the land he loved. Would it always be so?

So he was on a rough ride to New Orleans. It rains every day in New Orleans in August. It is hurricane season. The flight from New York gets in every day at five o'clock, which is exactly when the height of the storm begins. It is as if you have to defy death to go there. Plus he had just seen *The Hurricane* with Dorothy Lamour several times in succession at three in the morning as they had played it over and over on TV in his hotel room in New York.

If you live in New Orleans, the biggest thing in your life is the weather. The entire theory of human conduct, some say, is governed by weather. Yankees are hardy and victorious because they have a brisk, invigorating climate and hard winters.

In August the weather is torrid, and in the afternoon it rains for two hours. In summer it rains every day. Then the water rises up from the pavement in steam. If the sky is gray, then all is relief, as a gray day is more gentle and offers respite.

Coming in amid the nerve-racked palms during a crashing tropic storm, he saw the Mississippi River dully glittering across the land of all his forebears. On the ground there was some flooding. "Is it bad?" he said to the taxi driver taking him uptown. "It's always bad here," he said with dark gaiety. There was a sense of ease, the gaiety in fact made more by the flood, the sentiment of nameless excitement as in hurricanes, the thrill of disaster.

Walter was reading *The Decline and Fall of the Roman Empire*. There was something in it, pertaining to Leontius Pilatus, that reminded him of Grace. The scholar's deportment was rustic, his temper gloomy and inconstant. Petrarch entertained him at Padua for a short time "but was justly offended with the gloomy and unsocial temper of the man. Discontented with the world and with himself, he depreciated his present enjoyments, while absent persons and objects were dear to his imagination. In Italy he was a Thessalian, in Greece a native of Calabria; in the company of Latins he disdained their language, religion, and manners; no sooner was he landed at Constantinople, then he again sighed for the wealth of Venice and the elegance of Florence."

In New York she was a Southerner, in the South an outsider who had forsaken the South. No sooner was she landed in New York than she pined for New Orleans; no sooner was she removed from Istanbul than she pined for Anatolia; in Italy she pined for Africa; in Africa remembered Sicily too fondly.

But it fascinated him.

Walter's father, who had the bad heart, was advised to retire at an early age. So he retired, and lived for forty-five years thereafter puttering around the house, retreating to the basement to look at his fishing tackle, tying flies, and fixing the plumbing. He became a failure, although he had never been a failure before. He had been a very eminent professor. He wasn't really a failure exactly in retirement, but it was just that he had never got the chance to flower or attain the limit of achievement. He seemed angst-ridden. He was a sort of shadow passing through the house. Walter's attitude to this was somewhat similar to Mrs. Stewart's attitude to her father—who had gone on a bender in the middle of his career and then the bender never ended. They were disillusioned with their fathers, though Mrs. Stewart was more fierce in her disillusion as she was in all things, and Walter was more dry and forbearing, as he also was in all things. But it may have accounted for the bond of understanding between them. They both saw the craven and the feckless and the ignoble, where Grace saw only gallantry and angst.

He expected to hear she was married. They had distant mutual acquaintances. Eventually he made inquiries. Then he heard that she was not. Being a man of action, he took up the gauntlet, to pay a last call on the unconstant Grace.

However he had first called her mother. He had a sort of bond with the psychoanalytical Mrs. Stewart. He might sound her out. He also wanted to determine Grace's whereabouts as he assumed she would have returned to her beloved and demented South, the land of her imaginings. He wanted to identify her exact locality. He wanted to surprise her. He always did things in that way, rather dramatically, and with a loping generosity.

He had called from New York, where he was stopping on a short sabbatical from the Italian desk in London. Mrs. Stewart answered, fiercely interested—her interest in all things was fierce. If only she could have diagnosed mental illness through the telephone, or administered a Rorschach test over the telephone, she would have been overjoyed. But she informed him where Grace was.

When you arrive at the airport this is the scene you will see. White-suited Southerners mopping their brows, but holding their tempers, for it is their way to be polite. They don't know another way. Perhaps they could conceive it or had heard about it or perhaps they too had once been Hey you in New York—but it wasn't polite. The minute you drive toward the river you will be struck by the unending green and monumental oaks. The atmosphere is very thick. The air will seem dark as though it were twilight but this is only because it is impending rain. The gods seem angry, but the residents forbear. Also, it will be sleazy.

He went to the address he had been given. The weather changed a lot, as if the town itself were having mood swings and malaise. There was an exhausted palm beside the entrance of the obscure hotel. He rang the bell and it was answered.

He stretched out his arms to her in his characteristic gesture; he held her closely and then before she could exactly tell what was happening, she was falling to the ground. He pulled her down onto the floor. She fell to the floor as if in slow motion, while Walter fell above her—he had somehow thrown her on the floor—and started kissing her; she began to weep. He stopped. He did not know why she wept. Marrying the man you love is strangely debilitating. One of the great campaigns of your life has been won. Lacking angst, Walter could not see all this. He had a hard moment. Here we go again, he thought. It's going to be some nutty rubric. Or men in white tie and tails. But from there it was not far.

From there it was not far to Walter's slow but inevitable ascent to the Fiery Pantheon.

She wept some more.

"Do you want me to go?" asked Walter.

He kept his arm around her. She seemed to be becoming hysterical. He said, "I think I'd better stay."

She started rambling about how she was older and wiser and sadder now. She had come to the end of the line. She was now twenty-nine, she would have to adapt, time would grow short, her life might soon be over, due to her fossilized age, and love required a struggle that she had endured and it would not be quite the same again; she had waited for him for a year, it had been like traveling far, but while traveling, it is a good feeling to know you love your country, and to know that you will one day see it again.

A wedding was planned anew. Her father immersed himself in etiquette and she constantly attended meetings with florists and caterers that her mother conducted as if they were World War II summit conferences.

For their honeymoon they went to the Italian lakes, where the paths among the gardens on Lake Como looked to Grace like the Bosphorus at the viceroy of Egypt's summer palace the year before. At the entrance to the hotel was a sign with its name lit up dashingly in bare bulbs. It was not opulent as European hotels go. It was even on a par with the Virginia Hotel, whose Great Hall was more gay, and it reminded her somewhat of Alabama.

The weather cleared and the lake was a bewitching dark green opaque color. There were abandoned crumbling villas, with overgrown gardens as lush as Palermo. It had the remoteness and abandoned air of Sicily. The abandoned mansions were the gorgeous remnant of another time, like plantations along the River Road in Louisiana, causing Grace to wonder at the former occupants, like the DeLords and the DeCourcys of Lord Hall. She wondered: Did they participate in glittering balls and dirges on the river and then lunge through the house lighting bonfires in mad grief and crash around the levee in grief-struck losses and defeats? No. They conducted business, they planted crops, they wrote business letters to Baton Rouge, and met with their accountants. As Walter pointed out.

There was always that trouble with her worldview, Walter always attempted to point out.

So on the drive from Cernobbio to Tremezzo along the east shore of Lake Como, from Walter's perspective as a capitalist, he thought they were passing a series of eighteenth- and nineteenth-century villas, classic examples of Palladian, Baroque, and neoclassical architecture. Only after observing it all through the highly trained and sensitive eyes of his wife, he professed, did he realize that the lake was lined with white-haired gents in white tie and tails and orchestras playing under palm trees.

She saw there the man she loved, who had the ability to make a joke of her demented visions. She saw his crazed youth, his industry, his valor. Mr. Stewart could not have parted with her if he had not seen it too. He had to fight a duel, but he had to grudgingly admit the excellence of his opponent, and over time actually came to admire it. Mrs. Stewart had psychoanalytical fodder for the rest of her life to mull over.

Walter thanked his father-in-law at their elaborate departure from New Orleans for the elaborate wedding he had thrown. "Take care of my daughter," repeated Mr. Stewart gruffly; "that's how you repay me," as he paced away.

After some months of traveling and doing everything he did in such a courtly manner, Walter finally collapsed. So she took him home—and she watched over him.

But where is home? Is it North or South, the Old World or the New, the East Coast or the West? Is it Monte Carlo? Trieste, perhaps. Or Beaufort, South Carolina.

Is it in the elegance of Istanbul, the gardens of Palermo, the unexpected palm trees at Lake Como, or the green and beleaguered coast of Mississippi? In lieu of home the matter becomes more abstract: Honor is home. Walter was made of that. She never doubted that the Fiery Pantheon would be his permanent address.

It isn't easy to uphold such high ideals. But her mind was filled with death or glory charges and last stands.

The Fiery Pantheon raged on.

9 780684 852058